An Invitation to Scandal

THE SINS & SCANDALS SERIES

KELLY BOYCE

For Pamela Callow, Julianne MacLean and Cathryn Fox – you ladies are the best!

And always, for John – sorry I couldn't fit in a car chase. Maybe next time.

Chapter One

"Oh, that horrid man! It is so unfair that he, of all people, can still show his face in polite society after what he has done."

Miss Abigail Laytham gave the oars of the small rowboat a hard pull, sending the vessel in the opposite direction from the loathsome monster. Perhaps she and Caelie should not have come to Hyde Park, but it was such a beautiful sunny day, and while most people might prefer to stay indoors away from the late June heat, Abigail had always hated being confined.

Despite the ton's newfound aversion to their presence, she refused to cower like a mouse in some dark corner of her home.

In truth, with the Season all but at an end, she had hoped the city would have thinned by now, its inhabitants departed for their country estates. A luxury her family could no longer afford.

"I am certain he has as much right to be here as we do," her cousin said, her quiet voice interrupting Abigail's thoughts.

She pursed her lips. Caelie maintained a most charitable

nature, but even she must find it difficult to turn the other cheek where Lord Roxton was concerned.

"The man destroyed our family's reputation," Abigail said, as if her cousin needed the reminder. As if she hadn't noticed she had been left fatherless due to Viscount Roxton's callous actions.

Caelie offered up a sad smile. "I cannot dwell on the past, Abby. I am afraid if I do, I will fall into a deep, dark hole and never find my way out. It is better to leave the past where it belongs and move forward as best we can." But in Abigail's estimation, Caelie had already fallen, and darkness had swallowed her bright light.

Abigail did not share her cousin's sanguine reasoning. She had loved her uncle. He had been the only family member willing to take her and her older brother in after fever had taken her Papa and younger brother and left her mother in a weakened state. Uncle Henry had raised her and Benedict as if they were his own and she would be forever grateful. He had not deserved such an end. Nor did her family deserve to suffer because of it. Eight months had passed and still the wound rubbed raw.

No, some crimes were unforgivable. And Lord Roxton had committed his fair share of them, yet paid for none. A travesty that gnawed at her bones.

Abigail took a deep breath and pulled on the oars once more. The muscles across her back strained with the effort. What had possessed her to take one of the boats out? She had wanted to protect Caelie from the stares and whispers that still followed them wherever they went, but could she not have found a secluded path to walk instead? Perspiration beaded her brow and the moisture from the Serpentine caused her perfectly tamed curls to frizz. She really had not thought this out well.

Caelie's swift intake of breath captured her attention. "I believe he is coming this way."

Abigail looked at the rowboat in the distance. It was indeed moving in their direction. "The man's audacity knows no bounds. For all the length of the Serpentine, he has to row near us?"

"I am sure it is unintentional, Abby. Perhaps it is time we returned home, anyway." What Caelie truly meant went unspoken. Despite having arrived before the fashionable hour, the position of the late afternoon sun told Abigail they had overstayed their welcome. The park had become crowded and Caelie did not care to be seen. Or pointed at. Or whispered about. Abigail couldn't blame her.

She watched Lord Roxton's gradual approach, a serpent slithering through the water toward its prey. Granted, he was more handsome than most serpents, with his shock of thick black hair and perfectly chiseled features.

Anger fueled her strength and she pulled on the oars, leading them toward the shore. The distance was disconcerting. She hadn't realized she'd rowed so far out. The other boat gained on them; Lord Roxton's slow, steady movements much more effective than her shorter, choppier ones. Did he not realize they were there? Or was he so caught up in seducing his latest conquest, sitting at the opposite end of his boat, that he lost track of those around him?

Abigail looked about. Within moments, he would be upon them. She had nowhere to hide, unless she planned on jumping into the Serpentine. Which she didn't. It would mean leaving Caelie behind, and she would never desert her cousin.

Well, she would not give him the satisfaction of acknowledging his presence. She would snub him as polite society now did her family. She would—

"Oh!"

The oar jerked in its mooring as she slapped the water with it. The sudden movement yanked it from her grip with a swift jolt that reverberated up her arm. She grasped at the handle, too late. The oar slipped out of her reach.

Caelie's concerned gaze swept from the drifting oar to Abigail, then back again, her bonnet blocking all but the profile of her straight nose and generous mouth—a mouth now pulled into a tight line of distress. One fiery lock of hair had escaped its confines and bounced gently in the breeze.

"This is not good, Abby."

Abigail winced. Her poor cousin had become a recluse after the despicable Lord Billingsworth, a horrid snake perhaps as wicked as Roxton, cried off their engagement shortly after the scandal over Caelie's father broke. They could have sought damages—Abigail wished they had—but Caelie had begged them not to and Aunt Edythe had, for once, agreed with her daughter. Aunt Edythe didn't want any more attention, and Caelie had been too broken-hearted on all fronts to try to hold onto a man whose affections were obviously not fully engaged.

"Do not worry," Abigail said. It had taken a Herculean effort on her part to convince Caelie to come out for the afternoon. She had promised it would be a quiet, leisurely outing. How wrong she had been. She would find a way out of this. She just needed a minute to think. To come up with a plan. To...to...

She reached for the oar. It floated beyond the tips of her fingers.

"Blast it!"

"Abby!"

Abigail ignored her cousin's admonishment. There was no time. She turned her attention to the remaining oar. "Help me get this loose. I can use it to retrieve the other one before it floats beyond our reach."

From the corner of her eye, she could see Lord Roxton's

boat drawing nearer. He had rowed close enough she could discern the well-tailored cut of his expensive clothing. Nothing but the best for Lord Roxton. While her family had to count every last shilling and hope it stretched far enough to accommodate their needs. A feat that became more and more impossible with her uncle's creditors banging on their door.

She and Caelie freed the remaining oar and Abigail reached out again.

Likely Lord Roxton would find great humor in their current predicament. The man had no conscience whatsoever. How had she been so foolish as to have once thought him worthy of her consideration? Perhaps it was for the best he'd changed his mind and dropped his suit without so much as a by your leave.

The small rowboat rocked and pitched at a precarious angle as she stretched over the side, working to retrieve the oar. Abigail stabbed at the water with the extended oar, creating enough waves to send its mate farther out of reach.

"This is not good," she muttered, echoing Caelie's earlier assessment.

"Do you require assistance?"

Lord Roxton's voice carried across the water, abrading Abigail with its masculine confidence and false sincerity. Such mockery. He did not care a fig about their dilemma. He was merely trying to impress the simpering miss in his boat, hiding beneath her parasol. What doxy did he cavort with this day? An actress? A young widow of low repute? Maybe the infamous Madame St. Augustine herself. Not that she cared. She didn't. Not even a little.

"No, I do not need your assistance," Abigail bit out. She kept her gaze averted, refusing to give him the satisfaction of looking his way.

She threw her arm out in one last vain attempt to retrieve the wayward oar. The boat dipped beneath her weight and she pitched forward, swallowing a scream as cold water rushed up to greet her. Her arm smacked against the oar she had been reaching for with bone-cracking force. Pain shot through her forearm, but the sensation paled in comparison to the humiliation that slapped her pride when she sputtered to the surface and found Lord Roxton's boat not ten feet away.

"Abby!" Caelie leaned against the side of the still teetering boat, her hands gripping the edge. With both oars now in the water, her cousin was left adrift.

"Miss Laytham, are you injured?"

Abigail treaded water, keeping her back to Lord Roxton. How she despised the sound of her name on his gilded tongue. "I am perfectly fine, thank you. Please, do not trouble yourself."

Although, she was rather troubled. How exactly did she intend on getting herself back into the boat without capsizing it and sending Caelie into the water with her?

Caelie obviously shared her thoughts, concern dipping her eyebrows downward. "Can you touch bottom?"

Abigail held onto one of the oars to help keep her head above water and stretched her foot as far as it would go. Nothing but more water.

"No, I'm afraid not."

Lord Roxton reached a hand toward her. "Swim over and take my hand. I will pull you up."

The man could not leave well enough alone.

"Do you honestly believe I would accept your assistance?"

"Do you have another choice?"

Had he smirked? The nerve!

"I would rather stay here until the lake dries up. Or until... until..." She huffed out a breath. The cold water froze her brain, preventing her from coming up with the perfect set down. "Oh! There is simply no scenario where your assistance would be wanted, required, or solicited. Go away."

Abigail lifted one hand from the water and swiped a handful of soaked curls away from her face. What a mess she must be. This was beyond mortifying!

She glanced at his rowing companion, sitting with her back straight and her cream-colored day dress perfectly unwrinkled. The woman shifted her parasol to block the sun at her back.

Shock rendered Abigail mute.

This was no actress or courtesan. Abigail had heard the rumor Lord Roxton courted Miss Eugenie Caldwell, but she had not believed it. Though only the daughter of a baron, Miss Caldwell exemplified propriety, her example held up for all the other young ladies to emulate. The very idea she would consider the suit of someone as debauched as Lord Roxton seemed inconceivable. And yet, there she was. Sitting in his boat. Staring down her perfectly shaped nose.

"Miss Laytham. It is...lovely to see you."

Abigail blinked. "Yes, indeed," she managed, as if Miss Caldwell had stopped by for tea. Not that such an event would ever happen now. Since Uncle Henry's death, their receiving room had remained quite empty. Society did not care to associate with a family they now considered beneath their contempt. Though Abigail suspected it wasn't so much that her uncle had fallen under the spell of Madame St. Augustine, but rather the extremes he went to win her back when she rejected him for the younger and more affluent, Lord Roxton.

Miss Caldwell offered Abigail a polite smile, but her large brown eyes glittered with distaste and revealed her true feelings. Uncle Henry had once told Abigail the truth always revealed itself in the eyes. And the oh-so proper Eugenie Caldwell's eyes indicated she would rather be anywhere else but where society's cast off treaded water in the middle of the Serpentine.

Abigail could hardly blame her. She didn't particularly want to be here either.

"Miss Laytham," Lord Roxton said, his tone filled with the condescending self-importance she had been too blind to hear when they were courting. "You cannot climb back into your own boat without capsizing it and it is too far to swim to shore. I cannot in good conscience leave you—"

"Good conscience?" She swiped at another waterlogged curl. "Are you mad?"

He drew his extended arm back slightly. "I beg your—"

"Oh, Abby, not now," Caelie groaned, covering her eyes with her hand.

But if not now, then when? She had waited eight months to face Lord Roxton and make him admit his wrongdoings, but the man had made himself scarce. It seemed he went out of his way to avoid her family. If she hadn't known better, she would think guilt provoked such evasion. But she did know better. He, like everyone else, simply preferred to ignore their existence.

"Since when have you ever had anything resembling a good conscience?" Abigail sucked in a deep breath. Her limbs ached from treading water and she desperately wanted to stop, but pent-up anger gave her the strength to carry on. "I am quite certain you would not recognize a good conscience if it waltzed up and sank its teeth into your be—"

"Abby, no!"

Caelie's shocked tone stopped her from finishing her rather improper remark, but she continued to glare up at Lord Roxton, clamping her teeth together to keep them from chattering.

"Miss Laytham, you are shivering. Give me your hand."

She stared at his hand. She knew the sad effect his touch had, even in the limited contact their brief courtship had allowed. It did strange things to her. She would rather drown than succumb to such foolhardiness.

"I will swim to shore, thank you." At least then she might be allowed to hold on to an ounce of her dignity. Provided she didn't drown first.

Lord Roxton's gaze slid to the shoreline and Abigail's followed. A small crowd gathered in the distance. Lovely. Had there been no witnesses, likely he would have paddled past her and continued on his way without sparing her a glance. But at this rate, everyone in town would be dissecting this newest indignity by the time the dinner bell rang.

That they would know Lord Roxton had saved her was a horror beyond measure.

"Nonsense," Lord Roxton said, interrupting her thoughts. "Your skirts will drag you down before you make it half way. Allow me to pull you up so we can be done with this."

"Abby, please. Accept Lord Roxton's help," Caelie said. A thin line of tension creased her cousin's brow. Guilt pinched Abigail's conscience. She had made a promise to Caelie to keep their outing quiet and calamity free. A promise she had, thus far, not kept. Why was it each time she tried to protect her family she failed miserably? Could she do nothing right?

"Take it." Lord Roxton thrust his hand toward her once again. She had drifted closer to his boat, the gentle current doing her no favors.

Swallowing her pride, a lump that did not go down easy, Abigail gritted her teeth and grabbed for it. This was beyond belief.

Lord Roxton drew her to the side of his boat until she found herself staring up into his handsome face. The sun hit at such an angle his silvery eyes sparkled as if diamonds hid beneath his irises. Was it any wonder the ladies of the ton tittered and swooned whenever he smiled at them? Well she was not a silly, simpering female to be undone by such nonsense. In fact, upon closer inspection, she decided it was all a trick of the light and, in fact, his eyes were nothing special at all. Quite ordinary, really.

His fingers curled around her hand, warm and solid. A niggling memory she thought long buried rushed to the surface. His hand on the small of her back as he whisked her around the dance floor. She had thought him the most handsome of men, then.

Now she recognized him for the beast he truly was.

He steadied his boat and kept the rocking to a minimum as he hauled her over the side and dropped her like a sack of potatoes at his feet. Abigail pushed herself into a sitting position with far less grace than she would have preferred. Her soaked skirts twisted around her legs and rode upward to an embarrassing degree. She grabbed at the hem and gave a quick yank to put things to rights, cringing at the sound of material tearing.

Oh, how the fates mocked her this day.

Lord Roxton unbuttoned his coat and struggled out of the sleeves. The motion rocked the boat slightly but not enough to concern Abigail. The command he had of his vessel irritated beyond measure.

"Put this around you." His coat swirled over her head and landed heavily around her shoulders. She hissed in pain, unable to stop the revealing sound. He leaned down and took her arm. "You have hurt yourself."

The pad of his thumb brushed lightly over the bruised area where the oar had accosted her. An uncomfortable sensation tripped up her arm and made her momentarily forget the throbbing.

"Kindly let go of me. I am fine." She tried to pull her arm away, but he held it firm. His warmth seeped into her skin. Her mind rebelled against the sensation as much as her body embraced it.

"You are not fine," he said. "You are injured." His dark eyebrows dipped and an expression she couldn't read crossed his face. It added an unexpected depth to his natural handsomeness.

"It is just a silly bruise." She did not like this side of him. His feigned concern existed only for the benefit of Miss Caldwell, to prevent her from seeing the wolf lurking beneath sheep's clothing. But she knew better. The man did not have an ounce of compassion housed within his lean, muscular frame.

Abigail jerked her arm away and this time he let it go.

"Did you walk to the park?"

She glared up at him. "Of course, we walked."

What other choice did they have? They were down to one carriage that Benedict had required for business that morning. Hailing a hansom cab was an extravagance they could ill afford. Besides, it was a perfectly lovely day, and they did not live far away, as Lord Roxton well knew; his bachelor residence was located only two houses down on the opposite side of the street. She could see his well-appointed townhouse from her bedroom window, if she chose to look.

Which she no longer did.

"You cannot walk back," he said. He sounded no less perturbed by this fact than she. "My carriage is at the end of the lane. I will convey you—"

"You will do no such thing."

Abigail tried to push herself up into the middle seat, but the boat pitched unsteadily with her sudden movement and she fell forward. He caught her about the waist and they stayed like that, nose to nose, until the boat steadied. This close, she could smell his scent.

He positively reeked of outdoors and masculinity.

His hands on her person left her disconcerted. They had touched like this only once before, during a waltz at Almack's.

But they had been in a room filled with people then, not sitting in a boat, soaking wet. She did not care for the way his hands on her waist injected heat into her body to battle the cold. She most certainly did not like the way said heat went deeper than just her skin and began to seep into areas where it had no business—

"Perhaps, Lord Roxton," Miss Caldwell's firm tone brought Abigail hurtling back to reality. "When we reach shore, someone else could assist Miss Laytham home?"

No doubt Miss Caldwell felt anxious to retreat from the embarrassing display Abigail provided before it colored her pristine reputation.

Lord Roxton gently settled her onto the middle seat then looked over her shoulder to address to Miss Caldwell. "I will take her."

Abigail did not care for being discussed as if she was not there. "You have done quite enough. We will make our own arrangements, thank you."

He raised one dark eyebrow. "If I do not assist you, who will?"

His question infuriated her, the truth behind it hitting a direct blow. Who indeed? There was not a lady or gentleman left who would even look them in the eye when they passed on the street. But to have Lord Roxton—the man who had created the circumstances that sent Uncle Henry into the emotional spiral that made him take his own life—point this out...well, it was beyond intolerable.

"Someone surely will."

"No," he said, with grave finality. "They will not."

Abigail wished to refute his claim, but she had no evidence to offer. He was right. No one would assist them. Even relatives of her father pretended the relation did not exist. Papa had been excommunicated from his family years before she was born and with his death long past, it seemed the newest scandal proved enough to keep their familial attachments at bay. Only Uncle Henry had acknowledged them. And now he was gone too.

She beat back the sense of shame and dismay that threatened. She could not allow Caelie to see her weaken. She was determined she would remain strong for her family. Looking over at her cousin, she could see the anxiety framing her pretty features. Her knuckles whitened where they gripped the edge of the boat.

"Abby, you cannot walk home as you are."

Abigail glanced down at the sodden mess she had become. A clear outline of her stays and undergarments showed through the soaked, pale blue muslin. Her skirts molded to her body and left little to the imagination. She hugged Lord Roxton's coat tighter and tried to ignore the male scent that wafted up from the superfine wool. Much as it grieved her, Caelie was right.

"Fine. We would be most...pleased," she stumbled over the word, "to accept your assistance."

"Good," he said, his manner turning brisk. "Lady Caelie, toss me the rope. I will tie your boat to mine and tow you to shore."

Caelie did as he requested and within minutes, they were underway. A few minutes after that, they reached the shore to the cheers of those standing along its edge. It did not go unnoticed by Abigail that the hearty congratulations were directed at Lord Roxton, while the most she and her cousin received were pitying glances.

She reached over and squeezed Caelie's hand. They would get through this. They had weathered worse.

Nicholas poured himself a stiff drink and tossed it back, letting the liquid hit his throat with a burn. The brandy did nothing to erase the image of Miss Laytham and the intense resentment rife in her light blue eyes. Amazing how a woman of such small stature could produce such an overwhelming amount of disdain.

But he deserved it, did he not? Yes, he more than deserved it.

Nicholas finished the glass and poured himself another. He had tried to avoid any contact with the Laythams since Lord Glenmor's death eight months earlier. It had proven a rather easy feat, despite the closeness of their homes. The Laythams rarely ventured out into society now. First, because of the mourning period and then...well, humiliation was a hard thing to face in one's peers.

His ability to walk away unscathed as if nothing had happened only made things worse. Except that something *had* happened. And while society may not hold him accountable, the Laythams did. Or rather one Laytham did. The one that meant the most.

And she was right to do so.

He had become so wrapped up in exacting his revenge against Glenmor, he had ignored what was happening right under his nose. If only he had not been so determined to show Glenmor how it felt to have something dear taken away. If only he'd recognized the man's desperation and taken his threats more seriously. If only—

Well, if only.

He could fill a book with that list. But Spence was right—he could not go back, only forward. Bit by bit, he'd reevaluated the mess his life had become, the level of debauchery he had sunk to, the lack of compassion he had shown.

What he'd seen had sickened him.

"Nicholas, do wipe that scowl from your face."

Nicholas looked up from his drink as his mother and sister joined him in the drawing room before the dinner bell rang. He set his drink on the counter and left it there. Getting sloshed would do him no good. He'd learned that the hard way.

He forced a smile and crossed the room, taking a seat next to the sofa. "Forgive me, Mother. I had something on my mind."

"The incident at the park, perhaps?"

Nicholas stiffened as the sound of his father's voice announced his arrival. He had hoped the old earl would not be joining them this evening. He had been ailing, and while Nicholas would not go so far as to wish him ill, he had expected the man would take his dinner in his room. Dinner with his heir had never been an event the earl cared to attend.

Nicholas stood and faced him. "What do you know of it?"

His father's stern features did not soften. They never did where Nicholas was concerned. "One cannot behave foolishly in front of others and not expect news of it to spread like wildfire. You know what this town is like."

Indeed, Nicholas did. He had once reveled in the discomfort that tales of his escapades caused the great Earl of Blackbourne. Now, however, he no longer had that luxury.

Nicholas adopted an air of indifference. He retook his seat and stretched his long legs out. He refused to let his father know he'd struck his mark yet again. "What is being said?"

Rebecca leaned forward on the sofa, her hands clasped in her lap. One dark curl bobbed near her temple. "They are saying you practically had to force your assistance on Miss Laytham when she did not wish it. No one blames you, of course. What else could you do? Leave her to drown? Eugenie insisted Miss Laytham behaved most rudely and in a very unladylike manner."

"Is that so?" Nicholas could not fault the accuracy of the claim. Miss Laytham had made it quite clear she would rather sink to the bottom of the Serpentine than accept his help. Had Lady Caelie not been present to impart reason to her, she likely would have. She'd always had a bit of a stubborn streak. There had been a time when he had found her spirited behavior quite amusing. Charming, even. Funny how it didn't feel quite the same when it was turned against him.

His father poured a drink and slowly walked over to where the others were seated, though he did not join them. Instead, he stared out the large bow window behind the sofa and took a slow draw on his drink.

"We have spoken about this, have we not?" The censure in his voice grated. "You cannot be seen to have contact with those people."

Those people. As if they were lepers who might infect others with their disease. Nicholas bristled at the suggestion. The Laythams had done nothing. He and Opal were the guilty parties.

"The Laythams are—"

"Social pariahs. Any interaction with them will only reignite the scandal. You can hardly afford that—especially now."

Meaning now that Miss Eugenie Caldwell had set her cap for him. Or rather for his bank account. Despite her family's vaunted respectability, their lack of an heir left the family's future in peril. They could no longer count on the income from the entailed property to continue after her father passed. And with three daughters to marry off, plans had to be made to ensure their future financial stability. And those plans included him.

Desperate times called for desperate measures.

He pushed his mind away from Miss Caldwell. An easy

accomplishment. He rarely gave her much thought when they were apart.

"Would you have preferred I left Miss Laytham and Lady Caelie to their own devices?"

"No, of course not," his mother said, jumping to his defense. An action sure to stoke his father's ire even further. "You did the right thing. You can hardly be blamed for the circumstances."

Rebecca cleared her throat. Her gaze darted between him and the earl. "Perhaps what Father is trying to say is that you have made such wonderful progress. It would be such a shame to lose it all now." His sweet sister. Always the diplomat. He wondered if she ever wearied of the role.

"Stop being so selfish and think of your family. We have worn the taint of your past behavior long enough. It ends now before it affects your sister's prospects," Blackbourne said. A faint smile played about his thin lips when he glanced down at his daughter, the only member of his family he considered deserving of his love.

"Father, please." Rebecca shot Nicholas an apologetic look. The dove gray of her gown brought out the silvery hue of her eyes, that and her dark hair were the only hint they had at least some of the same blood running through their veins. Beyond that, every aspect of her resembled their mother, while he...

Well, he did not exactly resemble anyone, did he?

"The thought of you returning to your old ways disgusts me," Blackbourne said. He delivered his harsh words to the window, rather than address Nicholas directly. An intended slight. A reminder he was beneath the earl's contempt.

"I have no intentions of returning to my old ways."

"Good." Rebecca issued the word with a relieved sigh. "See, Father, there is nothing to be concerned about."

Nicholas remembered a time when his little sister had

worshipped the ground he walked on. How she had tagged along behind him like a shadow he could not shake. Now she was a woman in her own right, and the brother she'd once adored had become less of a hero and more of a hindrance as she developed aspirations of her own. Aspirations that included snagging Lord Selward as a husband.

What she saw in that stick in the mud, he would never understand, but she had her heart and mind set on him, and only now that Nicholas had begun to turn his life around had Lord Selward bothered to look in his sister's direction.

Not a point in the man's favor.

His mother reached out and placed a hand over his. "I would hate to see you lose your chance at happiness."

Happiness. Nicholas twisted his mouth to one side. At one time, he thought he'd had it within his grasp, but it had been taken away. Now, the concept was completely foreign to him. He had not turned his life around to find happiness.

He did not deserve it.

It was redemption he sought, though even that seemed far beyond his reach at the moment.

"I will be on my best behavior." He displayed a confidence he did not feel. He had suppressed his natural desires for eight very long months. Surely, he could do it a while longer until he married the very proper Miss Caldwell. Though, seeing Miss Laytham with her dress plastered to her body, revealing the curves of her body, had stoked a fire inside of him Miss Caldwell's cool perfection never could. A clear reminder of the tenuous hold he had on his desires. "Please do not trouble yourself."

Nicholas shifted uncomfortably in his seat and forced thoughts of Miss Laytham out of his mind. Perhaps it would be best if he spent the night at his parents' house rather than returning to his own lodgings, with its clear view of Miss Laytham's bedroom window.

Chapter Two

Abigail leafed through the letters on the silver salver in the main hall. Her arm felt much improved today, though her pride still stung over having allowed Lord Roxton to convey her and Caelie home like errant children.

The conversation during the carriage ride had been stilted and awkward, a situation she did nothing to alleviate. She did not care if the always-virtuous Miss Caldwell suggested to others her behavior was rude and peevish. What did it matter? Society had already made up their collective minds about her family and seemed disinclined to change them.

She picked up a letter addressed to her, recognizing Lord Tarrington's shaky penmanship.

Lovely. No doubt another lengthy missive describing the progress of his gardens. Heavens, how she dreaded a life with this man. The age gap between them was so staggering they shared no common ground. He rambled on about botany while she responded with descriptions of her latest watercolors. A bold-faced lie if she'd ever told one. Her watercolors were abysmal and in truth, she had given up the pursuit years ago. But she had to write something, and she doubted the true thoughts and feelings of a young woman just one and twenty would be of any interest to a man well into his sixtieth year.

Besides, they both knew he did not want her for conversation. He needed an heir, and as he had already outlived two wives who had failed in that respect, he hoped a third would prove the charm.

A shudder coursed through her at the mere thought of what that entailed. Papery thin hands touching her bare skin; his aging body covering hers, pushing his withered manhood into her.

Bile roiled in her stomach and threatened to rage upward.

She was not a prude. She knew what went on between a man and woman. She and Caelie had spent enough time eavesdropping on the maids to have a proper idea of the mechanics involved. Unfortunately, she did not share the maids' exuberance over the act when she thought of her betrothed.

If only things could be different. Just once, she wanted to experience that kind of giddy enthusiasm before she must play the part of the dutiful wife, her independence stripped away and along with it any hope for love. Was there a more tragic circumstance than to live out one's life never experiencing true love or passion? She could not think of one.

She'd had the chance once, or so she thought. But Lord Roxton's interest had cooled, and he'd dropped his suit. Abigail had fretted for months over his sudden indifference. Had she done something to turn him away? Yes, he'd always been a bit of a rake, but no more so than most young men his age and she'd been certain he was worth reforming, that he had *wanted* to be reformed. What a fool she'd been! Without warning, he had turned his attentions away from her and toward Uncle Henry's mistress. She had watched helplessly as he went from a rake to a reprobate. He had changed from the man she knew. Or at least from the man she'd thought she knew. His sudden rejection still stung, but better she had learned of his true nature earlier, rather than later.

Perhaps the sting would have faded away in time, if Lord Roxton hadn't re-entered their lives, but he had. And thanks to his callous actions and the scandal that ensued, her choices in the marriage mart had disappeared like a wisp of smoke caught on the wind. Now, instead of entering a marriage based on affection, she must make the best match she could to keep her family afloat.

Heaviness settled upon her shoulders. Abigail placed Lord Tarrington's letter back on the plate and rummaged through the others. Was there not even one measly invitation? In the last week only Lord and Lady Doddington had dared to issue an invite to their masquerade one week hence, though it was clear in the note sent to her brother, Benedict, they did so only due to their familial connection with Aunt Edythe. When one read between the lines, it became evident they expected their invitation to be declined. The insinuation had been enough to anger Mother, who had quickly instructed Benedict to send back their acceptance, instead.

The impending masquerade notwithstanding, it would have been nice to receive a genuine invitation where the people issuing it actually wanted you to attend. Abigail let out a short breath. How long must they put up with this shunning?

Her fingers bumped against something cool and hard. Feeling around for the object buried beneath the letters, she pulled out a shiny skeleton key with an ornately designed head. Attached to the head was a length of red velvet ribbon, and at the end of that, a vellum tag.

Abigail's hand shook as she turned the tag over. On it, written in a clear script, was an address, date and time. Nothing else.

But she did not need anything else. She recognized the key immediately. She had seen it once before. It had come for

Uncle Henry, though at the time, she did not understand what it represented. She could no longer make such a claim.

The key was an invitation—though not just any invitation. This one provided entry to one of the most scandalous parties of the demimonde, hosted by none other than Madame Opal St. Augustine, her uncle's former mistress.

She shook her head. She had loved Uncle Henry dearly. He had been their savior after Father's untimely death. Warm and affectionate, he was filled with life—the exact opposite of his cold and shrewish wife, Aunt Edythe. Could she really blame him for seeking affection elsewhere? She did not condone his behavior, but a part of her understood it.

But why was the key here, now? She turned the tag over. Her heart lurched in her chest. The delivery address had the correct street name, but the wrong number. It read eighty-seven. Their house number was seventy-eight. Number eighty-seven sat across the street and two houses down.

And belonged to Lord Roxton.

Footsteps echoed down the marble hallway. Abigail hurriedly pocketed the key, then took a deep breath to quell the pounding of her heart.

"Good morning, sister." Benedict strode into the room and stopped at her shoulder, reaching around her for the remaining letters.

"Good morning, Ben." She offered him a warm smile, which he half-heartedly returned.

Once, he had been so quick to smile; now it appeared he had forgotten how. Since inheriting the title of Earl of Glenmor upon her uncle's death, only tension pulled at the corners of his mouth. Between Ben and Caelie, she would be hard pressed to say who had changed more. A depressing pall had claimed them both. Ben's due to the responsibility of taking on an earldom on the brink of ruin; Caelie's due to heartbreak. Abigail had tried to cheer them both up, but to no avail.

Her heart twisted. They had all had such bright futures before Lord Roxton and Madame St. Augustine crossed their paths. One could not expect more from the Queen of the Demimonde, but from a gentleman? As a gentleman, Lord Roxton, future Earl of Blackbourne, should have shown more compassion for her uncle's plight. Even if his interest in her had waned, she would have thought some small bit of good-will remained.

It hadn't. Had it, Lord Roxton would surely have accepted responsibility for his actions and deflected the worst of the scandal away from her family and put it where it belonged—at his doorstep. Instead, he walked away from the scandal as quickly as he had walked away from her, and her family was left to wear the stain of his wrongdoings.

Well, she wouldn't stand for it. She had failed to save her family once before, but she would not fail again. She would do whatever she must to ensure Lord Roxton accepted his role in her family's downfall, and that he did so with the full ear of their peers. Only then would her family be vindicated and able to regain their rightful place in society. Benedict could stop worrying. Caelie could return to her once vivacious self and find happiness again.

Benedict handed her the letter she'd ignored earlier. "Another letter from Lord Tarrington, I take it?"

"Yes." She took the vellum envelope and held it to her fore-head like a mesmerist. "I sense it is filled in great detail about how his crocuses are very much in bloom and that he has high hopes for his rose bushes this summer."

Benedict sighed and the tightness around his mouth inten-sified. "There must be another way—"

She placed a hand upon his arm, stopping him. "There

isn't. I do this of my own free will. You have never asked anything of me and you do not now. This is my choice."

"Abby—"

She forced a bright smile, hoping the lie did not show in her eyes. She loved her family. She would not see them suffer when she possessed the ability to prevent it. Nodding at the letters in his hand, she asked, "Who do you hear from today? Anyone of interest?"

He allowed her to redirect the conversation but guilt tainted his eyes. He glanced down at the letters in his hand and grimaced.

"Creditors. The wolves are howling at the gates."

It was a familiar refrain. If they didn't act fast, they would lose everything but the title, and a fat lot of good that would do them when they faced an empty table.

But now…

She squeezed the key inside her pocket. Cool metal indented her palm. Providence had given her the opportunity to confront Lord Roxton privately and convince him to publicly acknowledge what he had done. If she convinced him, she could regain her family's honor. She could save them.

All she required was the courage to see the opportunity through.

———

"Is it…?" Caelie rose from the writing table in her bedchamber and turned the key over in her hand, letting her words fall away.

"It is an invitation to one of Madame St. Augustine's parties," Abigail supplied, though she didn't really need to. They both knew what it was.

The key dropped from Caelie's fingers as if it bore the taint of the courtesan's reputation. Her cousin paled considerably. Guilt pinched Abigail's conscience. Perhaps she should not have dredged up the bad memories, but she could find no other way around it. If she planned on pursuing this opportunity, she would require Caelie's assistance. Her cousin rarely did anything without thinking it through thoroughly beforehand, whereas Abigail tended to barrel into things with no thought at all. She liked to think of it as spontaneity, though Benedict insisted the correct term was foolhardiness.

Either way, her plan required a careful approach. She would have one opportunity to confront Lord Roxton. She could not squander it with brash action.

"What is it doing here?" Caelie whispered, motioning toward the offending item. "Madame St. Augustine knows all too well Father is dead. Even she couldn't be so cruel as to mock us by sending this." Fire flashed in her green eyes and for a brief moment, Abigail saw the spirit she missed so much. Perhaps her cousin wasn't beyond reach after all.

Abigail bent down and picked up the key. "It was sent in error."

"In error?"

"It should have gone to number eighty-seven." She held up the tag dangling from the key for Caelie's inspection.

Her cousin glanced up sharply. "Lord Roxton's home?"

"Yes."

A brief scratch sounded at the door. Abigail called an invitation to enter and Muri bustled into the room, carrying a tray of hot chocolate and biscuits. This type of situation called for tasty reinforcements. One could not plan properly on an empty stomach.

Muri set the tray down on the small table near the writing desk and turned around. "You said you needed my 'elp with somethin', miss?"

"Yes, Muri, but first you must swear to keep what I am

about to tell you strictly between us. No one else must know." Abigail fixed the maid with a stern look. "Absolutely no one."

"Of course, miss. Take it to the grave, I will."

Abigail shifted the key in her hand then held it out. The metal object unfurled and dangled from the velvet ribbon.

Muri's eyes widened.

"Do you know what this is?" It was a ridiculous question. No doubt everyone below stairs knew far more details than anyone above as to exactly what the key stood for. The destruction it had caused.

"Oh yes, miss." Her head bobbed up and down as she spoke. "It's for them scandalous parties that Madame St. Augustine throws for gentlemen that's got a particular itch and ladies that likes to scratch it for 'em. Beggin' your pardon, my lady."

Caelie blushed and turned away, walking toward the window that overlooked the rose bushes. It was not a pretty sight. Since Uncle Henry's death, they had gone mostly unattended. Their gardener had been one of the first casualties of their restricted finances and though Abigail's mother tried to keep things up, she did not possess much of a green thumb.

"Exactly. I need you to help me prepare for such a party."

Caelie swung back around. "Abby, no! Absolutely not. You will be ruined!"

Abigail shook her head. "On the contrary. No one will even know I am there. Tell her, Muri."

"She's right, Lady Caelie," the maid said. "All the ladies wear masks and turbans and the men dress as highwaymen or pirates and such. 'Tis important that no one knows who's who so's as no one can try 'an use it against them."

"See? I can slip in and out with no one the wiser. Save for Lord Roxton."

"Have you gone mad, Abby? What makes you so sure Lord Roxton will even be there if we have his invitation?"

Abigail dismissed Caelie's concern with a wave of her hand. "Of course, he'll be there. The invitation is proof he still partakes in that lifestyle, despite outward appearances to the contrary. Even without receiving the invitation, I am certain he knows when these parties occur and can easily gain entrance." He may have fooled the rest of London with his newly turned leaf, but he didn't fool her. She had experienced his mercurial nature firsthand. The only difference was now he would have to be more careful with his behavior, a wary attitude that only worked in her favor. "He will not dare whisper a word about my presence. If he did, the ton would know he has returned to his old ways. A fact he seems determined to cover up."

"Regardless," Caelie said. "What can you possibly hope to accomplish by confronting him? The damage is done, Abby. Lord Roxton cannot change that."

Abigail went to her wardrobe and swung open the doors. She needed the perfect dress to catch Lord Roxton's attention. "He can take responsibility," she said. She sifted through the dresses. "In doing so, the ton will see how Lord Roxton's callous actions tormented poor Uncle Henry. They can't possibly continue to blame him—and by extension us—once they know where the true blame lies."

"Do you honestly believe that will happen?" The hint of bitterness in Caelie's voice revealed her lack of conviction. Abigail didn't blame her, but nor did she agree with her. Of course, it would happen. It had to.

Abigail poked her head out of the wardrobe. "What should I wear? He once mentioned a penchant for red. Crimson, I believe he said. Or do you think it would matter? Perhaps he simply chases anything that moves?"

Caelie sat on the bed. The fire Abigail had seen earlier drained out of her. "Are you so certain Lord Roxton hasn't mended his ways? He is courting Miss Caldwell. One would hardly consider that rakish behavior."

Abigail stared at Caelie, momentarily rendered speechless. "It is all an act, I assure you. How could you think otherwise?"

"I don't know anymore. Perhaps Father's death has had an impact on him. Yesterday, there was something different about him. He reminded me of the man who courted you, only... more subdued, I think." Caelie shrugged.

Abigail snorted in a rather unladylike fashion. "The man who courted me was nothing more than a wolf in sheep's clothing. The man who made it his goal to ruin Uncle Henry for no good reason—that is the *real* Lord Roxton. One cannot deny he threw himself into the role with relish."

Caelie gave a sad smile that broke Abigail's heart. Whatever she had suffered, Caelie had lost so much more: her father, her fiancé, even her ability to show her face in public without being scalded by shame and humiliation. It broke Abigail's heart. She would risk everything to put things back to rights. To see her family happy once more.

"I am convinced if Lord Roxton publicly accepts his responsibility for the scandal, people will see it was his fault and not Uncle Henry's," she said.

"Do you think my father holds no culpability for his actions, Abby? He is the one—"

"No!" She cut Caelie off, unwilling to hear it. She owed him that much, if not more. "Uncle Henry was the best of men with a generous heart. He took us in when no one else would. Yes, he strayed and shouldn't have, but that does not mean he deserved what happened to him. Lord Roxton waited until he was in a vulnerable state and then he pounced. His actions were deplorable. But this—" she held up the key she had looped around her wrist, "this is our key to salvation."

Caelie shook her head. "No, Abby. That key is nothing more than an invitation to scandal."

Abigail turned to her maid. "Thank you, Muri. That will be all."

"Yes, miss." Muri curtsied and gave Abigail a cheeky grin. Abigail experienced a second's hesitation—would her maid keep their secret? She hoped her trust was not misplaced. She did not need the entire below stairs gossiping about her plan, especially if the gossiping reached the ears of Titus, their rather old, stuffy butler. He would not hesitate to take the information directly to her brother and who knew what that would result in. Nothing good, that was for certain.

She waited for the door to her bedchamber to close behind Muri before turning back to Caelie.

"You know I am expected to marry Lord Tarrington?"

Her cousin nodded.

"And you know the man is sixty if he is a day."

"Yes, but Benedict says you don't—"

"And being that he is old and...and..."

"Disgusting?"

Abigail sighed; Caelie had never bothered to hide her distaste for the aging lord. "Yes, disgusting. Once I marry him, my fate is sealed. There will be no chance of me convincing Lord Roxton to take responsibility for what he has done. Lord Tarrington rarely comes to London, and Lord Roxton rarely leaves it."

"Abby—"

Abigail held up her hand to stay Caelie's protests. She did not want to hear it. She had made up her mind. Desperate times called for desperate measures.

"Madame St. Augustine and Lord Roxton have brought this family to social ruin and they used your poor father to do it. Benedict struggles each day just to keep us from falling into bankruptcy. You lost your fiancé, and I have no choice but to marry a man nearly thrice my age!"

"But, Abby!"

Abigail sat on the bed next to Caelie, the key clutched tightly in her hand until its ridges dug into the soft flesh of her palm. "My mind is set. I will attend the party, confront Lord Roxton with my demands, then leave."

"What possible reason would Lord Roxton have to agree to such demands?"

Abigail took a deep breath. In truth, she had nothing. Nothing she could threaten him with or hold over his head. Nothing except the belief that perhaps somewhere, deep inside of him, a hint of the man she once believed him to be might truly exist. It was to that aspect she would appeal, and pray with all her might she could breathe life into it once again. Because if she couldn't...

"I will apply sound reasoning for him to do so. I will remind him that a man of honor, as he seems determined to show himself as now, would do the right thing."

Caelie raised a skeptical eyebrow. "What if someone recognizes you?"

"You heard Muri. My identity will be carefully concealed. But I will need your help in keeping Mother from discovering my absence."

"What if someone approaches you and expects you to...to..."

Abigail smiled. She had considered the possibility, and if she were honest, she would admit to a small thrill at the notion of indulging in a little bit of passion before marriage to Lord Tarrington destroyed any hope of ever experiencing such a luxury. But she was not so foolish as to believe the kind of passion she sought could be found at such a party. And even if it could, she did not dare. She had but one objective—to find Lord Roxton and convince him to repent.

Abigail pushed off the bed and strode to the middle of the room. "I will be safe, Caelie. No one would force me to do anything against my will. I will be in and out before I am even noticed. I promise."

"But how will you know which gentleman is Lord Roxton

if everyone is in costume?"

Abigail scowled. The only wrinkle in an otherwise well thought out plan. But only a small wrinkle. After all, had she not spent the better part of two years watching him, studying him? First as a smitten young girl, then later as a rejected fool. Surely, she would be able to pick him out of a crowd. Wouldn't she?

She shook off the creeping doubt. "I will just know."

This was her one and only chance. Failure was not an option.

"Oh, Abigail," Caelie rose from the bed and crossed the room. Her hand pressed against Abigail's cheek, cool and firm. "Can you not leave well enough alone? The scandal will pass in time. People will forget—"

"You don't believe that any more than I do. The ton's memory is long and unforgiving. If we do not prove their scorn is undeserved, we will forever wear its stain." She covered Caelie's hand with her own. "Please say you will help me, Caelie. I cannot bear to stand by and do nothing while my family suffers."

"You are determined to do this?"

"I am."

Caelie sighed and her eyes dimmed with resignation—a far cry from the conspiratorial spark Abigail had hoped for. "Fine. What do you need from me?"

S pencer, Lord Huntsleigh, smiled as he raised his glass. His tanned face stood out among the paler complexions surrounding the tables at White's.

"I am telling you, Nick, you should have come to the Caribbean with us. It was a beauty to behold. The bluest of skies, the warmest of water and the loveliest of women. And best of all, no one insisting upon some ridiculous state of propriety—except of course our friend, Bowen, here."

Nicholas turned his gaze to Marcus Bowen who sat quietly reading the morning paper.

Bowen folded down one edge of his newspaper and peered over it. "I merely suggested running amuck on the beach in nothing but your shorts was a less than ideal way to spend your time."

Spence raised one eyebrow, bleached golden by the sun. "Did you have a better way to spend it?"

"Your grandfather sent us there to determine the viability of the coffee plant. Not to run about playing like a child who had not a care in the world."

Spence shook his head. "All work and no play make for a very dull life, Bowen. You should break out of your shell and give it a go, old chum."

Bowen smiled. "I like my shell just fine, thank you. And your grandfather doesn't pay me to play. He pays me to work."

The reminder of Bowen's status as employee was enough to dampen Spence's teasing. Though the Marquess of Ellesmere had raised their friend, he was not family. He bore no title or familial connections. Spence turned his attention back to Nicholas. "How have things been in our absence? Is it true you are courting Miss Eugenie Caldwell?"

"Indeed." He didn't bother including any enthusiasm in his answer. He had known Spence and Bowen since they were boys. They would detect the lie for what it was.

"And how does that fair?"

Nicholas took a slow draw on his brandy; the aged vintage slid smoothly down his throat.

"I believe she is expecting an offer shortly."

Bowen's dark eyebrows lifted above the edge of the newspaper, a quiet telling of what he thought of the situation. "Will she receive one?"

Nicholas shrugged. "Of course."

"Bloody hell, Nick!" Spence threw an arm up in disgust, nearly spilling his drink. Several heads turned in their direction. "How can you do this? We are too young to be thinking of marriage."

"We are eight and twenty, Spence. And your grandfather has been crowing about you picking a wife for the past three Seasons."

"A crowing I have pointedly ignored. I have no interest in marriage. It ties a man down. I much prefer a life of freedom and adventure and you well know it. Marriage would be akin to death for me." He placed a hand over his heart and leaned back in his chair. "I should have been born a pirate."

Bowen folded his newspaper and set it on the table. "I don't believe one is born a pirate, Spence. I believe one becomes a pirate."

Spence made a face. "Such a stickler for details, Bowen. Perhaps you should marry. I think the institution would suit you admirably."

"No, thank you," Bowen said, coloring slightly. "The women I am exposed to do not find me suitable and the others do not suit me. I'm afraid I am destined to bachelorhood."

He seemed the only one of them remotely put off by this outcome.

"Pardon the intrusion, Lord Roxton."

The three men glanced up. White's major domo stood at Nicholas's shoulder.

"Yes, Farnley, what is it?"

"There is a..." he hesitated, clearing his throat. "There is a lady here to see you, my lord." He extended a hand, gnarled by arthritis, a card caught between two bent fingers. Nicholas recognized it instantly.

"Please tell the lady in question I am otherwise engaged," he said, without taking the card.

Farnley swallowed. His Adam's apple bobbed in his narrow throat. "She was quite insistent, my lord. She indicated that should you decline to see her, she would haunt the entrance until she was received, creating quite a ruckus if need be."

A fire crackled in the hearth while the din created by conversation from the club's members droned on in the background. The heads that had turned to them after Spence's outburst had gone back to their own business, but Nicholas knew it would take little to recapture their attention. Not so long ago he would have reveled in such theatrics. Now he avoided them at all costs.

He closed his eyes and pinched the bridge of his nose. Why was she doing this? Why now? After the debacle in the park with Miss Laytham, tongues were already wagging. He could ill afford another scene and give his father further proof to his claim that he was beyond redemption. He let out a slow breath. "Have my carriage brought around. Tell her to get into it. I will be out shortly."

"Yes, my lord."

Nicholas waited until Farnley left before answering the question in Spence and Bowen's respective gazes.

"Opal."

Spence shook his head. "The woman has no shame. Does she honestly think you would take her back as mistress after all that has happened?"

Nicholas shrugged. "I do not know what she wants, nor do I care. A fact I plan on making perfectly clear to her. Again."

He had allowed Opal St. Augustine's beauty and carnal expertise to rule his life once, to play on his need for revenge, resulting in tragedy and disaster. He would not make the same mistake again.

Chapter Three

N icholas climbed into the carriage. Thankfully, Opal had possessed the good sense to pull the drapery on the windows closed, leaving only a crack to allow light to pass into the spacious cab. Though how much of that had to do with wanting their meeting to take place shrouded in privacy, and how much of it had to do with the fact the dim light helped hide the signs of aging that had begun to creep up, he couldn't say.

The past year had not been kind to her. He had never thought much about the gap in their ages until the veneer began to crack. And while Opal remained a beautiful and seductive woman, her standing had slipped significantly since the late Earl of Glenmor's death. Now, younger women of her chosen profession took advantage of her downfall and climbed upward, overtaking her. A reality Opal could not avoid, and yet she fought it tooth and nail with a stark desperation Nicholas found most telling.

Her days were numbered. Without a protector and with limited funds, she would be left destitute and alone. Perhaps he should feel sorry for her, but Opal had made her bed and for years, she had been content to lie in it. Let her do so now when the sheets were stained with the blood of her actions. It served her right. Nicholas would reserve his compassion for those who truly deserved it. Like the Laythams.

"What do you want?" He didn't bother with a polite preamble. They were well past that.

She smiled at him; a coquettish smile that had worked once, but now left him cold. Seeing it held no sway, she packed it away and her hazel eyes turned hard.

"I sent you an invitation. The key was to be delivered to number eighty-seven yesterday."

The key. He gritted his teeth. She could not seriously think— But no. Of course, she would. Opal did not slink away in defeat. She had licked her wounds for a sufficient amount of time and had come out swinging. She was a survivor if nothing else and she needed to court the good favor of those amongst the ton who craved the services her key parties provided, no doubt hoping to find a new protector in their midst.

"I have no interest in your invitation, Opal. I believe I have made myself perfectly clear in that regard. Either way, I have received no key."

Nor did he care to, but he did not say this aloud. The cold tone of his voice conveyed his thoughts well enough.

"I know you didn't," Opal said. Her tongue flicked out and touched her bottom lip before she dragged the plump flesh slowly between her teeth. "There was a slight mix up."

He did not like the sound of that. Still, he failed to see what it had to do with him.

"Mix up?"

"Percy resigned his position. I've had to employ a new man."

It didn't surprise him. Nicholas had heard through the grapevine Opal's sudden lack of income had forced her to tighten her purse strings, a situation that must have had her seeing red. She loved her little luxuries. But with no gentleman to pay for them, the expensive retainers she'd once held in abundance had soon been let go, or left of their own accord, leaving her with a skeleton staff.

"I care little about your staffing issues, Opal. Or your parties. As far as I am concerned this conversation, and any further need we might once have had to see each other, has ended."

Nicholas leaned forward to open the door and usher her out of his carriage, but before he could grip the handle, Opal's thin fingers wound around his wrist.

"I think you will find this of interest."

Nicholas froze. He recognized the mercenary gaze in Opal's eyes. He had seen it directed at him enough times, although at the time it had been tempered by carnal pleasure. Now...now it was filled with something else. Something he couldn't name.

Or didn't want to.

It made his blood run cold.

"What is it?"

"My new man is not as learned as I would like. But this is what one is forced to employ when one does not have the means to do better." The unspoken accusation, as if somehow this was his fault, rested heavy in the air. "You see, my man delivered the key not to number eighty-seven, but to number seventy-eight."

The drink Nicholas had consumed only moments earlier soured in his gut.

Number seventy-eight.

The Laythams.

He willed his guilt back. This was not his problem. Besides, the new Lord Glenmor had never been to any of the parties Nicholas had frequented. He didn't seem the sort to revel in such debauchery. Then again, neither had the previous Lord Glenmor. But it wasn't debauchery that had sent the late Lord Glenmor to Opal's bed, was it? No. It had been, of all things, love.

"How does this affect me?"

"How it affects you is this—" Opal smiled, but no such warmth lingered in the depths of her eyes. She was the Cheshire cat, canary feathers poking out from a wide, sensual mouth. He pulled his arm away from her touch.

"Someone returned the RSVP." When one accepted the invitation, they simply dropped the numbered tag into an envelope and returned it to the address written upon it. "At first I thought you had finally come to your senses and realized this life of propriety was not for you."

She tossed out the word propriety as if it left a bad taste in her mouth. The illegitimate daughter of a baron and a French courtesan, Opal held the ton in contempt, yet at the same time, she craved their acceptance. An acceptance that would never come.

"I have no intention of returning to my old life." He couldn't afford to. His conscience would no longer allow it.

"You may want to change your mind. You see, I don't believe it was the young Lord Glenmor who returned the invitation. More's the pity." She pouted. "He's a most handsome man. I would have welcomed him most warmly."

Heat rose up Nicholas's neck. He wanted to reach out and grab his former mistress by the throat. Had she not brought enough pain and suffering down upon the Laythams?

"Leave that family be."

Her smile increased yet again. "It is hardly my fault that one of them accepted the invitation."

His heart pounded in his chest, yet his skin turned cold. "Who?"

"It was a ladies' maid. Miss Abigail Laytham's maid, to be exact. My man recognized her when she came to the door."

Nicholas shook his head. "You lie."

Opal laughed, a light, airy sound underscored by a throaty nuance. "Rumor has it, Miss Laytham is expected to marry Lord Tarrington. Perhaps she wants to be bedded by a real man before submitting to some doddering old fool's fumbling attempts to breed an heir. Whatever her reasons, she will be arriving at my soiree in two nights hence."

P reparations kept Abigail busy over the next two days while nerves kept her stomach twisted into a tight knot. A part of her could not believe she had decided to do something so daring, so crazy, so...so...scandalous! For her to even be caught walking past Madame St. Augustine's home would be enough to set tongues wagging. For the past eight months, her family's every move had been watched and analyzed and whispered about until no one but Benedict dared even leave the house most days. The confinement had driven Abigail to the brink of madness. When she'd finally convinced Caelie to join her in the park, however, she'd only managed to make more of a spectacle.

Aunt Edythe continued to demand they retire to the country, though whether she meant for good or only for a little while was difficult to determine. Thankfully, Benedict had let the country estate out to a gaudy American family to help pay expenses, and the other three estates to lesser-noted families with larger coffers than theirs. They had nowhere else to go, trapping them in London for the time being. The news did not sit well with Aunt Edythe. Abigail almost wished they could have sent her aunt to the country. Her grim demeanor had grown even more hostile since Uncle Henry's death. She possessed the ability to suck the joy out of a room simply by walking into it.

Abigail could not help the uncharitable thought. As much as Uncle Henry had welcomed her family into his home with open arms, Aunt Edythe had never warmed to them. If anything, she seemed to resent their very existence. Worse still, she treated her own daughter with bitter indifference for not being born a son. What a humiliation it must be for her to find herself at the mercy of Benedict's good favor now that he was the new Earl of Glenmor. Not that he would ever turn her away. She was Caelie's mother, after all.

She had hoped time would cause the ton to forget about her family and move onto other things. It hadn't.

Oh, there were other scandals to grab their notice. The Duke of Franklyn had caught his duchess in a rather compromising position with Lord Huntsleigh, and Miss Shelton had run off with her father's coachman, reaching Gretna Green before anyone could stop them. Unfortunately, none of these scandals refocused the ton's attention for more than a week before it swung back onto them.

But enough was enough. Abigail refused to hide any longer, to scurry away like a cockroach from the light. She had done nothing wrong. Her family had done nothing wrong. Even Uncle Henry, who had taken up with a mistress of infamous ill repute, had done nothing out of the ordinary. Plenty of gentlemen of the ton had mistresses. Her uncle's only mistake was falling in love with his. Was Abigail to fault him for that? Was she to sit back and allow his memory to be destroyed because his heart led him astray?

"Can I do nothing to talk you out of this?" Caelie asked, sitting on Abigail's bed. She had tried to be the voice of reason for the past two days to no avail, but Abigail had made her decision. It was fraught with danger, but she had to at least try, didn't she? Was it not providence that had shined down upon them when the key had been inadvertently delivered to their door, beckoning her to take up the charge?

"Nothing will go wrong, Caelie. Please do not fret."

In truth, any number of things could go wrong. She must travel to an end of town most ladies of quality would not be caught dead in. And she traveled alone, unless one counted the driver of the hired hansom cab. She risked being recognized despite the trouble she had taken to ensure her face and hair well covered. It was a dangerous quest, but the only chance she had to confront Lord Roxton. She must take it.

"What if one of the men propositions you?"

Abigail leaned forward and peered into the mirror over her vanity. She adjusted the mask covered everything but her mouth and chin. It was encrusted with pearls and feathers flowed up and away from its edges. A tight chignon kept her hair in place and Muri pinned more long feathers, these ones red, into her hair until barely any of her blonde locks showed through.

"Caelie, we have gone over this. I will simply tell him I am not interested."

"You are at a party where being interested is your only reason for being there. You don't think it will look suspicious if you behave otherwise?"

The idea of being propositioned by a handsome gentleman did hold a certain amount of thrill to it. She stood on the precipice of a future with Lord Tarrington, who cared little for her beyond her ability to produce heirs. The thought of him touching her made her skin crawl. Their marriage would never be a love match, or hold anything resembling warmth and affection. Much like Uncle Henry and Aunt Edythe's marriage and look what misery that had produced.

Would it be so wrong if she indulged in just one passionate kiss before—

"Abby? Abby, are you even listening to me?"

Abigail shook her head and blinked at the masked reflection in the mirror. A flush had spread across her chest—a chest that revealed enough cleavage to send her mother into a deep, wailing swoon. Which was saying something given her mother had never swooned a day in her life. Nor wailed for that matter. Not even during the worst of it, when Papa and Roddy were taken by the fever, and they'd lost their home forcing Benedict to beg shelter with Papa's estranged family.

"Of course, I'm listening." Abigail pushed the dark thoughts away. She rarely let them out. The pain and guilt of being the one who'd brought the sickness into their home was too great. "You do not have to worry, Caelie. If a gentleman propositions me, I shall simply tell him he is not to my liking. Or that I am waiting on someone else." Not a complete untruth, since Lord Roxton was the only one she wished to see.

And kissing him was the furthest thing from her mind.

Abigail stepped away from the vanity and picked up the hooded black cape draped across her bed, settling it about her shoulders. Only a hint of red silk peeked out from the bottom. It was a bold choice, with the deep claret setting off the paleness of her skin. The dress had been one of Caelie's, purchased shortly after her engagement to Lord Billingsworth as part of her trousseau. When he broke it off, the dress had gone into her wardrobe and had not come back out.

Until now.

Muri had made a few modifications to the dress to remove the lacing around the neckline, leaving it to plunge dangerously low. Abigail feared she might spill out of it given how tightly Muri had laced her stays, forcing what cleavage she had upward. She had to force herself to not check repeatedly to affirm everything remained in place.

"How do I look?"

"You look beautiful. Scandalous." Defeat slumped Caelie's shoulders. "I still wish you would reconsider this folly."

"It is not folly. It is a chance for us to reclaim our lives," Abigail assured her. "I have taken great pains to disguise myself. Have I not succeeded?"

Caelie sighed. "Yes, I suppose you have."

"Good. Now I must go."

Arrangements had been made for the driver to wait two houses away. Abigail would slip out the servants' entrance and keep to the shadows as best she could. At this time of night, the streets were quiet and chances of running into anyone she knew were slim to none. But she had to be careful no one spied her from their windows, and if they did, that they thought her a servant, and not a member of the family.

Abigail pulled the hood of her cape over her head, careful not to crush the feathers. "Everything will be fine, Caelie. Do not fret. The next time you see me, Lord Roxton will have agreed to make amends and our family will be well on its way to regaining our good name."

"Or you will be steeped in regret," her cousin warned. "Believe me when I tell you that is not something so easily washed away."

"I will not fail." She could not. "Please, will you not wish me luck?"

Caelie grasped both of Abigail's hands tightly in her own, giving her a meaningful look. "I will wish you safe return."

N icholas had no intention of going to Opal's party. That part of his life had ended and he was content to let it go. Content to give up passion for propriety. Desire for duty.

He needed none of that.

It did not matter if his body cried out in denial and his needs went unfulfilled, keeping him up at all hours of the night, leaving him no other alternative but to satisfy himself, which proved no satisfaction at all. He craved the warmth of another body. A body ripe with feminine curves, scented with roses or jasmine or lavender. Skin so soft it was like silk against his touch. Full lips that would take him in—

He groaned and rested his head against the windowpane. It did little to cool the heat pooling in his groin. Damn Opal for putting even the slightest hint of an idea in his head. For reminding him of the way his life used to be, where his every sexual whim was satisfied.

He did not want her. Of that, he had no doubts. But he could not deny he longed for the fulfillment he found in the arms of a woman. At least physically. There had been no fulfillment beyond emotionally. Nor had Nicholas looked for any. He'd had that once. Or thought he had. But Lord Glenmor had taken it away, refusing to consider a match between his niece and a man of his questionable parentage and rakish reputation.

Granted, he had not always behaved the proper gentleman. He had sown his wild oats and had a good time doing so, especially when his behavior sent Lord Blackbourne into fits. But he suspected it was not his rakish behavior the late earl had taken true exception to, but rather the whispers that his claim to the Blackbourne title came to him only by default. When it came down to it, Glenmor did not want his beloved niece affianced to a man who was, in effect, a bastard.

The rejection had cut deep. The succor he found in Opal's bed had been part sexual release and part retaliation. Lord Glenmor had taken something from him—no, *someone*—he had truly wanted. And in turn, Nicholas thought it only fair to repay him in kind and steal his mistress. He had enjoyed the game in the beginning; it diverted his thoughts from the loss of Miss Laytham's company.

Though near the end—

Nicholas shook his head and pulled it away from where it rested on the window, looking through the paned glass. Near the end, winning Opal became a hollow victory, leaving him empty. But instead of walking away, he spiraled downward. Bitterness twisted around his heart and any goodness Miss Laytham had once coaxed out of him became lost in the darkness of his soul.

A flash of movement caught his attention farther down the street. Nicholas trained his gaze near the corner of the street. He could see the Laythams' house clearly, a beacon in the night mocking him, reminding him of everything he'd lost and all he'd destroyed. He could not escape it, nor did he try.

It was his penance to bear.

And because of that, he stood at his window tonight, waiting.

The movement came again. Nicholas squinted and leaned forward until his forehead touched the glass. A hansom cab waited near the corner.

There!

His heart shuddered to a stop. He had hoped it had been nothing more than a ploy to lure him back, but—

No. He glanced back at the Laythams' house, then to the pathway where the movement occurred.

"No," he whispered. "No, no, no. Don't do it."

The lithe figure climbed into the hansom cab and a moment later the carriage pulled away. One of the ladies in the Laytham household had accepted the invitation. And Nicholas had no doubt as to which one it was. Lady Caelie barely showed her face in public any longer, a mere shadow of her former vibrancy. No, it was Miss Laytham. It had to be. Only she would be so bold as to take such a risk. But why?

What was she about, going where no innocent lady of quality should be seen? And whether or not she would return an innocent, was a different question entirely.

"Dammit!"

He strode to the bell pull and rang for his valet. It appeared as though he would be going out this evening after all.

Chapter Four

ntry into the party proved a simple affair. One merely inserted the key into the front door and entered a small vestibule. There, a large, towering man with ebony skin greeted Abigail. He took the key from her and, with a sweeping gesture, silently ushered her into the inner sanctum.

The hum of conversation greeted her arrival, punctuated with raucous laughter and the clinking of glasses. Somewhere in the background, a quartet of strings played a bawdy tune she doubted would ever be heard at Almack's.

She stepped a little farther into the main room, skirting the crowd. The room was extravagantly appointed, if rather gauchely decorated. Hints of shabbiness, however, were evident. Little telltale signs betrayed the truth, that the owner was not quite as flush as she may appear on the surface, such as the ill-fitted livery worn by the servants that were obviously handed down and not custom cut.

The rooms were all connected and Abigail, making a cursory check for Lord Roxton in one and not finding him, simply moved from one into the next.

Her nerves balanced on a jagged edge, waiting for someone to find her out, to realize she did not belong here. But so far, she'd been left alone, though the looks she received from some of the men present as she walked about let her know she was not invisible.

She tugged self-consciously at the bodice of her dress, wishing she had not allowed Muri to lower it to such a degree, or cinch her stays so tightly her normally small chest practically popped up to twice its normal dimensions. Despite her disguise, she felt hideously exposed. Did no one worry their secret would be revealed? Then again, perhaps it served in everyone's best interest to turn a blind eye. After all, the success of these parties depended upon their secrecy and discretion. Anyone could expose anyone else at any time, and vice versa. Perhaps the threat of retaliation kept everyone from wagging their tongues. In order to acknowledge you knew of someone else's attendance, you would have to reveal your own.

Still, knowing this did little to ease Abigail's misgivings. Most men had dressed as either a pirate or a highwayman, just as Muri predicted. Some wore basic black silk masks over their nose and eyes; others wore extravagant headpieces that made Abigail's feathery confection look positively dull in comparison.

How in the world was she to pick out Lord Roxton? Her confidence dimmed. She had been certain she would simply *know*, but now she wasn't so sure. Oh, some men were easy to rule out as candidates. Several were overly rotund, their need for indulgence obviously extending beyond their amorous appetites. Others were simply too short, or too thin, or too tall. In fact, there were very few that appeared to possess the combined assets of broad shoulders, trim hips and long, muscular legs of Lord Roxton.

And those that did had disguised themselves so well, she couldn't see beyond their masks and head coverings to determine if their hair held the inky blackness of Lord Roxton's. Or the small dimple in his left cheek.

What if—

No. She shook her head, refusing to finish the thought. For if Lord Roxton had in fact chosen not to attend, then she...well, she was the biggest fool of all, wasn't she? Risking her reputation, and that of her family's, for nothing.

A wrinkle of disquiet rippled across her conviction. Why hadn't she listened to Caelie's counsel? Why must she always act so rashly? And why in heaven's name wasn't Lord Roxton here? She had been so certain his recent behavior had all been for show. Leopards did not change their spots...did they?

Abigail grabbed a glass of champagne as a tray passed by her line of vision. The bubbly liquid made her want to sneeze as she downed it quickly with several large gulps. Her mother would be horrified. Then again, if her mother knew where she was, gulping champagne would be the least of her worries.

The thought of facing Mother if she was discovered made her reach for yet another glass. This one went down much smoother than the last. A giddy warmth crept over her, bringing with it the boldness she had lacked since handing her key to the large footman and stepping into this den of inequity.

She could do this. She straightened her backbone, a move- ment that caused her chest to jut out at a precarious angle. Lord Roxton had to be here. She couldn't be wrong. Too much rode on her success. She would simply have to take another turn through the rooms and—

"Oh!"

A firm hand on her elbow interrupted her newly formed bravado and propelled her from the room.

"Come with me," a dark voice growled near her ear.

Abigail glanced up, trying to identify her kidnapper, but he hurried her along a dimly lit hallway and she had to keep her eyes forward to prevent herself from stumbling over the hem of her dress.

But that didn't mean her vocal cords could not be put to good use. "What do you think—"

"Hush," the voice whispered harshly, direct and forceful. He manipulated her up a narrow staircase to the third floor.

"Take your hands off me. You have no right to—"

The hand in question spun her around to face him, but the sparse candlelight from a distant wall sconce wavered, casting murky shadows over the dark figure looming above her. Like the others, he wore a mask, black silk that left only his mouth exposed. A matching black scarf covered most of his hair, which in the poor lighting could have been anywhere from brown to black to dark blonde. Unrelenting black made up the rest of his outfit, right down to his cravat and shirt collar.

He reminded her of a well-dressed pirate.

"Is this not what you came for?" He leaned in closer and pressed her back into the wall. His voice was low and husky like a whisper dragged over a rough surface.

"To be manhandled? Certainly not!" She struggled against him, but she might as well have pushed against a brick wall.

"No?" His voice slithered over her as his arm came around her. She froze. Was that footsteps she heard in the stairwell? She wasn't sure what frightened her more. The man who held her, or the threat of being found in such a compromising position. Should she call out for help?

Something clicked behind her and the wall fell away. She stumbled backward and would have fallen had he not caught her in his arms and pulled her against him.

The door shut behind him and locked with an unmistakable click.

Abigail's heart accelerated and all the warnings Caelie had given her raged in her ears, berating her stupidity at thinking such a thing would not happen. No light penetrated the room. Only a small fire burned in the hearth as if someone had been expecting them. Its meager glow did not reach far enough to give her any hint to her captor's identity as he kept to the shadows.

"Then why did you come here? Did you think to sneak in and see what all the fuss was about?"

Her brain sputtered. What could she tell this man without giving herself away? "I was invited."

"Were you now?"

A shiver coursed through her. Something about his voice... a strange accent she couldn't place. It mesmerized her. She suddenly wished she had not imbibed the second glass of champagne. It made her head fuzzy and her thinking muddled.

He took a step closer. His broad shoulders blocked the door.

"I—I am looking for someone."

He stopped, remaining in shadow. "Indeed? And who is it you're looking for? Or will anyone do?"

"Anyone—? No! You misunderstand. I am not here for *that*." She could not even say the word, and though she knew he could not tell through the darkness and the coverage of her mask, her face flamed. No doubt if she were to look in a mirror, she would find her skin matched the color of her gown. She took a deep breath to calm herself. She must keep her wits about her. "I am looking for Lord Roxton. That is what I'm doing here."

The man had started toward her but stopped at her announcement. His boot hit the floor with a thud.

"I beg your pardon?"

Abigail swallowed. Her answer had stolen the wind from the pirate's sails. Likely one did not speak names in such a place, but he'd left her little choice. "Lord Roxton. I am here to speak to Lord Roxton."

Outside, clouds shifted and moonlight filtered through the cracks in the heavy drapes, cutting a shard of light across the man's chest.

"Is he a particular friend of yours?"

Abigail choked back a cutting response. It would be in her best interests if he thought she was a particular friend of Lord Roxton's. If he believed such, he would be less likely to accost her for fear of reprisal. And it wasn't a complete lie. For a brief moment in time, they had been friends. Perhaps even a bit more.

"Yes, he is. I am to meet him here."

"Are you now?" The doorknob rattled. "Ssh," he commanded but Abigail had already clamped a hand over her mouth.

It rattled again then fell silent. She had no idea how long she stood frozen in the spot until her captor let out a long breath and spoke again in his strange accent. "If you are here to meet with Lord Roxton, then you are to be disappointed. Roxton declined the invitation."

Abigail shook her head, and then remembered the man could not see her clearly in the dark. "That's impossible." Well, perhaps not impossible, but highly improbable. It was Lord Roxton, after all. Consummate debaucher. Rakehell of the first order. A man with no conscience.

"It is not. Lord Roxton has turned his back on such things. He is determined to become a respectable gentleman."

She answered with an inelegant snort of disbelief. "Oh, please!"

The sliver of moonlight showed the shrug of the man's shoulders. "It is true."

"I do not believe you. Now, if you will kindly escort me back to the main rooms, I will continue my search."

"I cannot do that."

"You cannot—why?" Fear beat a hasty path up her spine. Behind her, the fire hissed and dimmed, conspiring with the darkness.

The man hesitated. "I will escort you to your carriage. It is not safe for you here."

"Not safe?" She really did need to stop repeating what the man said. She might as well be a parrot perched on his shoulder to complete his ensemble.

"You do not belong here." His words were clipped with anger.

What did he care about where she belonged?

"Of course, I do." But the words rang false even to her. The stranger took a step closer. His commanding presence enveloped the air around her. He had the strength and size to do to her what he wished.

"Do you know the pleasures sought here? The depths of depravity some will sink to within these walls?"

Her face reached a new level of heat. "I...I..."

His height forced her gaze upward in an attempt to see him, though he had stepped outside the shard of moonlight and was now little more than an opaque shadow.

What to do? Should she try to beat a hasty retreat? Scream for help? If she did, would anyone come to her aid? Whoever had been at the door was now long gone and she somehow doubted she would find a white knight in the crowd below.

"What are you going to do to me?" She tried not to fidget or show fear, but her heart pounded in her chest. Could he hear it?

"What do you want me to do?" His voice slid over her like liquid heat.

Caelie's warnings resurrected in her head, but none of Abigail's pithy responses applied. That had all been in theory, an intangible what if. But there was nothing theoretical about what was happening now. This went far beyond her experience. She stepped back until her bottom bumped against a hard surface. "I do not know." And she didn't. She had no idea.

Part of the entire situation excited her, which was utterly ridiculous. She should fear for her innocence, her very life even. She did not know this man. But while he possessed a dangerous edge, he had not hurt her. In truth, he had encouraged her to leave and even offered to see her safely home. Perhaps her current whereabouts skewed her judgment—she had, after all, thought coming here a grand idea—but she did not think the man meant to harm her.

He grabbed her wrist and pulled her toward him, eliciting a shocked gasp. "You should not be here, you little fool."

She jerked her arm from his hold and indignation lifted her chin. What right did he have to chastise her? He knew nothing about her. Nothing about the wrongs she needed to right. "I beg your pardon. I have a key."

His sensuous mouth pulled into a tight line. "Indeed. And how did you come to possess this key?"

"It was sent to me. I—I was invited. Just as you were."

She had not stepped away from him. The virile scent of masculinity and tangible hint of the outdoors clung to his skin.

"I doubt that."

"Well, if you do not want me here, then why do you have me cornered in this room?"

He did not answer her. "Is your innocence such an expendable commodity that you are willing to throw it away?"

"How dare you!" Such things were not discussed, especially not with strange men in dark rooms. She quickly turned a blind eye to the irony of that thought, given she shouldn't be in a dark room with a strange man to begin with.

"How dare I? How dare you, to come in here as if this

were some game. What did you hope to accomplish here tonight?"

Fear was quickly giving way to irritation. "I told you I came to meet Lord Roxton."

Nicholas gritted his teeth at her stubborn refusal to leave. It took every ounce of will to control his anger. At her foolishness. At himself. She had no idea what could happen to her here. Innocence was not something that passed through these doors. The men here would see her reticence as some kind of coquettish game, and not one that would end well in her favor. He had barely gotten her inside the room before Opal reached the top of the stairs. He knew it was she. The scent of her perfume was unmistakable. He didn't want to think what would have happened if she had discovered them together. Or worse, cornered Miss Laytham alone.

He glared down at her. She stood in the thin pool of moonlight and its soft light illuminated the contours of her jaw, her generous mouth. Even dressed as she was, she stood out in this crowd of fallen women, widows, and unhappy wives. Her virtue shone like a beacon through the mire of desperation where pleasure was a game and innocence held no value.

And she had come here because of him.

How was he to get her out without making a scene or revealing his own identity? Or worse, before Opal returned with the key to this room.

Opal blamed Abigail's uncle for her own downfall. His death at one of her parties had sent her worth among the demimonde spiraling downward. She cared little for Glenmor while he lived, outside of what he could provide for her, and she had not softened in this regard after his passing. The glee she had taken when telling Nicholas that a member of the Laytham family planned on attending her party made that obvious. As if their presence validated the late Lord Glenmor's own debauchery and absolved her from any responsibility in his death.

"As I told you, Lord Roxton no longer attends these parties." He struggled to keep his tone modulated, using an accent so she wouldn't recognize his voice.

"I find that very hard to believe. Lord Roxton lacks the morals required to give up his wickedness. This newfound sense of propriety is nothing more than a sham."

Her low opinion did not surprise him. What surprised him was how much it still stung. He had courted her, thought he had won her good favor, only to be told by her uncle any proposal he offered would not be considered. He was not a suitable candidate for Miss Laytham.

He—a future earl, a peer of the realm—was not good enough for the only daughter of a youngest son and a vicar's daughter, both of whom had been disowned by their families when they'd wed.

The set down had galled him. How could he have ever known his bruised ego would lead to such tragedy? He had wanted to hurt Lord Glenmor and he had succeeded. But he had hurt Miss Laytham in the process, as well as the rest of her family who were nothing more than innocent bystanders in the whole debacle.

Could he just stand by now and allow the Laythams to be dealt another blow should she be discovered here?

No, not if he held the power to stop it.

"Come, I am getting you out of here." He reached for her arm but she evaded him.

"No. I came here of my own free will, invited, and I will not leave until I have done what I came here to do."

"Lord Roxton is not here." He bit out. Did her stubbornness know no bounds? "There is nothing else—"

"Then I will stay for...for...pleasure." The word burst out of her and hurtled toward him.

"Pleasure? Are you mad?"

Could pleasure be found here? Certainly. But not the kind she sought. Her virginal mind could not even begin to comprehend what passed for pleasure here. For once one reached a certain level of gratification, it became passé, and one had to struggle to find a new level. In the beginning it had been a game, a great way to bury one's injured pride and wounded heart, but eventually...

Nicholas shook his head. He would not let her go there.

"Why not? I am to marry a man three times my age. He is dull and old and...and old!" She shivered. "If Lord Roxton is not here, then perhaps I shall wait until he arrives, for I am certain he will, despite what you say. In the meantime, why shouldn't I see what all the fuss is about? Wouldn't you want to know at least a little passion before you were consigned to a life without it?"

Her words hit their mark, though she would never know. Marriage to Miss Caldwell would serve a purpose, but that purpose had nothing to do with passion. He had turned his back on that part of his life before it destroyed anyone else.

"The kind of passion you seek will not be found here."

"How could you possibly know what I seek?" She pulled her shoulders back and stuck her stubborn little nose into the air in a show of bravado so false it would have been laughable under different circumstances.

Weariness seeped into his bones. By all rights she should have run long ago, not stood there and argued with him. But Miss Laytham had never been faint of heart. He had admired that about her once. Now it proved a great impediment.

"You want hearts and romance and love. But such things

do not exist within these four walls. The pleasure found here is desperate and depraved, doled out by men and women who have lost touch with anything of value, including themselves. Is that what you want?"

"I—" She stopped, wavered.

"Trust me."

"Trust you," she scoffed, in a tone he had become all too familiar with. "I don't even know you. You've pulled me into this room, insist I leave, and why? What do you care? You do not know me. Perhaps I am one of those desperate and depraved."

"You are not—"

She cut him off. "I came here to speak to Lord Roxton and I am not leaving until I convince him—"

Nicholas growled. He'd have better luck reasoning with a mule. He reached out and grabbed her around the waist. With one quick movement, he yanked her against him. "This is what is waiting for you out there."

She let out a gasp before he captured her mouth in his. Her hands fisted into the silk of his shirt. Her body molded to his, fitting perfectly against his burgeoning erection, the one that had begun the moment he'd stepped close enough to revel in her sweet scent. She reminded him of a meadow imbued with the promise of spring and awaiting full bloom.

Pain fused with pleasure. He wanted her, had wanted her since the moment he saw her at her coming out four years ago. He had bided his time, then, not yet ready to give up his wild ways, but by her second Season he could no longer resist her allure. The other women he knew paled in comparison to her spirited nature. He courted her in earnest and soon discovered she had been more than worth the wait. Sweet and sharp, bold and intelligent. A woman well worth giving up all others for.

It had all been for naught. Even after Glenmor had refused him, he had thought Miss Laytham would argue on his behalf and change her uncle's mind. But as the days passed and no word came, he realized he had overestimated her feelings.

He deepened the kiss, expecting her to shove him away. Slap him. Finally see reason and demand he escort her from this horrid place.

She did none of those things.

Instead, she tried to keep up with the hunger of his kiss. Something in the way she innocently bumbled her way through it touched him. Deeply. In a place he no longer thought available to him. And that was most surprising of all.

Instinctively, he gentled the kiss. He had meant to punish, to teach. To frighten. The lesson he'd meant to teach her had turned on its ear, and he realized he still had much to learn. The control he'd thought he possessed over his passions dangled from a tenuous string, and this woman—this woman that reviled him—plucked it until it vibrated painfully, bringing all his nerves to life.

If he had any sense at all, he would let her go. End this.

But he had no sense. Not where she was concerned.

He explored the confines of her sweet mouth with his tongue. She tasted of champagne. Heat seared through him as she tentatively did the same. Soft and willing as a courtesan, what she lacked in skill, she made up for with innocent exuberance.

He had meant to frighten her. Instead, he was the one who was frightened. By his body's response to her, by how good it felt to hold her in his arms, by the intoxicating feel of her body pressed against his own.

He had once dreamed of this. Once, a long time ago.

Much had changed since then.

With great reluctance, he lifted his mouth from hers, stopping only to drop one last, quick kiss on her swollen lips. He reached up and straightened her mask their passion had knocked askew. "Forgive me."

For a long moment, she said nothing. He stood silently, still holding her, feeling the vibrations of their heartbeats where their bodies met. She had been as affected as he by the rush of passion that had burned between them, a truth that offered him little solace.

"I will see you to your carriage," he said.

Still, she did not move. After a quiet moment, she spoke. "Are you married, my lord?"

The question surprised him. For a brief moment, he had forgotten she did not know who he was. The fact she did not know who she had kissed saddened him. "No."

"When you do marry, do you expect to have an affection for your wife?"

He thought of Miss Caldwell, her perfect beauty, her perfect manners, and her perfect sense of propriety.

"No," he finally answered. He did not love Eugenie Caldwell. He did not even know if he liked her. He did not know her at all. How did you get to know someone when they kept all conversations to topics so banal, they lacked any interest or depth?

"No," she echoed. "But I suppose it is different for men, isn't it? You can marry and seek your pleasure elsewhere if you so wish."

He shrugged. "As could you. Taking a lover is not the sole providence of men." He thought of his mother, but quickly pushed the thought away.

"Perhaps not." She shifted in his arms. He longed to catch a glimpse of her pale blue eyes, to know what she thought, felt. "I do not intend to do so. When I take my vows, I mean to honor them. But I have not taken them as yet. I have made no promises to anyone."

His heart thudded painfully in his chest. What was she saying?

"Do you swear to me Lord Roxton will not be attending this evening?"

"Yes," he lied.

A small puff of air escaped her and her body sagged in his arms. "How do you know? Who are you?"

He could not tell her. She hated him, despised his very existence. If she knew whose arms held her, whose mouth she had kissed with such passion, she would never forgive herself.

Or him.

"You know I cannot say."

"Then tell me this and be truthful—did you feel it when we kissed? Did it not feel...magical? Or is that always the way?"

He lifted his hand and touched her face. Such innocence. His thumb trailed along the line of her lower lip. He could not help himself. She trembled beneath his touch. "No. It is not always like this."

He should have lied again, but the words would not come. It had been magical. And foolish. And a million other things. It was like nothing he had ever experienced before.

"I thought not." Then, almost sadly, she whispered, "I quite liked it."

He closed his eyes. He played with fire. He must convince her to leave before he debased them both.

"Please allow me to escort you to your carriage. You must leave here. Whatever your intention in meeting with Lord Roxton, you will not meet with success. Not here. Not tonight. I know a back way out. You can leave the premises and no one will be the wiser."

Why had she wanted to meet him? And why here of all places? But he could not ask her. Not without forcing her to reveal her identity, and he would not do that. Her name must never be spoken within these walls. There were too many ears. But if he expected her to slink away in defeat, he was wrong.

"I will leave on one condition."

Relief rushed through him. He wanted her out of here then he wanted a very large, stiff drink to cool the heated ardor burning through his veins. Oh, how Spence would laugh to see him now, brought down by an innocent in the most debauched of places.

"What condition?"

A bead of sweat made a hasty path down his spine. Please do not let it be another kiss. Should his lips touch hers again he did not think he possessed the power to stop it there. Her effect on him proved too strong, too uncontrollable. He did not have enough goodness in him to combat it a second time, and not take everything it offered.

"Lord and Lady Doddington have their annual masquerade ball next week. Will you be attending?"

The masquerade was one of the last big fetes of the Season. He had received his invitation weeks ago. "I am not certain." A lie. Miss Caldwell had indicated to his father she looked forward to his attendance, and that had been the end of that.

"If you promise to attend, I will leave this place now."

"Why?"

She smiled slyly; he could hear it in her voice. "If you know Lord Roxton well enough to know he is not here tonight, despite everyone being in costume, then you should have no difficulty picking him out at the masquerade."

"Why is it so important for you to speak with him?" He could not hold the question back any longer. She had risked her reputation and her virtue to confront him here tonight. But why? What had she hoped to accomplish?

"I cannot say. It is a personal matter. Will you accept my condition?"

His mind worked furiously. It was dark; she did not know what he looked like. If she saw him at Lord and Lady Doddington's masquerade, likely she would look right through him and not even realize he was the man who'd kissed her senseless and longed for more.

"It is dark. You will not recognize me."

"But you will recognize me. You saw me before you pulled me into this room. I shall wear the same feathered plumage as tonight." The feathers brushed his chin as she looked down. "But not the same dress."

He issued a silent prayer of gratitude for small favors. He'd seen enough of her as she made her way through the rooms of Opal's home to bring his blood to a boil. It would not be wise to set her loose upon the ton where any slobbering idiot could ogle her at will. Inhibitions were notoriously lowered at such events. Masking one's face seemed a license for risqué behavior. A fact Opal understood and exploited to no end. "Very well," he agreed, hoping she could not detect the deception in his voice. "I accept your conditions."

Chapter Five

Abigail fingered the silk ribbon spread out on the table at Madame Gaston's. It matched the sapphire gown from two Seasons ago perfectly. The dress, though beautiful, needed to be updated.

"It's pretty," her mother said, coming up behind her. "You should buy it."

Abigail let out a slow breath. She had just enough pin money left for a length of ribbon to use along the hem of the dress. She had stopped taking an allowance from Benedict several months earlier. They had larger financial concerns than enhancing her wardrobe and she could not justify such frivolity in the face of their current situation. Better he used the money toward their uncle's debts. The amount she'd had left, she held onto religiously, determined to make it last and only use it for the most important of items.

Did this qualify?

"You will need to begin building a trousseau, Abigail," her mother continued. "I know we don't have much, but surely Benedict will allow you a few new items. After all, a bride cannot go into marriage without one."

Abigail scanned the shop. Thankfully, only a few patrons perused the fabrics, while one discussed design with the proprietor herself. Every now and again their gazes would flit toward her before racing away. "Lord Tarrington has not yet made an offer, Mother. And we cannot afford—"

"We will find a way, Abigail. It is the least we can do for you. Whether Lord Tarrington or another gentleman."

A mix of guilt and responsibility weighed upon her heart. Her family counted on her, and yet she knew they wished it otherwise. She could see the pain in her mother's eyes whenever the subject of her expected engagement to Lord Tarrington came up. Abigail did her best to convince her mother she wanted it, but they both recognized the lie, though neither chose to acknowledge it as such.

It was easier that way.

"The wardrobe I have is fine."

Her mother picked up the spool of ribbon from the table. "The wardrobe you have needs updating. I will not allow my only daughter to be shabbily dressed. You deserve more than—"

"Lorena?"

Her mother stopped mid-sentence and turned around. "Gloria..."

Abigail tried to get her mouth to work a proper greeting but her throat constricted and nothing came out. In front of her stood her arch-nemesis's mother, the beautiful Lady Blackbourne and her darkly stunning daughter, Lady Rebecca.

"It has been so long." Lady Blackbourne smiled, but pain glittered through her silvery eyes. Eyes identical to her son's save for the tender emotion Abigail saw there. Any emotion Lord Roxton exhibited was nothing more than a ruse. Something used to lure in unsuspecting young ladies before he broke their hearts.

"Indeed. Too long," her mother replied, surprising Abigail

with the tremor in her voice. Her mother was a pillar of strength. Always had been. From the time little Roddy and Papa had died, leaving her family without protection, to when she had brought them to Uncle Henry to start a new life, straight through the scandal her uncle's death had created. To see her now, on the verge of tears by a simple greeting...well, it only served to solidify how deep the damage Lord Roxton had wrought.

There had been a time when Lady Blackbourne and her mother had been particular friends. In fact, had it not been for Lady Blackbourne's friendship when they had first arrived in town, many of the ton would not have paid her family much heed at all. The ton had a long and lingering memory. They had not forgotten her mother was the daughter of a poor country vicar. Or that her father, Uncle Henry's youngest brother, had possessed the audacity to run off and marry her despite stringent family objections. But something about their story had touched Lady Blackbourne and she had reached out.

Had she not deigned to cultivate a friendship likely they would have remained on the outskirts of acceptability. Perhaps Uncle Henry's support and Benedict being set to inherit the earldom would have helped their cause, but who knew how long it would have taken. With Lady Blackbourne's help, they never had to learn.

But Lord Roxton had destroyed all of that.

In the beginning, the two women had tried to maintain their friendship while Uncle Henry and Lord Roxton battled for the affections and rights to Madame St. Augustine's bed, but eventually it became the elephant in the room. An elephant too large to ignore. Lady Blackbourne stopped coming by. As did most everyone else.

"We haven't been getting out much," Abigail stated flatly, her anger loosening the constriction on her throat and letting the words pass. In truth, other than the invitation to the

Doddingtons' masquerade, their social calendar remained dismally empty.

"Of course." Pink stained Lady Blackbourne's cheeks and Lady Rebecca glanced down at the floor. Too late, regret filled Abigail. That had been unkind. Lady Blackbourne had not been the one at fault.

"But we will be attending Lord and Lady Doddington's masquerade," Mother added, a proud lift to her chin.

Lady Blackbourne's smile, and her relief, gave her face vitality and enhanced her beauty. A beauty that still retained a strong, youthful quality. How young she must have been when she married the much older Lord Blackbourne. It made one wonder if there was truth to the rumor of her affair. Not that it mattered. Whether Lord Roxton was the true heir or not changed nothing. Where Lord Blackbourne recognized him as such, he would bear the title either way upon the earl's death.

"Rebecca and I will be attending as well."

"Perhaps we will see you there?" her mother asked, hope lighting her face.

Lady Blackbourne stepped forward, bridging the chasm between them and took Abigail's mother's hands in her own. "I would love that. I truly would."

As she watched Lady Blackbourne and her daughter leave the shop, a thought nudged her. If Lady Blackbourne planned to attend the masquerade, would Lord Roxton accompany them? If so, it would eliminate the need to meet up with her mystery man. Her shoulders drooped. She'd rather been looking forward to seeing him as more than a dark shadow.

Then again, Lady Blackbourne had not specifically said Lord Roxton would be there and therefore, it would be better to err on the side of caution and continue to enlist the help of said mystery man. Just in case.

She smiled and lost herself in the memory of his kiss while

Mother plied her with ribbons and excited chatter about renewing her friendship with an old friend.

N icholas let his gaze roam the sitting room while he waited for Miss Caldwell and her mother, the baroness, to arrive. His father had insisted he pay a visit, asserting he not neglect his duties to the young lady whose hand he planned on requesting in marriage. He was not to do anything to jeopardize his chances.

His father had far less faith in his abilities than Nicholas did. Though in truth, Miss Caldwell's acceptance of his proposal had absolutely nothing to do with his persuasive abilities and everything to do with his bank account—a bank account that had swelled considerably over the past several years. Despite his debauched lifestyle, he had paid particular interest to the markets and investments with Bowen's help and expertise. He'd had little choice.

While he would inherit the title and the entailed property upon his father's death, the bulk of the earl's unentailed estate would go to Rebecca. As it should be. She carried his blood after all.

Nicholas was just an interloper. A pretender to the crown.

"Roxton, my good man! They told me you had come to pay a visit. Keeping you waiting, are they?"

Lord Caldwell entered through the open door, his short, portly stature filling the room with a jovial air.

Nicholas stood and accepted the man's outstretched hand and friendly cuff to the shoulder. "Good afternoon, Caldwell. I thought I would drop by and pay my respects."

"Lovely to hear. Lovely to hear. Sit." He ushered Nicholas back into his seat and took the one across from him. He turned to their butler, Gordon. "Is someone coming with refreshments?"

"Right away, sir." Gordon inclined his bald head and disappeared in swift silence.

"The ladies are all a twitter about the masquerade, save for Rosalind who has made herself scarce," Lord Caldwell said. "I've been awash in talk of ribbons and frills and such for an entire week. It is nice to have another man about to converse with."

Nicholas didn't know how the baron did it. With a wife and three daughters, it was a wonder he remained sane. Or solvent. Then again, the last part was only partly true. Lord Caldwell struggled. With three dowries to supply and no son, he found himself in a bit of a pickle. He had to marry his daughters off to men of means to secure their futures. Yet he had not the means to procure such men.

Unless one of those men had buggered his own reputation to such a degree most parents corralled their daughters away from him, with only the most desperate considering him marriage material. While his title was impressive, it was well known that his sister would inherit the bulk of the fortune. Though the why of it remained a mystery to most.

But Caldwell was desperate. Despite his eldest daughter's much exalted reputation, she was still only the daughter of a baron. Her family had never amassed a fortune, never made a name for themselves. They had lived quietly and somewhat frugally and managed to get by.

Of course, all of the families before theirs had had sons. Lord Caldwell, an only child, had produced only daughters.

And daughters were, as any man knew, an expensive proposition.

The quiet swish of dresses and soft lilt of female voices preceded the women's entrance, giving the baron and Nicholas time to rise to their feet to greet them.

A close copy of her husband, small and portly, the baroness possessed a sense of jolliness their eldest daughter had not inherited.

Nicholas bowed slightly. "Lady Caldwell. Miss Caldwell. It is lovely to see you again. You both look particularly beautiful this afternoon."

Indeed, Miss Caldwell did. Her appearance was a study in perfection. That she was beautiful was never in question. In truth, she was quite stunning. Her dark hair and large brown eyes complimented her ivory skin. Only her mouth, slightly wider than fashion dictated, kept her from utter flawlessness. And yet no warmth lived within those features. Nothing welcomed a man in and made him feel he had found a home. Every attempt he had made to cultivate closeness had been rebuffed. She never looked at him as if she wanted him. Or even liked him.

He could have been anyone, so long as he came with a large enough purse.

Nicholas found it difficult to believe someone so beautiful could be so mercenary. Where she derived this particular trait from, he could not fathom. Neither parent appeared to possess it.

Then again, they had allowed him to court their daughter. Perhaps they simply hid it better than she.

"Shall I assume you will be attending Lord and Lady Doddington's masquerade, Lord Roxton?" The baroness asked him the question. Caldwell rolled his eyes and Nicholas struggled to suppress a grin.

"I have not yet decided." While he had promised he would be there, in retrospect, he'd been a fool to agree. He could not risk Miss Laytham discovering who he was. He certainly could not risk what the gossips would say if they were caught together. His father would pitch a fit. A wry smile twisted his lips. That alone would almost make it worth it.

"You find indecision amusing?" Miss Caldwell folded her hands in her lap, her own generous mouth turning up at the corners, though Nicholas would never go so far as to call it a smile. In retrospect, he wasn't sure he had ever seen her smile. Certainly not with the abandon Miss Laytham—

He cleared his throat. No. Best to stay off that particular road.

"Forgive me, Miss Caldwell. My mind merely entertained a thought that pleased me."

"I see."

This was not going well. Charming Miss Caldwell was akin to crossing frozen ice. One never knew if their next step would crack it and send them plunging into frigid water or if the ice would hold and see them safely to shore.

The thought of landing in water, brought forth another memory. A sodden Miss Laytham sitting at his feet staring up at him with a fiery anger that left little doubt in his mind as to what she thought. Though in truth, her thoughts were no more distracting than the soaked muslin clinging to her skin, or the plump lips pulled into a tight line of disapproval that begged to be kissed.

Lips he had kissed. Lips that tasted like an exotic fruit so sweet few words existed that could describe such a—

Nicholas slammed the door on the memory before evidence of what that kiss had done to him showed on his body, mortifying them all. He pulled his attention back to the situation at hand. He would not entertain thoughts of Miss Laytham. He no longer had that right. And if the late Lord Glenmor was to be believed, he never had.

He picked up the thread of their conversation. "What pleased me was the thought of seeing you at the masquerade. Your father tells me you and your sisters have been hard at work fashioning your costumes. I think that alone would be worth my attendance."

"Oh, how wonderful." The baroness clapped her hands and saved Nicholas from the frigid waters with the arrival of a steaming pot of tea. He relaxed. Marriage to Miss Caldwell would never be a comfortable existence but he could not withdraw now. His family would never forgive him. And he had much to atone for.

"Yes, wonderful indeed." He forced a smile.

Now he must attend this godforsaken masquerade, which he had dearly hoped to avoid, spend the evening doting on Miss Caldwell, while doing his best to avoid Miss Laytham. When in truth, he would much rather avoid Miss Caldwell, and spend the evening with Miss Laytham, sampling one or more of her delectable kisses.

So much for simplicity.

"Abigail, you must reconsider this. It is madness. You are playing with fire and yes, it seems exciting now, but eventually you will get burned. Honestly, I feel like a parrot!"

Caelie followed Abigail around the room as she ferreted through her armoire. The masquerade fast approached and she wanted—no needed—to look spectacular. She had to stand out among all the others so he could find her.

He. Him. Her mystery lover. Of course, it had never gone so far as that, it had just been a kiss after all. But oh, what a kiss it had been. She had never thought something as simple as two pairs of lips meeting in the dark could create such a thrill through every inch of her body. It had almost made her forget why she had gone there in the first place.

Almost. She'd remembered herself at the last moment and managed to convince the stranger to meet her once again.

Quite a brilliant piece of thinking, if she did say so herself. Though Caelie had other thoughts on the matter.

"Have you even stopped to consider why this man attended *that* party in the first place?"

Indeed, the thought had crossed her mind, but she chose not to explore it with any great depth. He'd been the perfect gentleman with her—well, almost. She smiled secretly as she pulled out a sage green silk that looked far better on Caelie than it ever had on her. In fact, when he'd warned her of what went on at such parties, he had sounded almost...disgusted. Angry.

"Are you listening to a word I am saying?" Caelie rounded to Abigail's left. She took the gown from her hands and tossed it back onto the bed.

Abigail shrugged. "Of course. Fire. Burning. Very bad things. Parrots. I have heard you, Caelie. I simply choose to take a different viewpoint."

"And that is?"

Abigail stopped for a moment and stared into space, trying to formulate something pithy that would convince her cousin she had not lost her mind. "Nothing ventured, nothing gained."

If Caelie found the humor in her flippancy, it did not show. "You do not know what you are doing. How can you be so cavalier about your reputation? You think it is something to play with, but I assure it is not. Once it is lost, it is lost forever, much like your innocence. And you will wish it back, I promise you. But there will be no retrieving it."

For an instant, Abigail thought Caelie spoke of herself, but she shook the idea away. Had Caelie ever done anything even remotely scandalous, Abigail would surely have known. She and her cousin had no secrets between them. Besides, as spirited as Caelie had once been, she would never do anything to risk her reputation. Not that it had mattered in the end.

Poor Caelie. At only two and twenty the life she had planned had come to a screeching halt, all her hopes and dreams thrown into the wind and scattered to the four corners. What would she do now; reduced to living as a captive in a town she could not escape, surrounded by people who no longer acknowledged her existence?

She had turned into a ghost. And Abigail would do anything to change that. Even if it destroyed her own reputation in the process. Her family was everything to her. There was no price so high she would not pay if it meant they could live easy once more.

Abigail took Caelie's hands in her own. "You're right, of course. And I promise I will take the utmost care to ensure nothing happens to damage my reputation. Or our family's. Yes, I kissed this man and perhaps I shouldn't have. And yes, it would be wonderful to be kissed like that again. But I shall not court disaster. I only wish to speak to Lord Roxton and convince him to publicly take the responsibility for what happened, so he carries the burden and not us. But I need this man's assistance to ferret him out from all the other masked gentlemen."

"And this stranger you kissed? What do you hope from him once he has pointed out Lord Roxton to you?"

Abigail pursed her lips. Were her secret desires so obvious? Perhaps she shouldn't have confided the kiss to Caelie, but it had been such an earth-shattering experience, she'd needed to tell someone, and she trusted no one as much as her cousin.

"I admit I would like to get to know the man behind the mask." She held up a hand when Caelie moved to protest. "It is foolish, I know. I am all but promised to Lord Tarrington. But I would be lying if I said the thought of spending the rest of my life in a loveless marriage with an old man didn't leave me cold. Is it truly such an awful thing to allow a few stolen kisses before my vows are spoken? To have the memory of such to sustain me through the years?"

"You will have your children to sustain you."

Abigail let go of Caelie's hand and returned to the armoire. "Lord Tarrington has already outlived two wives, neither of whom bore him any children. What if the problem is with him? What if I too, remain barren? Then not only have I given up passion, but nor will I have children to fill my days. I need something." She turned to face Caelie. "Can you not understand?"

Caelie bowed her head. A silken lock brushed against her cheek. "I do understand, Abigail. Believe me, I do. But I fear what you are wishing for will not come about the way you envision. You know nothing of this mystery gentleman, after all. What if he threatens to expose you?"

"Why would he? It is in his own best interests to keep it quiet unless he wants a hasty trip to the altar."

Caelie shook her head. "I cannot help but feel there is more to this than meets the eye. Why would he care so much about getting you away from that party?"

Abigail had thought the same thing. "He said he could tell someone of such innocence did not belong there."

"And how did he determine this? The dress you wore was a far cry from innocent."

Caelie made a good argument, but Abigail preferred the fantasy. That he had swooped in to keep her safe, to claim her for his own, and, in doing so, promised to help her confront Lord Roxton.

Granted, it hadn't happened quite that way. He'd actually been rather arrogant and heavy-handed in his actions at first. He hadn't swooped so much as dragged her into the room like an errant child. And *promised* to help might be a bit of a stretch. More like been coerced, as a condition upon her leaving.

"It does not matter how he determined my innocence," Abigail said, holding up a cream-colored gown with dark brown stripes and looking to Caelie for approval. Her cousin shrugged. "The point is he did. And he has agreed to help me."

Caelie stood silent in the middle of the room for a moment before letting out a long sigh of defeat. "Then you should go with the sapphire gown you chose earlier. With the added ribbon it will look quite lovely, and the color brings out your eyes to their best advantage. If you are intent on ruining your future, the least you can do is look fabulous in the process."

Chapter Six

"Tell me again why we are here," Spence said, scratching at the mask he'd been forced to don for the masquerade. He had kicked up a stink about going, throwing out every excuse in the book until Nicholas had reminded Spence that he owed him a favor.

Shortly before leaving for the Caribbean, he'd helped extricate Spence from a rather sticky situation with an unhappy duchess and an even unhappier duke who had caught his wife in a rather compromising position with an inebriated Spence. Had Nicholas not quickly intervened and pointed out the fact that Spence lacked the coherency to understand the gravity of his actions; the evening might have had a much different outcome. The duke, after all, had a reputation for calling out young gentlemen who showed undue interest in his wayward wife.

"You are here because I need to keep a certain lady from doing something she will regret." He planned on sending Spence to meet with Miss Laytham in his place, hoping she would not know the difference. While not of identical height and build, they were close enough that she should not notice.

The room, after all, had been quite dark and he'd deliberately avoided the moonlight.

He loathed getting Spence involved. But he did not trust himself to be near her. Not after the kiss they had shared. Not after her passionate nature spurred desires he'd thought well under his control.

How wrong he had been.

"Why is this your responsibility? Who is she again?"

"Stop asking, I have told you I have no intention of revealing her identity. We met at Opal's party the other night and—"

"Opal's party? Why, you old dog! I knew you wouldn't stay—"

"It wasn't like that. My only purpose for being there was to prevent—" Nicholas waved a hand. "Never mind. Suffice to say, I need your assistance."

Spence scowled and tugged at the mask again. "How horribly chivalrous of you. Fine then, we shall call her Lady X. So, explain again how you plan on playing the white knight when you already have another young maiden, one Miss Caldwell in case you have forgotten her name, to attend to this evening?"

Nicholas's eyes drifted over to where Miss Caldwell and her mother stood. She had come dressed as a Grecian goddess, her white gown draped in threads of gold, accentuating her gentle curves. She was a beautiful sight, yet it stirred nothing in him, leading him to believe he had finally suppressed his baser instincts and conquered his demons. One kiss from Miss Laytham had proved how wrong he had been on that account. Now he could not get the taste of her out of his mind. Her generous mouth and eager lips haunted his memory, teasing his control until it threatened to snap.

"I plan on having you play the white knight, that's how. All you need to do is make her aware you received word Lord

Roxton had an urgent business matter arise and therefore will not be in attendance. Hopefully that will squelch her quest to find me."

"What does it matter if Lady X finds you?"

"You will not wheedle any more information out of me. I told you, her identity must remain a secret."

"Very well," Spence agreed. His tone made it clear he cared little for the arrangement. A masquerade, he'd pointed out, was like a license to behave improperly without the consequences of doing so. Being forced to curb his own fun to attend to an unknown young lady he was not allowed to dabble with hardly seemed like a good use of his time or skills.

"I don't see why Bowen can't do it. He's far more the chivalrous sort."

"Because," Nicholas pointed out, "Bowen has a strict aversion to subterfuge. You on the other hand, excel at it. I need you to make her believe you are the man she met at Opal's."

"I think Bowen pretends such an aversion for instances such as this so he will not be called upon to do such mundane tasks."

"Bowen," Nicholas reminded his friend, "is not the one who was found with his britches around his ankles at the Plankford soiree, servicing Her Grace while her husband played billiards in the next room."

Spence cleared his throat and crossed his arms. His scowl deepened. "Hardly my fault. She seduced me, and the duke interrupted us before anything could happen."

Nicholas opened his mouth to respond to Spence's ridiculous assertion when a flash of deep blue caught his eye and held it.

She had arrived. As promised, she wore the same mask from before. A royal blue silk ribbon had been threaded through the pearls and feathers. Her dress shone like sapphires and silver lace teased the swell of her breasts.

His fingers flexed. He burned to feel her skin. He imagined she would be softer than the silk draping her body, and slide just as effortlessly against his own.

"I will assume from the ridiculous expression on your face that this is the lady in question?"

Nicholas quickly schooled his emotions. "It is. Now remember, you are not to compromise her in any way. Simply tell her Lord Roxton is unavailable this evening and then leave before she realizes you are not the same man she met previously. Understood?"

Spence shrugged beneath his tailored jacket and smiled. "Of course. Perfectly. Very simple. What could go wrong?"

Nicholas pursed his lips. He did not wish to contemplate.

Abigail skirted the edges of the party. How strange to be back amongst the ton, knowing the only reason they did not shy away was because they did not recognize her. It was perfectly ridiculous that a mask was the only thing that kept her from being shunned, as if each one of them did not wear their own masks. Every day they put on the polite veneer society dictated as fashionable, decorating it with false sincerity and inane conversations that meant nothing. Yet once you turned your back, they did not hesitate to stab you with rumors and innuendo and gossip.

The sudden release from convention, the constant need to always ensure she did the right thing at the right time with the right person while wearing the right outfit, was the only welcomed benefit of her family's denunciation from polite society.

Still, she would take it back in a heartbeat if it meant seeing her family whole again. If it healed Caelie's broken spirit, wiped the loneliness from her mother's eyes, and erased the worry lines creasing Benedict's face, she would wear the hypocrisy until her dying day and not bat an eye.

But it wasn't that easy. For eight months, she had tried to worm her way back into society with the hopes it would ease the path for Caelie, but to no avail. Most barely tolerated her presence, others completely ignored her. It was as if she was contagious.

Lady Blackbourne found them within the crowd and approached with her daughter in tow, a generous smile on her face.

"How glad I am to see you," she said, reaching out with both her hands to clasp Abigail's mother's hand.

"We wouldn't have missed it," her mother replied. Abigail looked at her and realized it was true. Relief lightened her mother's hazel eyes and smoothed the lines around them. Despite her affiliation to the horrid Lord Roxton, Abigail could not help but feel a sense of gratitude toward his mother for her public acceptance of her family.

After a quick exchange of pleasantries, and a determination that Lord Roxton had indeed come, Abigail extricated herself from their group with the excuse of taking care of personal business. She started toward the ladies' room then veered off, doubling back into the crowd to search for her accomplice from the other night.

Her efforts proved fruitless, and after a second cursory look, she left the crush and sauntered out onto the terrace overlooking the gardens. A gentle breeze caressed her skin, but the gooseflesh that followed had little to do with the weather and everything to do with anticipation. He'd promised he would come, and for reasons she could not pinpoint or make good sense of, she trusted him.

She stared out over the gardens and prayed she would not be disappointed. Time trickled away. Soon Lord Tarrington would make his offer, and once she accepted, her chance to face down Lord Roxton would be gone.

"Lady X?"

The touch at her elbow startled her and for a fleeting second, her heart roared to life, only to settle back down when she realized it was not her mystery man from the other night.

"What did you call me?"

He smiled. A lovely smile, really. Most engaging. Her mystery man, however, did not smile. Or if he had, the darkness had hidden it from her. Curiosity overrode any sense of trepidation. Though the terrace was sparsely populated, she remained in full view of the ballroom through the open French doors, and there were others within shouting distance, should she require assistance.

Though he was close to the same height, and wore the same mask and black attire as her mystery man, something was off. "I called you Lady X. We did not exchange names the other evening, so I thought to name you such." The quick, engaging smile came again. Definitely not her mystery man.

"We did not meet the other evening."

"At the *party*," he said, stressing the last word then leaned in and whispered. "At Madame St. Augustine's."

Her heart pounded beneath her breast. Had he seen her there and recognized her mask and now thought to play with her? Oh, why had she not thought of that? And if he recognized it, were there others here who would as well? Caelie's warnings came back to haunt her. Denial was her only option.

"I am afraid you have me confused with someone else."

He took a step back. "I do?"

"Indeed, you must. For I have no knowledge of a Madame St. Augustine." She tried to put as much effrontery in her tone as she could muster.

"But you requested that I meet you here."

"I did no such thing."

This was not her mystery man. He wore the same type of mask and dressed in the same unrelenting black. But it was not he. No hint of the strange accent existed. And his scent—this man reminded her of exotic spices and sunshine. If she kissed this man, it would feel different. She didn't know how she knew, but somewhere beneath her skin, deeper than muscle and bone, she could feel it.

This man was an imposter. But why?

"But I..." His words trailed off and he looked behind him as if searching for something, or someone.

Was this an awful trick? Had someone discovered her identity and thought to have some fun at her expense? Anger burned inside of her. How cruel. How completely, utterly cruel!

"I do not know who you are, or what you think—" Her words were abruptly cut off.

"There you are, you smarmy little bastard!"

Their heads swiveled in unison at the booming voice. The bulky frame of Lord Franklyn lumbered toward them, his fist hammering the air. He'd pushed his mask off his face as if he cared little about revealing his identity.

"Oh dear." The imposter swallowed. "Not good."

"Do not even think of trying to escape. I heard you were back in town and I know damn well it is you beneath that ridiculous mask. We have not yet settled our differences, young man, and I mean to—"

"Y-Your Grace. How lovely to see you again." The imposter's well-formed mouth stretched it into a false smile. "And how is your lovely wife?"

"Why you little—" The older man charged forward but was briefly thwarted by a group of revelers.

"My apologies, Lady X. I am to tell you Lord Roxton will not be in attendance this evening." He quickly lifted her hand to his mouth and dropped a quick kiss before letting go and sprinting across the balcony, vaulting over the balustrade into the gardens below. The Duke of Franklyn brushed past her without so much as a glance, huffing as he ran after the much spryer younger man, with no hope at all of ever catching him.

Abigail stared after them, too stunned to speak or think.

How did that man know about her search for Lord Roxton? And why was he sent to tell her something she knew to be false? Lord Roxton *was* in attendance. Lady Blackbourne had said as much. Unable to come up with any plausible answers, Abigail returned to the ballroom and resumed her search. She would find her mystery man, or Lord Roxton, before the night ended.

Another full hour passed before her determination came to fruition. After checking in with her mother who was happily ensconced in Lady Blackbourne's circle, she excused herself once again, this time under the guise of getting punch and reintroducing herself to a group of old friends. Abigail sensed him first, as if his presence reached out and caressed some deep, instinctual part of her. Several moments later, she laid eyes on him, and oh, the wait had been worth it. Even though she was unable to see his face, covered as it was, she knew he would be handsome. How could he not when his mouth alone held such delights?

Did she dare seek out another kiss? She didn't did not require his assistance in finding Lord Roxton. She well knew it would be easier to simply have Lady Blackbourne point him out. But need and want were two entirely different things. His kiss haunted her dreams, and more of her waking moments than she cared to acknowledge. Would it be so wrong? She would be discreet. No one would know. Just one more kiss filled with passion and desire before she consigned herself to a life with a man old enough to be her grandfather. A man who only saw her as a means to procure an heir. Maybe a little more than a kiss—

No! She gave herself a shake. Tonight was not about stolen kisses in dark corners. It was about resurrecting her family's reputation from the ashes.

Abigail walked the edge of the crowd, then came up behind him to stand on her tiptoes and whisper near his ear. "I worried you had reneged on our deal."

His shoulders tensed, then he turned slowly. The mask he wore was more elaborate than the other night and yet still covered all but his tantalizing mouth. Dressed as a swashbuckling hero, he had covered his head with a silk scarf and his hair had been tied back in a queue.

Something tugged at her memory, but he interrupted her thoughts before she could pay too much attention.

"What are you doing here?" His greeting held far less enthusiasm than she had hoped for. "Come with me." He took her by the elbow and directed her firmly through the crowd until they came out at the entrance to the gardens. He kept to the shadows and led her through the narrow maze of hedges and flowerbeds.

"Where are you taking me?"

"Hush!"

She clamped her mouth shut, more out of surprise than from any plan of acquiescence. His manners had not improved since their last meeting. At the far end of the house, he marched her back up onto the terrace before stopping at another set of doors. They opened easily and he pulled her inside, shutting the door behind them. Abigail looked around, staring through the shadows. It appeared to be a music room, but without enough light, she couldn't be certain. In the distance, she could hear the muted din of the other guests, but they felt a million miles away from them. And from Lord Roxton.

She turned on him. "I do not feel this silly cloak and

dagger behavior is necessary. And I don't appreciate being manhandled in such a fashion. Anyone could have seen us."

"Exactly," he said, his voice abrading her nerves until they sizzled to life. How could someone's voice do that? Make her react like a physical touch? "I sent my...my man to find you. To give you a message. Did you not get it?"

Her eyes widened. That explained how the imposter knew to look for her, but it did not explain why he'd sent someone instead of telling her himself. "That gentleman pretended to be you. Really, did you think I would not know the difference?"

He ignored her question but his refusal to meet her gaze was as much an admission as she needed.

"I discovered Lord Roxton would not be attending this evening. I merely wished to convey that information to you."

"You could not do it yourself?" She had so looked forward to seeing him again. To have him purposely try to avoid her... well, it stung. More than it should have.

He turned away from her. "I thought perhaps after my behavior the other night, you may have wished not to see me."

"Oh." A blush crept upward, warming her throat and cheeks. "No. That is not the case at all. I...I quite enjoyed it."

He shot a sideways glance in her direction and the heat of her blush raged through the rest of her body. "That's rather bold of you."

She had no response. What she had said pressed the far edge of propriety, but what did it matter? He did not know her. She did not know him. Neither of them intended to take this strange relationship beyond this night. No expectations and their hidden identities offered a sense of freedom to speak one's mind.

Abigail smiled. "Did I offend?"

A low chuckle rumbled deep in his chest. She quite liked the sound of his laugh. It reminded her of someone, but she couldn't say whom. Being near him made thinking of anything beyond the moment difficult. "No. You did not offend."

"Good. And you needn't worry about Lord Roxton's attendance. Your source provided faulty information. Lady Blackbourne has already confirmed his attendance. And given the way he's been doting on Miss Caldwell, who is also present, I have no doubt if we watch her, we will find him." She bit her tongue. Her admission highlighted the truth—she did not require his assistance. But she had wanted it nonetheless, if for no other reason than to see him one last time.

"And when you find Lord Roxton, what then?"

"Then I will—" She clamped her mouth shut. She could not tell him her plans. If she did, it would divulge who she was, and she couldn't chance it. Perhaps her instincts about this man were correct, and he would keep her secret. But given she had nothing to base this instinct on except two clandestine meetings she could not take the risk. If she was wrong, it could ruin everything. "Lord Roxton owes my family a debt and I mean to see that he pays."

He stepped back, farther into the shadows. "And you're willing to jeopardize your own reputation in order to achieve this end?"

"I would do anything for my family," she whispered. Harnessing the boldness he had accused her of, she followed him until the distance between them disappeared. If she wanted, she could reach out and rest her hand on his solid chest, to feel if his heart beat as rapidly as hers. The closer she stood, the more she wanted to do just that. To experience the heady sensation of his arms around her, his thighs pressed into hers, his mouth and tongue hungrily invading her own. She had never experienced anything like it. "Please tell me you will help."

"I do not think that wise."

"I would have thought someone who attended Madame St. Augustine's parties would be more adventurous."

He straightened. Her comment seemed to hit a nerve, though which one she could not rightly say. The mask and the darkness conspired against her, making him impossible to read.

"Adventure is not always what it is cracked up to be. Sometimes it is nothing more than a road to perdition."

"And sometimes it is a road to untold riches."

He shook his head. "Does anyone ever win an argument with you?"

"Rarely. Most have stopped trying." She moved toward him.

"Hardly surprising."

She mustered her courage, reached out, and laid a hand on his chest. The fine linen of his shirt slid smoothly beneath her fingers. He braved the edges of propriety with his lack of coat, and his waistcoat left unbuttoned. But that was the wonderful thing about a masquerade. One could tiptoe outside the restrictive boundaries and not be taken to task for it. "Will you help me?"

His hand came up to cover hers. Strong fingers caressed her own, sending little shivers quivering down her arm. She had only meant to touch and retreat, but he held her there, and she made no move to pull back. When he spoke, it came in a hushed whisper, urgent and pleading.

"You've already indicated you do not need my help. Either way, I caution you to reconsider what you are doing. It will come to naught."

"You don't know that."

"I know you are on the wrong path. Confronting Lord Roxton will do you no good. The man is a cad of the first order. He has done despicable things and is not worthy of your time, or your trouble. He certainly is not worth risking your reputation over. I urge you to reconsider."

He spoke so forcefully. Did he have a close association with Lord Roxton, one that had not ended well? If so, it could mean only one thing.

She had found herself a true ally.

"If you know Lord Roxton, and if you have been the recipient of his special brand of deceit, then you must understand I cannot let this slight pass. He will get what is coming to him."

She had moved closer to him until her body rested lightly against his. She should be shocked by her behavior, yet everything about it felt natural, as did the longing for more. To know the feel of him again. To be caught in the maelstrom of his kiss.

"Can I ask one more favor?"

He stared down at her, his mouth turned downward at the corners, his intense eyes unfathomable. She wished she could discern their color, but the darkness had washed such details away.

"You may."

Beyond the music room, the sound of a lively tune filtered up the hallway, mixed with the din of conversation. She wondered if anyone had missed her yet. Her mother had been deep in conversation with Lady Blackbourne. Likely, it would be a little while before she realized Abigail had not yet returned. She had time. The question was, did she have the courage?

"Will you kiss me once more?"

Chapter Seven

~∞~

Her reckless request bordered on madness, but Abigail could not resist. She had been unable to get their first kiss out of her mind. He had stirred in her such desires she could barely go more than a minute without some part of her mind or body reminiscing about that one perfect moment.

Once married to Lord Tarrington, this part of her life would be over before it began. Was it so wrong she wished to experience the sensations this mystery man provoked in her just one more time? Did that make her a wanton?

A muscle in his jaw twitched and the hands around her waist tightened, pulling her into him a little more until the hard contours of his body could be felt through the layers of her skirts.

"I do not have that right." The words were strained, as if speaking them caused him great discomfort.

"I am giving you that right," she said. "Did you not feel something when we kissed before?"

For a fleeting moment, she thought he would deny it, but he didn't. Closing his eyes, he answered her with a curt nod.

She rushed ahead before he could speak, before he could talk sense into her, because in truth what she asked was preposterous in so many ways, yet in one way, in the only way that counted, it made perfect sense.

"If you were in my situation, forced by circumstance to marry someone who would never love you, would you not want to grab a brief moment of happiness, of pleasure, before time ran out and you were consigned to a life without it? Is a kiss so much to ask for?"

He shook his head, lifting a hand to her lips. She trembled beneath the light touch of his calloused finger, letting the shivers course through her body and awaken it to possibility. To hope.

"Shall I give you a kiss to remember then?" His voice grew husky, its roughness making her insides heat.

"Please."

His mouth descended upon hers, his touch tentative as their lips met. She could feel his restraint in the tightening of his muscles. She wanted to toss off her mask, hating the barrier between them, but she dared not. Though she had the sense if she did, he would keep her secret. How foolish to put such trust in a man she had met only once before, whom she knew nothing about, but her heart told her she could. Of course, her heart had also told her she could trust Lord Roxton, once upon a time. The sobering thought gave her pause, not enough to dampen the heat his touch inflamed within her, but enough to keep her mask in place.

He teased her mouth with small butterfly kisses building a need that made her keen for more. She wanted to give herself over to him. She wanted—oh devil take it!—she wanted him to peel away every last layer of clothing and cover her body with those kisses. The very thought of such decadence flushed her with a desire she could not control and when he deepened their kiss, encompassing her in his arms, she did not object.

Nor did she voice any concern when he guided her backward with his body until the edge of a small table bumped her from behind.

Yearning roared through her like a tempest and assaulted her body and mind with wants and needs until she was helpless to stop it, even if she wanted to. Which, she quickly discovered, she did not.

"Close your eyes," he whispered.

Her heart pumped, but she did as he bade, relinquishing control for the sake of pleasure. Oh, and there would be pleasure. Already her body sang from his kiss, the sound of his voice, the strength of his hands around her waist.

"Keep them closed," he instructed.

She nodded forcing herself to comply, even as his hand reached downward and the hem of her skirt began to rise. His body shifted and she sensed he had knelt down in front of her.

"What are you doing?"

"Should I stop?"

Abigail shook her head fervently and his hand slid upward over her silk stockings, up her calf, over her knee, until his touch teased the edge of her garter. The sensation of his bare skin grazing hers sent shivers through her and a deep ache pooled between her thighs.

"Oh!" The word rushed out on a breath.

How could a touch be so seductive? But it was. His hand touching a part of her body only she had touched. Warm flesh against warm flesh. His hands inched farther upward, continuing their sensual journey. They brushed over her hips and began to move inward. Abigail held her breath, part of her wishing with all her might his hand would dispel the ache. How, she didn't know. She didn't care. She only knew he could.

And that she desperately wanted him to.

But the other part of her, the sensible part that had been

trained year upon year to behave properly, to not give into temptation and desire, that part wanted her to run away. It was too much. But temptation and desire proved stronger, rooting her to the spot. When the ties of her drawers loosened and he tugged them gently over her hips until they slid down to her feet, she did not stop him. She did not run away, or demand he release her.

Abigail trembled, her body shaking from a mix of nervousness and desire. It was all so wrong, yet nothing had ever felt more right. She needed to stop this. She needed to—

"Do you want me to kiss you now?" he asked. She opened her eyes to find him looking up at her from where he knelt upon the ground. Darkness shrouded them and he was little more than shadow and sensation.

"Oh yes," she breathed. She craved his mouth. That intoxicating mouth that could send her mind reeling and her body singing.

"Very well then."

While she had indeed desired a kiss, the one she received was far removed from what she had been expecting. She had never had a man this close to her before, in this manner, and certainly not with his mouth so near her...well, needless to say, this was an uncommon occurrence.

Perhaps that was why she did not cry out when he disappeared beneath her skirts. Or refused him when his hands gently guided her legs apart. She remained silent when his lips placed a soft kiss on the inside of her thigh, so close to where she ached. So close to where a pulsing need had grown into a roaring desire she could no longer control or deny.

His mouth pressed against the nest of soft curls at the juncture of her thighs. Heat spiraled through and up and around until it permeated every aspect of her being and left nothing untouched.

Sinful. It had to be, but she did not stop him. She

couldn't. She needed release, and she needed him to be the one to release her.

The tip of his tongue flicked out and slid along her opening, now slick with the desire coursing through her. She gasped and her hands gripped his broad shoulders beneath her skirts.

"No, you mustn't—"

But he did. Had it not been for the grip she had on his shoulders or his hands cupping her bare bottom, she would have collapsed onto the floor. Her legs shook. No, her whole body shook.

He kissed her again, teasing with his lips and his tongue, deeply, wantonly. She could not stand it. She perched on the brink of something cataclysmic and though she could not understand it, she did not want to run from it. Rather she wanted to run to it, fully, completely.

He did not remove his mouth this time. Instead, he pulled her closer, shifted position until her legs spread wider, giving him more access. It proved her undoing. His mouth, his tongue, his hands upon her. The sensations built inside of her until she could no longer contain them. It rushed upon her like a crescendo and pulled her under. Abigail bit down on her bottom lip to keep from crying out, but she was too far-gone in the sensations rolling over her to know if she succeeded.

She had no recollection of time, or how long it took before her faculties returned. But when they did, she realized, with such clarity, she had just experienced passion.

And she wanted more.

Nicholas pressed his mouth against her one last time, taking one final taste before he reached down and pulled her drawers back up, tying them in place. His hands shook. He could not believe he had allowed himself to get this carried away. Guilt clawed at him the instant she found release. Had he not done enough to this family that he now must debauch Miss Laytham as well?

That she had been the one to request the kiss mattered not, as the kiss he gave her was a far cry from what she asked for, or expected.

He had broken the promise he had made to himself. And he had done it in the worst possible way.

He should tell her the truth; reveal his identity, but to do so would only make things worse. If she knew who had given her the passion she had craved it would destroy any happy memory she had hoped to create. She would despise him even more. And she would never forgive herself.

Nicholas could not add to the gravity of the situation by allowing that.

No, he would bear the weight of this on his own shoulders. He would not see her again, at least not like this. The mystery man of her romantic fantasies would disappear, and hopefully she would be satisfied with the pleasure and passion she'd experienced this night and not seek it—or him—out again.

"I have never..." She did not finish her sentence, but merely stared at him with half-sated desire still simmering in her blue eyes.

"I am glad it pleased you," he said, wishing things could be different. That he was different. What might their courtship have led to had it not been abruptly ended by Lord Glenmor? Would they have had a lifetime filled with these moments?

"Pleased me?" She smiled. "It more than pleased me." She moved closer and rested her weight against his chest. His arms automatically encircled her. She fit perfectly, more so than he had ever experienced. The thought had not occurred to him before. But he thought about it now, and it disturbed him almost as much as his behavior. He wanted to hold her there forever, keep her safe, and be the only one who ever touched her.

But that could never happen. He must let her go. Now, before he lost the will to do so.

"Is it horrible I do not feel ashamed? I know I should. But..." her words trailed away.

He stroked the back of her neck and she shivered. "You did nothing to be ashamed of. It is I who should be ashamed. You asked for a simple kiss and I...I took it too far."

"No, don't say you regret it." She pulled away slightly and placed a gloved hand over his lips. Pristine white against the dark. The color of innocence. He removed her hand and tucked her back under his chin. Better she not look too closely, even in the unlit room he risked her recognizing him.

His heart lurched. How close he had come to allowing his base instincts to take him further. To ruin her forever. What was wrong with him? Even at his worst, he'd had better control over his passion and desires than this. Was it because she was the forbidden fruit? The one woman he could never truly have?

"I must leave London," he told her, before the words deserted him.

"L-leave? Why?"

His mind worked feverishly. He had to put an end to this once and for all. "Family business. It is difficult to say when I will return."

"I could wait—"

"You will be married," he reminded her, then wished he had tempered his words when he felt her shoulders droop. "Forgive me. I do not mean to be so blunt. But this—" His hand touched her cheek. "It can be nothing more than what it is right now. A pleasant, pleasurable interlude. As you said, you must marry this other man, and I...I too have commitments elsewhere."

"Will I never see you again?"

He shook his head. "Not like this."

She pulled away and a shard of moonlight cut across her. He took a step back into the darkness. Even from that distance, he could feel her disappointment as a living, palpable thing. He longed to reach out and kiss her one last time, but he did not dare. As if sensing his intent, she straightened her shoulders and drew in a deep breath, pressing her breasts upward against the strain of her stays.

"I should go then." She looked around her, as if noticing her surroundings for the first time. "Mama will be wondering where I've gone off to."

Nicholas nodded. He could not escort her back. It would raise too many questions. He must make his excuses to his mother and Miss Caldwell then leave the party immediately before she laid eyes on him again.

Her voice turned businesslike. "You will still point out Lord Roxton to me?"

He had to admire her strength. Most women would be reduced to a sobbing mess by now, given the situation. Or demand on recompense. What had happened in Miss Laytham's life to give her this core of strength that would not allow her to resort to such measures? Surely, the scandal had intensified it, but he had witnessed it before. It was in the way she carried herself, the way she spoke her mind regardless of what others thought. It was one of the things that attracted him most to her. It saddened him they'd never had the time to delve farther into their pasts, to reveal their secrets and desires.

"If I see him." An event easily avoided by a hasty exit. He must end this now.

"Thank you," she said, her voice a soft whisper. They stood there a moment, then she turned away and walked to the French doors. She hesitated upon opening them. A sliver of moonlight illuminated her like an avenging angel.

Look back, his thoughts begged. *Just this once, do not forsake me.*

But she didn't. Instead, her narrow shoulders squared as she slipped through the door without so much as a glance in his direction.

Nicholas slumped back against a nearby chair, her scent still imprinted on his clothing, her taste still on his tongue, and the heat in his groin still not abated.

There would be a price for what he had done this night, of that he was certain.

"Where have you been? I have been looking for you everywhere."

"Forgive me Mama, I needed some air and I lost track of time."

Abigail took a deep breath. She had taken several gulps of air since walking from the music room, turning her back on the unbridled passion that had erupted there. It had taken every ounce of her strength not to turn back and beg him to change his mind, to stay in London, to throw caution to the wind and claim her for his own.

But such foolishness was not to be borne. Besides, in all likelihood, when she removed her mask and revealed her true identity, he would run away in horror, leaving not just London, but England itself to avoid an association with her or her family.

Perhaps that was a gross exaggeration, but regardless, she could not deny suitors had beaten a hasty path away from her door since the scandal. And not one had asked to fill her dance card at any of the few events she had attended since. No doubt, her mystery man would be no different. It was all well and good to be lost in the moment and pretend otherwise, but reality tended to intrude with its heavy feet and trample such imaginings before they had a chance to grow.

Abigail snapped her fan open to cool the flush of her skin, hoping her mother didn't notice.

"Have you seen all the costumes, Mama?" she asked, to prevent further questioning on her whereabouts. "There is no telling who is who."

Her mother scanned the room. "Don't be silly. Of course, you can. Why look, that's Lord Slottingly next to the potted plant. You can tell by his portly belly busting out of his overly ornate waist jacket. And over there, that is Miss Chaucer holding court with all the young bucks. It is said she has turned down several proposals already this Season. Lady Blackbourne and Lady Rebecca are speaking with Miss Caldwell. You can tell her by her stiff upright posture. And I believe standing with them is—" Her mother squinted behind her mask. "—ah, yes, Lord Huntsleigh, if I'm not mistaken."

Abigail's eyes widened. "L-Lord Huntsleigh?"

"Yes," her mother nodded with a smile. "You can practically feel his charm from across the room. He's quite the devil, that one. Gives his grandfather no end of grief, according to Lady Blackbourne. He has been a particular friend of Lord Roxton's since childhood."

Abigail stared at the man standing next to Lady Rebecca. The same man who'd approached her on the balcony calling her Lady X and claiming to be her mystery man—before the Duke of Franklyn chased him into the gardens. As he looked unaffected by the event, she could only assume he'd survived the encounter unscathed.

"And you're certain it is him?"

"Of course. Look at how he stands. Brash and confident. His laugh is unmistakable. He throws his head back with abandon, as if he had not a single care in the world." Her mother turned to her. "It really isn't difficult to tell who is who, dear, if you look close enough. Most people just don't. It's more fun to turn a blind eye and get lost in the mystery and the masks. But one cannot truly disguise who they are simply by covering a portion of their face. It doesn't cover their eyes, or their mouths, the sound of their voice, their mannerisms. There are so many more things that make up a person."

"Indeed," Abigail said, the word coming weakly as an uncomfortable knowledge roiled in her belly. She thought of her mystery man's eyes. Pale beneath his black silk mask. And his hair, the color of midnight. She swallowed. No, she imagined things. It was dark. His hair could have been brown for all she knew.

But her conscience would not be silenced.

He had sent his man to tell her Lord Roxton was not attending this evening. That man being Lord Huntsleigh. Lord Huntsleigh who was a particular friend of...

Abigail shook her head. No. *No.* She jumped to foolish conclusions, surely. She would know if it had been him, wouldn't she? Besides, her mystery man's hair was longer. And his voice, the accent she couldn't quite place—

A man approached Miss Caldwell and executed a brief bow. Her man. Reality clenched her heart.

The flitting of her fan increased despite the chill that swept through her body. This was not happening. It was not. How could she have been so foolish? So duped by blind stupidity? How could he—how could he so boldly lie to her about his identity and then kiss her and...and...

"Abigail, are you all right? You look rather pale." Her mother laid a hand on her arm but Abigail could barely feel it. Her body had gone numb. Her mind raced and darted in an effort to avoid making the final connection.

Her mystery man and Lord Roxton were one and the same.

"I—I'm feeling slightly ill all of a sudden, Mama. I think I need some air."

But there was not enough air in the atmosphere to help her now. She did not need air. She needed to turn back time, to change the truth now falling about her in bits and bobs, chipping away at the romantic fantasy she had concocted in her mind like an infatuated school girl intoxicated on the hope that things could get better. The illusion where she waited for her mystery man to return to London, knowing he could not stay away from her. He would be wealthy and titled and he would save her from marriage to Lord Tarrington, rescue her family's name, and help her bring Lord Roxton down.

Nowhere in her silly fantasy had her mystery man *been* Lord Roxton. For, how could he? His very existence set her teeth on edge. He embodied every bad thing that had happened to her family in the past year. And he had...she had let him...oh dear heaven, she really was going to be sick.

"Perhaps we should leave." Her mother pulled on Abigail's arm.

Before she could be led away, Lord Roxton turned and his gaze met hers.

She couldn't move. Couldn't speak, or breathe. She could only stand and stare, watching her reaction, as it became his.

In that moment, she knew.

Even more, she knew that *he* knew she knew.

A group of guests passed through the space between them, briefly blocking her view, breaking the hold he had on her. She allowed her mother to lead her away, her legs like heavy wooden objects jutting out from her hips.

She glanced back only once, but Lord Roxton had vanished. Much like her hopes.

Chapter Eight

"You have not seemed yourself since the masquerade." Caelie lowered the book she had been reading and stared across the small rounded table in the breakfast room. Abigail's mother was still abed. Benedict hid away in his study, likely going over ledgers in the vain hope the numbers would change in their favor, and Aunt Edythe remained in her rooms, as she was inclined to do these days. She and Caelie had the room to themselves.

It was Abigail's favorite room of the house. Morning light poured in through the windows and gave the bright yellow walls a golden glow. But today, her usual joy had abandoned her. Today, she wished she could emulate her aunt—hide away in the darkness and wish it all away.

Caelie closed her book, a clear signal she did not intend to leave the subject alone. "Did something happen at the masquerade? Did your mystery man not show up?"

Did something happen? How did she answer? Yes, something happened. Something so devastating she did not know where to begin. The pain too raw, the humiliation too deep. Still, she couldn't keep it bottled up inside. She'd die if she did.

"Have you ever done something so blindly foolish it was as if, for a brief moment, you were someone else entirely? And then afterward, when you looked back at what you had done, you wondered who that person was and how you could have been so reckless? So...so, stupid?"

Something changed in Caelie's sea green eyes, darkening their hue. A muscle twitched near the corner of her mouth. "I suspect there are few among us who have not found themselves in such a predicament. We are all fallible, Abby. What did you do?"

Abigail glanced down at her hands folded in her lap. She could not utter the words. To admit to Caelie she had allowed her archenemy to...to...oh! She couldn't even think it without shame racing through her like wildfire. She had allowed his kiss. His touch. His mouth on her most private parts while she behaved like a wanton, practically begging for more!

Her skin burned with the memory.

How effective a ruse Lord Roxton had pulled off, for she could never face him now. Never demand he make amends to her family. Suddenly, London felt too small for the both of them. Had they not let out their country seat to help with expenses, she would join her aunt in insisting the family retire there for the rest of the Season. Maybe even the next.

"Abby?"

The sharp click of heels on the polished wood floors cut off any answer Abigail may have formed. She recognized the bitter, angry stride before Aunt Edythe reached the doorway of the room, filling it with her severe presence.

Caelie slid the book behind her and fell silent. Aunt Edythe did not approve of what her cousin read. Then again, her aunt approved of very little regardless, especially where Caelie was concerned.

"Good morning, Mother." Abigail noted the forced smile on Caelie's face. She did not bother an attempt. She didn't have it in her this morning to tiptoe around her aunt's dour mood.

Aunt Edythe glanced at Caelie, looking down her long, straight nose at her daughter before turning toward the table at the back and walking stiffly across the room. Caelie and Abigail shared a look, both wishing for escape but knowing it was impossible. Aunt Edythe would expect them to stay. They would not be excused until she had completed her meal. A meal she would eat slowly, each bite chewed with meticulous intent.

Abigail poked at her coddled egg with a fork, pushing it around on her plate.

"Do not play with your food, Abigail. You are not a child." Aunt Edythe's strident tones raked across her nerves. Her aunt rarely spoke, but when she did nothing positive or pleasant ever passed her lips. Only censure and condemnation resided inside of her. It had grown worse since Uncle Henry's death, and she had lost her standing as mistress of the household. That honor had passed to Abigail's mother until her brother married.

"I understand you and your mother attended my cousins' masked ball."

"Yes, Aunt. It was a lovely affair," Abigail tried not to choke on her words.

"I am certain it was anything but. Why my cousin insists on throwing such a fete every year is beyond me. It is nothing more than an opportunity for debauchery. Your mother should be ashamed for exposing you to such a thing. But what can one expect?" She left off saying 'from a poor vicar's daughter', but the implication hung heavy in the air. Aunt Edythe's opinions of her mother's origins had never been a secret. She had resented their presence in this house since the first day Uncle Henry opened his doors, and his heart, to them.

Abigail pushed back a harsh retort. What was the point?

Aunt Edythe held to her opinion as if it was the word of God and no one would sway her from it regardless of how sound the reasoning. And Abigail didn't have the strength this morning to try.

Aunt Edythe took a small bite of toast and slowly chewed, waiting until she had fully swallowed before fixing her hard, brown eyes on Abigail once again. "I understand you had another letter from my cousin, Lord Tarrington?"

Abigail's stomach twisted further. She did not need the reminder of him this morning. "Indeed, I did. He believes his roses will be quite the thing this year." At least she thought that's what he'd written. She'd only skimmed the pages briefly.

"I have invited him to visit. We must push this alliance post haste. Your brother is doing a dismal job at managing the finances. It is only a matter of time before he runs us into the ground without the assistance of my cousin to stop him."

"Mother, Benedict is doing a fine job. It is not his fault Papa—"

"Did I direct my comment to you, daughter?"

Caelie visibly winced at her mother's strident tone. So sharp and caustic it surprised Abigail that her words didn't peel the paper off the walls. "No, Mother."

"Then I suggest you hold your tongue until you are addressed." Caelie shot Abigail an apologetic glance. Abigail shook her head. She had tried. A valiant effort given Aunt Edythe reserved her most hateful treatment for her only child. Penance for Caelie not being born a son. Had she been, Aunt Edythe claimed she would have been spared the horror of poor relations taking possession of her home.

Abigail often wondered if Aunt Edythe hadn't been such a cold, bitter woman, perhaps Uncle Henry would not have looked elsewhere for affection, becoming so desperate for it he would do almost anything, even pay the ultimate price when faced with losing it.

"When is Lord Tarrington expected to arrive?" Abigail asked, pulling Aunt Edythe's attention away from Caelie. She would try to make herself as absent as possible. If she had to marry the man to save her family from financial ruin then so be it, but until such a day arrived, she preferred to avoid his company. Lord Tarrington was about as entertaining as a pound of dirt.

"He should arrive next week. I expect you will be on your best behavior and treat him with the respect and deference that is his due."

Abigail forced a smile as her hands clenched in her lap. "Of course, Aunt. I look forward to his arrival."

Dread pooled in her belly. How had this become her life? She bit the inside of her cheek to hold back the tears. She feared if they started, they might never end.

"If I have to repeat myself one more time, I am going to start talking to the ferns," Lord Huntsleigh muttered. He jabbed Nicholas in the ribs with a sharp elbow as they approached the steps that led up to his stately family home. "Whatever you have on your mind, leave it at the door. I need you to have your wits about you or Grandfather will eat us alive."

Nicholas gave himself a mental shake and waved off Spence's concerns. The Marquess and Marchioness of Ellesmere were hardly the dragons Spence made them out to be. Given that their grandson stood to inherit an old and respected title along with a vast fortune in land and holdings, it seemed appropriate they would be concerned about continuing the lineage. As the only male heir left in the Kingsley line, his grandfather expected Spence to marry—well and soon.

The marquess, as he kept reminding his grandson, was not

getting any younger and would not be around forever. He wanted to see the family lineage preserved before he met his maker. That meant Spence had to not only marry, but also produce his own heir.

Unfortunately for the marquess, Spence considered anything that shackled him, especially marriage, akin to death. As such, he always brought reinforcements with him whenever summoned to the family's London home.

Bowen, though often in residence, proved no help. As the marquess's chief man of business, he could hardly contradict his employer and tell him he should leave Spence to his own devices. Especially since no one believed leaving Spence to his own devices was the best option. When left unchecked, he immersed himself in no amount of trouble.

Still, Nicholas needed something to keep his mind off the other night and everything he'd done thus far had proven miserably inadequate.

Abigail—for he could no longer think of her as Miss Laytham after what had transpired between them—had discovered his true identity. He did not know what had given it away, though standing on the edge of the dance floor next to his family while he tried to excuse himself from the party had likely not been the wisest of choices. Abigail was an intelligent woman. If she recognized any one of them, the pieces would begin to fall into place. As obviously, they had. Nicholas had stood there, frozen, watching her put the puzzle together. Seeing the devastation in her eyes as his ruse became clear.

No. He didn't see it. He'd felt it. Like a punch to the gut, it had sucked the wind out of him and rooted his feet to the floor so he couldn't move. Instead, he stood and stared like a mute idiot. He wished he could have pushed through the crowd as they exited the dance floor and explained why he had perpetrated such deception.

But what explanation was there? He had lost his head.

Something about her made his blood heat and his good sense catch the first carriage out of town. He'd lost control. She made him lose control. Not that it was her fault. It wasn't. The guilt rested solely at his feet.

As usual.

By the time he found a clear path around the crowd of guests, Abigail had disappeared.

Fingers snapped in front of his face. "What the devil, Nick? You've been brooding for three days now. Whatever it is, snap out of it. It's most unbecoming in a reprehensible rake such as yourself."

Nicholas scowled. "I am reformed," he reminded his friend. The lie burned on his tongue like acid.

"A temporary aberration. You'll come to your senses soon enough. Now remember, when my grandfather brings up marriage, you remind him I am much too young to be confined to such an antiquated institution and that if I am, I may well go crazy and have to be committed to Bedlam, thereby making it impossible for me to secure an heir."

"And why do you think he will take my word for it?"

"He won't." A charming grin cut across Spence's face. "But the man loves a good debate and arguing with you over the merits of my sanity will take his attention away from me."

The door to the marquess's stately home swung open and Felton, the ancient butler on the other side, ushered them into a well-appointed receiving room. Dark brocaded curtains draped either side of the large windows, held back with golden, coiled ropes to let in the afternoon light. The walls and upholstery were a light spring green and patterned with rose and yellow flowers to keep the room from feeling oppressive.

The Marquess of Ellesmere entered the room moments later, his walking stick more for affectation than necessity. Though the man was well into his seventies, he still possessed a sharp mind and sound body, albeit slower than it had once been. Though not large in stature or loud of voice, the marquess remained an imposing figure. He commanded attention and obedience, and suddenly Nicholas had the impression of being a young boy again, brought before the marquess for some mischief he and Spence had gotten themselves caught up in.

"Good day, gentlemen. It was thoughtful of you to stop by."

Nicholas waited for the older man to take his seat before reclaiming his own. Spence continued to pace near the fireplace. He reminded Nicholas of a caged tiger he'd once seen at a traveling carnival.

"I was summoned, Grandfather."

The older man smiled. One eyebrow lifted in amusement.

"Cook has prepared your favorite ginger biscuits, my boy. Perhaps that will help alleviate your suffering."

For a fleeting moment, Spence's eyes brightened, before he caught himself and resumed his scowl. Nicholas shook his head. The two men were more alike than they gave each other credit for. Both strong-willed and stubborn. Both determined to get their own way. Neither willing to budge or compromise enough to see the other's side. Yet the bond between them remained strong, and Nicholas knew without hesitation both grandfather and grandson loved the other fiercely.

He envied them their relationship, even if at present it caused them both pain and frustration. He often wished growing up he and his father had shared something similar, instead of the hate and resentment that simmered beneath the ever-thinning veneer of civility.

"Roxton, good of you to come and play the part of the buffer again. Can we offer you a drink for your trouble?"

"Tea is fine, Lord Ellesmere." He had tried drinking his

troubles away two nights previous and spent most of the next day abed, paying the price.

The door behind them opened and Mrs. Faraday bustled in; her jolly cheeks and sparkling eyes bringing a warmth to the room that couldn't help but make Nicholas smile. She had been with the family for as far back as he could remember, a surrogate mother of sorts who filled their bellies with biscuits and hugged them to her ample bosom every chance she got. Her own children, eight in all that had lived past infancy, had been regular playmates until he and Spence were sent away to school.

"Good afternoon, men." She set a tray filled with tea and biscuits on the table in front of the sofa and poured three cups. "I've made those ginger biscuits y'like, Lord Huntsleigh."

"Thank you, Mrs. Faraday." Spence smiled. Not even he could maintain his scowl in the housekeeper's presence. "And how is Jimmy faring these days?"

Jimmy had been the son closest in age to them. "Oh, he's a fine thing, he is. Onto his third baby come Christmas." Mrs. Faraday beamed with pride and Nicholas had to hide his grin. Spence had walked directly into the lion's den.

"His third." Lord Ellesmere took the teacup offered him. "That is quite impressive, Mrs. Faraday. Please send him our best wishes. It is always good to see a family grow and thrive. Is it not, Huntsleigh?"

Spence glanced at Nicholas for assistance, but he had none to give. It was a straightforward question. Spence forced his grimace into a smile and turned his attention to Mrs. Faraday, ignoring his grandfather completely.

"Please wish him happy for us."

"Oh, I will. I will. He'll be most pleased to know you think well of 'im. Now you just give me a shout if you gentlemen need anythin' else."

Mrs. Faraday bustled out of the room much in the way she had bustled in, leaving Spence staring after her. The door closed behind her and sealed his friend's fate with a definitive click.

Lord Ellesmere took a sip from the steaming cup of tea and set it aside on the table next to his chair. "I understand we can expect to soon hear an announcement from you as well, Roxton, if the rumors are accurate."

"I expect there will be," Nicholas replied, unable to muster any real joy at the answer.

"And do you feel such an announcement will send you round the bend?" Lord Ellesmere tapped at his temple.

"I would hope not, sir." Though after what had transpired at the masked ball, he could not say for certain. How could he marry one woman when he could not divert his thoughts from another?

Out of the corner of his eye, he saw Spence's shoulders slump with a huff of displeasure over his answer.

"Then it would seem entirely possible a rake can be reformed and do so without losing his mind or being reduced to a gibbering idiot, wouldn't you say?"

Nicholas opened his mouth, unsure of what to reply. He did not want to betray Spence, but at the same time, lying to the marquess proved near impossible, especially when the man stared you directly in the eye.

"I think, sir, that uh—"

Lord Ellesmere waved him silent. "Please do not strain yourself trying to find an answer to appease the two of us, Roxton. My grandson has brought you here with the hopes you will have some pithy comment which will dissuade me from my course to see him married, convinced it will cause him to lose his mind and other such rot. But given you are on the verge of making your own proposal, I daresay you don't believe a word of it."

Except that Nicholas did. Not the going crazy part, of course, but that a forced marriage was not a recipe for happiness. He knew people of his ilk married for money and position, not love. It was the accepted norm. But Nicholas had watched such a marriage destroy his family. His mother had been forced to give up the love of her life, a man considered beneath her social standing, to marry the earl. The ensuing affair, when her true love re-entered the picture, left a wake of devastation a mile wide. His mother had never truly recovered from losing the man a second time and the earl had never forgiven her for the constant reminder left behind.

Him.

No. He could not support the marquess's assertion an arranged marriage was the best course of action. It did not bring happiness, save for those atypical occasions where a husband and wife grew to love each other after the fact. It rarely bred contentment, if the turn out for Opal's parties were any indication.

Yet he intended to engage in such a marriage. But happiness and contentment were never his goal. He did not deserve them after all he had done.

"You are correct, Lord Ellesmere," Nicholas allowed. "I am indeed on the verge of proposing to Miss Caldwell. And while it is a match approved by both our families, and one I willingly enter into, I do not believe the same type of union would benefit Huntsleigh, save for the heir it may provide."

"What other true purpose to marriage is there?" The marquess lifted a stark white eyebrow. "You are not going to tell me love, are you, my boy?"

"What is wrong with love?" Spence stopped pacing and plunked himself down onto the sofa. "Would it not be preferable that I love my wife?"

The marquess's eyebrow lifted a little higher. "It is immaterial. Love will grow over time."

Spence's mouth twisted. "As it did with my parents?"

The marquess flinched, the movement nearly imperceptible. For all of the mess Nicholas's parents had made of marriage, Spence's mother and father had done an even worse job. Hardly any wonder he avoided the institution as one would the plague.

"Your parents were not the best example of anything, let alone marriage. Do not judge the institution on their behavior. If you wish to judge an example, use your grandmother and me. We barely knew each other when we married, but it was an advantageous match on both our parts and it turned out to be a wonderful union, where love grew true and deep after the vows were spoken."

"That is not a fair example. Anyone would be foolish not to love Grandmama," Spence said, and Nicholas could not argue the sentiment. The marchioness reminded him of a statelier, more elegant version of Mrs. Faraday, as strong-minded as her husband and equally as formidable, yet warm and engaging, a trait passed on to her grandson.

The marquess rose to his feet with the aid of his walking stick and for a long moment looked at his grandson until the younger man squirmed in his seat and averted his gaze to a nearby window.

"Marriage is what you make of it, my son."

"I do not know how I can make anything of it if it is not something I wish to be a part of. How do you expect me to produce this all-important heir if I cannot stand my wife and the thought of bedding her sends me running into the arms of my mistress?"

Spence didn't actually have a mistress as far as Nicholas knew. He had only recently returned from his travels. He hoped he hadn't taken back up with the Duchess of Franklyn. That was a disaster best avoided.

"I expect you will do your duty."

"It is not my intent to cause you grief, Grandfather. But I will not be boxed into a life I do not want."

"You may have little choice."

With that, the marquess strode to the door. Once it closed behind him, Spence turned to Nicholas. "Did you ever feel as if you were being forced into someone else's skin?"

"Every day," Nicholas answered. "Every day."

Abigail had met Lord Tarrington on a number of occasions. As second cousin to Aunt Edythe, he would pay a call on his rare visits to London from his country estate in Sussex. According to her aunt, he had arrived in town the day before and, after a night's rest, looked forward to becoming reacquainted.

Reacquainted. As if she had ever truly known the man. Or he, her.

Lord Tarrington spoke of nothing but his gardens and Maynerly, his estate. On occasion, he broached the subject of horseflesh, and on his last visit, politics. However, when Abigail ventured an opinion on the state of workhouses, Lord Tarrington quickly quelled her, declaring women had no business having an opinion on anything of a political nature. Women, he indicated with a rather pompous amount of authority, simply didn't possess the mind for it.

Indeed.

Abigail rose from the sofa and walked to the window. How would she ever manage marriage to this man?

"That is the sixth time in the past ten minutes you have paced to the window," Benedict pointed out, keeping his voice low enough so as not to disturb Aunt Edythe who worked diligently on her needlepoint closer to the fire. "Please sit down. He will be here when he gets here. You know Tarrington keeps his own timetable."

"Which I find abominably rude," she stated flatly, glancing over her shoulder at her brother. He hated these visits as much as she did. Both found the old man antiquated and hard to get along with. She knew it bothered Benedict to consider a marriage proposal between the old man and her, but really, what other option did they have?

Benedict could marry, of course, but with the taint of scandal still clinging to their name, finding an available bride with a sizeable dowry willing to marry into their family had proven a Herculean feat. Why it had become so desperate, Benedict had even broached the idea of marrying an American heiress. Imagine!

No, Benedict carried enough on his shoulders. It was up to her. She understood her duty, and while she did not like it, little could be done to change it. Her brother had never asked anything of her. He had allowed her a degree of independence most young women her age did not have and had given her every opportunity to educate herself in areas often reserved for men.

Perhaps if he hadn't done those things, marriage to Lord Tarrington would be a little easier to swallow. Perhaps she would be a little less headstrong and have thought twice before she rushed into sharing such a humiliatingly intimate interlude with her sworn enemy.

But she could not change who she was, or what she had done, any more than she could erase the memories of the pleasures to be had between a man and a woman. To know such pleasure existed, to taste it, and then know you would never experience it again...could anything be crueler? Perhaps only knowing whom she had shared the pleasure with.

Her skin scalded with heat. Since his rejection of her two years previous, Abigail had done everything to put Lord

Roxton and the hopes she had built around him out of her mind. When he had dropped his suit, without even the courtesy of an explanation, she had been heart sore for months. She had turned down other suitors, too bruised from her encounter with Roxton to even consider someone new. Only when the scandal with Uncle Henry broke did she turn her feelings of hurt into a more useful emotion—retribution.

Now he had even robbed her of that. How would she face him without expiring from humiliation? A carriage stopped outside their townhouse, the Tarrington crest emblazoned on the side in gold and blue. A moment later, a footman assisted Lord Tarrington out. He walked up the steps on spindly legs, his walking stick clutched in a gnarled hand. Though sixty, he looked much older.

"He is here," she said, her voice void of enthusiasm. She took a deep breath and turned to face her future.

Ben rose from his chair and glanced out the window, squeezing her shoulder as he went to greet Lord Tarrington at the door.

"Pinch your cheeks," Aunt Edythe instructed, setting aside her needlepoint. "You look like death."

Abigail pursed her lips to keep her tongue silent. Aunt Edythe, with her mourning wardrobe, severe hair, and dour countenance that could scare off the Grim Reaper, was hardly in a position to judge.

Lord Tarrington walked into the room moments later, Benedict in tow, and greeted Aunt Edythe before addressing Abigail.

"Miss Laytham. It is lovely to see you again. You grow more beautiful with each passing visit."

She offered a brief curtsey. When she straightened, he took her hand and bowed over it, his dry lips resting briefly against her skin. Abigail suppressed a shudder. She should have worn gloves. The very notion of allowing this man access to her body seemed inconceivable.

Abigail forced a smile. "My lord, I trust you are keeping well. Won't you please sit down? We have ordered tea and Cook has made those jelly biscuits you so love."

Lord Tarrington smiled, revealing a full set of teeth, albeit yellowed with age and those awful cigars he loved to puff on. She imagined his estate reeked of them. He released her hand and lowered himself into a nearby chair.

"Such a good girl. Lovely manners."

Her smile became harder to hold. His idea of a compliment was hardly what a lady wished to hear from her supposed intended. "How kind of you to notice. Tell us, how do things fare at Maynerly?"

"My gardens are beginning to bloom. I think I shall have an exceptional assortment of roses this year. I am working diligently on a hybrid that I have the highest hopes for."

"How wonderful. I am pleased to hear it." Abigail cut him off before he launched into a soliloquy on botany that left her bored to tears.

"Glenmor, my good man, I wonder if you would allow me the privilege of escorting your sister to Lady Perth's garden party tomorrow afternoon. Did you receive an invite?"

Benedict slid a glance in Abigail's direction. Their social calendar remained dismally empty. "I am unsure," he hedged. "My mother usually attends to our social calendar and she is indisposed at the moment."

If one could call hiding in her room to avoid facing her daughter's decision of allowing herself to be married off to a doddering old man, indisposed.

"I see. Well, it is of no consequence. I would like Miss Laytham to come as my guest."

"Ah," Benedict stalled once again, drawing the word out.

"I am most certain my niece will be more than pleased to attend," Aunt Edythe said.

Abigail gave Benedict a small shrug. What did it matter, after all? Despite the inevitability of the marriage, she supposed a certain amount of courtship was to be expected. The sooner she resigned herself to the fact, the better off they would all be. Besides, perhaps the more she was seen out in society, the less shocking it would be and smooth the way for Caelie to return as well.

Or so she kept telling herself.

Perhaps one day soon she would even believe it.

"I would be pleased to accompany you to Lady Perth's tomorrow, Lord Tarrington. Indeed, I look forward to it."

He smiled his yellow-toothed smile and Abigail suppressed another shudder. But this time it had little to do with Lord Tarrington and everything to do with the question of whether or not Lord Roxton would be in attendance at this same event.

I t was a beautiful day for a garden party. A warm June afternoon where the rain had dissipated, leaving the grass a brilliant green and the early summer flowers bursting from their buds. The full power of the sun had not quite reached its zenith and those families who had not yet escaped to the comfort of their country estates tried to squeeze the last drop out of the Season before they left. The garden party made for a pleasant diversion, if one subscribed to that sort of entertainment.

Which Nicholas decidedly did not.

However, Miss Caldwell's family had requested he attend and he had little choice but to go. After the debacle at the masquerade, he needed all the help he could get to keep his passions in check. Being around Miss Caldwell helped him do just that. He did not experience even the smallest stirring of desire when in her company.

Despite her uncommon beauty, she held little interest for him. There were no long looks, or sly sideways glances. No inappropriate touches when attentions were diverted away from them. She appeared to have no feelings whatsoever—for him, or for anything else.

For all intents and purposes, she appeared a pretty package with nothing inside.

And someday she would be his wife.

His mother turned to him, interrupting his thoughts. "Darling, Miss Caldwell is over by the rose arbor. Why don't you pay your respects to her? I see an old friend I would like to speak with."

He forced a smile. "Of course, Mother."

"Do not look so dismal," Rebecca whispered, looping her arm through his and leaning against him as their mother walked away. "It cannot be as bad as all that."

"Perhaps I should stay here with you," Nicholas suggested hopefully.

His sister had been thrilled with the invitation to Lady Perth's party, knowing Lord Selward planned to attend. She saw this as a good opportunity to gauge his true interest. Nicholas found it hard to believe any man could not be thoroughly engaged by his sister, but for some reason Lord Selward continued to drag his feet when it came to declaring his intentions. Nicholas wanted to press the man, but Rebecca forbade him from doing any such thing, insisting true love would unfold in its natural course, one only had to have faith.

But Nicholas didn't put much stock in faith. Or true love. Not anymore.

Rebecca gave him a little push. "Do not be silly. I have Mr. Bowen here to keep me company. Go and do your duty."

Nicholas and Bowen exchanged a look, his friend's expression conveying his sympathy. Though Bowen was a man of few words, he possessed a level of perception Nicholas often found uncanny.

"Take care of my sister," he told him.

"I shall fend off all unsuitable suitors."

"See that you do. I am rather fond of her and would hate to see—"

"You're stalling." Rebecca gave him another small shove. "Go."

Nicholas scowled, then quickly schooled his features and made his way across the lawn to the rose arbor where his inevitable future stood. As he crossed the well-manicured lawn, Miss Caldwell was joined by an old man and—

He froze in his tracks.

Devil take it!

She was not supposed to be here.

Chapter Nine

Abigail stood at the elbow of the aging lord; her spring green dress pressed against her lithe body by the soft breeze. Nicholas tried to avert his gaze, but his strength failed him and his eyes greedily gulped up the sight of her. The material outlined the sweet curve of her hips and gentle slope of her thighs. He had touched her there. He had run his hands and mouth along the smooth, soft skin. Tasted her—

He faltered, the toe of his boot catching a tuft of grass.

Dammit, man, get your wits about you!

He pulled his gaze upward and realized Abigail, who had yet to see his approach, looked decidedly miserable beneath the pasted-on smile curving the corners of her mouth. No great wonder. Tarrington was sixty, if he was a day, and in no way able to pleasure a woman of Abigail's fiery passions. Nicholas wouldn't be surprised if the man expired on his wedding night. Then again, that might be the best thing that could happen to Abigail. At least then she would be free of the backward thinking old goat.

"Good afternoon, Lord Roxton," Miss Caldwell said,

though her smile never quite made it to her dark eyes. Nicholas forced one of his own and wondered which would be the first to falter—his or Abigail's.

Next to Tarrington, Abigail stiffened, the already pinched corners of her mouth growing more pronounced. She avoided his direct gaze, looking off in the distance somewhere just beyond his shoulder.

"Good day, Tarrington, Miss Laytham." He gave a brief bow before turning his attention to his soon to be fiancée. "It is lovely to see you again, Miss Caldwell. I trust the day finds you well?"

"Well enough." Her voice flowed placid and plain, as if showing any hint of emotion was a strict breach of etiquette.

If so, Abigail had apparently skipped that lesson. Her pale skin flushed to a rosy hue that had nothing to do with the warm sun and everything to do with his arrival. Even without words—she likely could not fit any past her clenched jaw—he could read anger and disgust, and a strong desire for the ground to open up and swallow him whole. Or in piecemeal. He doubted she would be particular about the process so long as the end result meant he disappeared completely, never to return. Not that he blamed her. He had experienced the same emotions each time he looked in the mirror since the night of the masquerade.

He struggled to fill the awkward silence that had descended upon their quartet and to keep Miss Caldwell from making some benign comment about the weather. "Tarrington, what brings you to town?"

"I have come to pay my respects to Miss Laytham and her family." He patted her hand, a motion that only seemed to intensify her discomfort. She pulled her bottom lip between her teeth and bit down. "It is unusual for me to leave my estate. This is a crucial time for my roses, but Miss Laytham requires my attention as well. It would not do to propose without a little courting first, I suppose."

Abigail's rosy blush turned into a blotchy crimson stain.

How horrified she must be to face him now. No, horrified did not even begin to do justice to what she must be feeling. Had Nicholas known Abigail planned to attend Lady Perth's tea, he would have begged off, regardless of Miss Caldwell's request of his presence. He could not avoid her forever, but he at least wanted to give her time to come to terms with what had happened. What he had done.

Though given the anger she harbored against him for her uncle's death, he wouldn't hold his breath and expect her to forgive one more grievance.

Especially when said grievance was so horribly unforgivable.

Yet, even now, feeling the fury rolling off her, he could not help but be stirred. He could still taste her. Still feel her body's eager response to his touch. The warmth of her skin. In that one brief interlude, she had emblazoned her image into his memory with such heat it had scorched his soul.

He hated this weakness, but he was helpless to do anything about it. He was a creature of passion. Regardless of how much he tried to suppress or ignore the base, sinful needs of his body, he could not deny their existence. Or the way her presence preyed upon them.

"Do you not think so, Roxton?"

Nicholas pulled himself out of his thoughts and forced his attention back to the conversation at hand. Tarrington had droned on about his flowers, likely assuming it impressed the ladies, though from their expressions, Abigail appeared far from impressed and Miss Caldwell...well who knew what she thought of it.

"I'm afraid roses are not my forte, Tarrington."

"No," the older gentleman said, a condescending smile

quirking one corner of his mouth until it reminded him of his father. "And what is your forte?"

Putting my mouth on your intended and making her cry out with pleasure, Nicholas wanted to say, but refrained. That was something the old Nicholas would have said with careless disregard for the consequences. The new Nicholas, however, had learned some consequences came with a hefty price, and that decorum and restraint were not always the enemy.

"I am a man of simple pleasures, Tarrington. I do not ascribe to any particular talent." At least none he could speak of in polite company.

"Is that so?" Much to his surprise, Abigail had found her tongue. "I've heard you have a particular talent for acting."

"Acting?" Miss Caldwell echoed the word with such derision Abigail might have said he liked to run down Bond Street wearing nothing but boots and a top hat.

"Yes," Abigail responded, before he had a chance to counter her claim. She turned her direct gaze upon him, and her light blue eyes drilled him with all the pain and humiliation she had experienced upon discovering his true identity. The emotion left him humbled. And wary. "I've heard Lord Roxton is quite adept at making others believe he is one thing, when in fact he is something else altogether. Is that not so, Lord Roxton? Is that not a talent you ascribe to?"

Nicholas's mind worked furiously to find an appropriate answer given their mixed company, but he came up empty. He had not expected this full-frontal assault. Any lady who had suffered the humiliation and betrayal she must have felt would be more likely to hide away and lick her wounds. He knew of very few, perhaps even less than that, who would practically call him out in front of others, twisting her words in such a way he could do little to combat them.

Not that he had a retaliatory leg to stand on.

"Is that a talent, Miss Laytham, or a fault?" He asked.

She lifted one shoulder in a shrug. "I suppose it all depends on how one uses it. How would you use this skill, Lord Roxton—for good or evil?"

He wished he could look away; he could not form a solid thought while her gaze held him captive. No answer he gave her could make up for what he had done. Honesty remained his only option. "I think it is a talent best left forgotten, as I have no intentions of using it in the future."

"Time will tell, Lord Roxton. But if you'll forgive me, I, for one, will not hold my breath waiting for such an unlikely event."

"Lord Roxton, I see my mother standing over by Lady Colbert," Miss Caldwell cut in. Her tight expression indicated she wished to extricate herself from the escalating tension their exchange had created. "Would you be so kind as to escort me to them?"

Miss Caldwell had once told him she did not like conflict of any kind. She found it gauche. It was one of the few opinions she had expressed. Nicholas had tried to argue a certain amount of tension should be expected in life and could indeed lead to some of the most stimulating debates, but Miss Caldwell did not engage him further on the topic. She had stated her opinion and, in her mind, the matter was closed.

Nicholas saw long nights spent at his club in the company of Spence and Bowen if he wanted to have any type of lively conversation in his future.

Provided Spence did not make sail for some uncharted territory to avoid the marriage noose, a threat he made more regularly with each passing day. An idea Nicholas was beginning to think held true merit.

"Indeed, Miss Caldwell, it would be my pleasure." He inclined his head at Lord Tarrington and Abigail. "Perhaps I will see you again soon."

"I would not hold out much hope on that account,"

Abigail said, her gaze turning flinty. "We don't go out in society much these days, as I am sure you are aware."

The barb hit its mark with searing accuracy and embedded itself deeply into his conscience where his guilt lay unabated. He had no words to offer to refute her claim or make what he had done better.

He bowed once and turned to leave, her remarks festering deep within him.

"Really, the nerve of that man to address me after what he has done to my family." Abigail's grip tightened on Lord Tarrington's arm as she watched Lord Roxton lead Miss Caldwell across the lawn to the Baroness.

"Hm," Lord Tarrington grunted. "One cannot necessarily blame him for the downfall of your uncle."

Lord Tarrington's quick dismissal of her feelings stoked Abigail's ire. How dare he take Lord Roxton's side on this matter!

"Lord Tarrington, you cannot possibly absolve Lord Roxton for his part in my uncle's death."

"My dear," Lord Tarrington placed a hand over her arm and led her away from the rose arbor toward the path that followed the length of the garden. "Your uncle chose his own end. Roxton had no hand in that."

Abigail tried to pull her arm away from Lord Tarrington but he held it firmly in place and continued to walk them away from the crowd.

"That is untrue! He played a very important part. He knew how my uncle felt about Madame St. Augustine and yet he goaded and thwarted him at every turn."

"Your uncle should not have made such a public display of his affections, nor should any lady of good reputation utter *that* woman's name." He shot her a look of censure. "Glenmor allowed his emotions to get the better of him. Any gentleman knows he should never allow his mistress to rule his emotions. Your uncle disregarded this rule and—"

"Rule?" Abigail managed to free herself of Lord Tarrington's hold. "My uncle was a sick man. His mind unbalanced by heartbreak. He should be pitied, not disparaged. Lord Roxton should not have antagonized the situation."

"Lord Roxton did nothing more than any young buck in his position would have done. If society had expected anything more from him, he would have suffered the same irreparable ruin your family did."

Lord Tarrington stopped and stared out over a bed of tulips that carpeted the landscape in a blanket of brilliant red and yellow.

Abigail fisted her hands at her sides in frustration. "Lord Roxton was the author of my family's downfall!"

Lord Tarrington held his arm out again for her to take. "Your uncle managed that one all on his own, I'm afraid, and in the process made you privy to topics no proper lady should know about. If we are to be married, I will expect you to carry yourself with more decorum befitting a lady of your station. You would do well to look to Miss Caldwell as an example. I will be sure to speak to my cousin in this regard."

Abigail ignored his proffered arm. She could not believe what she heard. How dare he absolve Lord Roxton and admonish her behavior for knowing of men's follies! Yes, of course she understood her uncle's obsession with his mistress did not rest at Lord Roxton's door, but the viscount's actions had only exacerbated the situation. If he'd had any compassion at all, or even an ounce of common decency, he would have let the woman go, and left her to Uncle Henry. Instead, he went out of his way to bate and antagonize her uncle, driving him to the brink and then over it.

Abigail did not condone her uncle keeping a mistress, but

marriage to Aunt Edythe must have been an unpleasant affair. Uncle Henry had obviously craved a woman's attention and affection. Madame St. Augustine must have sensed this and used her powers of seduction to pull him into her clutches. Once there, he had changed. He became more secretive and closed off, his manner more erratic. His spending habits had spiraled out of control and strained their already thin coffers. When he began to lose her to the younger, more affluent Lord Roxton, Uncle Henry grew despondent, desperate to hang on to a woman who sold her affections to the highest bidder. Unfortunately for her uncle, Lord Roxton had the bigger purse.

Abigail despised the woman, but understood to some degree her lot in life. Women without protection and family had little recourse in the world. While she didn't condone the woman's behavior, she understood the instinct for survival. And her uncle, his mind fevered with lust and desperation, wanted only love and affection.

Lord Roxton, on the other hand, was the one person within that sullied triangle who could have changed the course of events. He could have stepped aside; he could have been a gentleman and realized his actions were not worth the pain and suffering they would cause. But compassion, unlike acting, was not a talent he possessed. He cared little of what happened to others, behaving with impunity, and cold disregard for the lives he ruined in the process.

And for what?

Some fancy whore.

The whole thing disgusted Abigail, but Lord Roxton's part in it disgusted her most of all. If he had stopped for one moment and looked at the bigger picture, he could have prevented what happened. It had been in his hands, and he'd crushed it in his fist, destroying everything. It turned out the man she thought him to be, kind and amusing, warm and engaging—had all been a ruse. He was a far better actor than she gave him credit for. He had deceived her not once, but twice now, making her two times a fool.

That she had a hand in her own downfall only made the pain greater.

"If you don't mind, Lord Tarrington, I am feeling rather unwell." Abigail lifted a hand and touched her temple. "Would you be so kind as to take me home now?"

Facing down Lord Roxton had required more energy than she possessed, given the sleepless nights she had suffered since the masquerade. The way her body had responded as he'd approached disturbed her most of all. The closer he'd come, the deeper the ache inside of her went, until she wanted to press a hand against it to ease the sensation. Worse still, she wanted his hand pressed against it. Or rather, the hand of the man she'd thought him to be before she'd discovered his true nature.

Her body flushed. Dear heavens, what had he done to her? Was she bewitched? Or, like Uncle Henry, had lust driven her to madness?

Regardless, unlike Uncle Henry, she refused to give in to such folly. Lord Roxton may be a sinfully handsome man with the ability to bring a woman's body to the heights of ecstasy, but he was also a man skilled at deception. She would not be so foolish a third time.

***

"Lord Tarrington has no inkling of what Lord Roxton did. He actually absolves him of all responsibility as if his behavior was perfectly normal!"

Abigail paced Benedict's study, her arms flailing in anger. She still could not believe what that decaying old man had said, or how she had stood there, mutely listening to it while he simultaneously suggested she be more like Miss Caldwell. And what did she do to counter his ridiculous claims? She insisted he take her home. Her anger had made her mute, a status not often achieved.

At least she'd had her say with Lord Roxton. She'd left no doubt about how she felt with respect to his behavior the night of the masquerade. Though his response had put her out of sorts. Perhaps if he had not appeared so chastened, it would have left her more satisfied. Instead, he had apologized. Apologized! Granted he had veiled his words so the others did not take his meaning, but she had understood him all too well.

Did the man think a mere apology would suffice? Or that she would believe it to be sincere? And why did his being sorry over what had transpired leave her empty inside?

"The man is insufferable!"

Benedict glanced up from his ledger. "Lord Tarrington?"

"No, Lord Roxton."

"Lord Roxton? Did you speak to him directly?"

Abigail waved a hand as if it were inconsequential. "Briefly."

Now she had her brother's full attention. He closed the ledger and leaned back in his chair. "And what did you say?"

"Nothing really."

Benedict raised an eyebrow.

Abigail huffed out a short breath. Her brother knew her too well. "Fine. I may have made reference to his past behavior."

Benedict groaned. "And what did he do?"

Abigail scowled, picking at a loose thread on the embroidered throw that lay atop one of the wingback chairs next to the fireplace. She could not count how many evenings she had spent curled up here, daydreaming of her future, a future that would now never come.

"He appeared to agree with me."

"Ah," Benedict returned to his accounts. "I am not surprised. He seems much changed since Uncle's death. I imagine the way in which it took place would have an effect on any man."

Abigail whirled around. "As it should! But it does not absolve him of what he did to precipitate it."

"Abby…" Benedict sighed and hung his head for a moment before pushing out of his chair and coming around his desk to stand in front of her. He put his hands on her shoulders and waited until she looked at him. Abigail hated what she saw. Strain and worry etched deeply where laughter and light used to be. He'd had a bright future once. They all had.

"Don't say it—"

"Lord Roxton is not to blame for what happened to Uncle Henry."

Why did everyone keep saying that? Could they not see? Were they all so blind to what he had done? "Yes, he—"

Benedict shook his head, cutting her off. "No, Abby. Opal St. Augustine is a mercenary woman who is always on the lookout for someone to give her protection. She had to have known Uncle's funds were running low, making him of no more use to her. That is the way of her sort."

"But Lord Roxton—"

"If it hadn't been Lord Roxton, it would have been some other gentleman. He was in the wrong place at the wrong time and paid the price."

"No, Uncle paid the price," Abigail said. Her brother's words cut deep. She pulled away from him to avoid the blade.

"Uncle chose the method of payment. Lord Roxton did not do that for him. Nor did his mistress. You know that. You are simply too hurt and angry to admit it."

Abigail turned and walked to the window. She stared out onto the quiet street. If she turned her head slightly to the right, she would have a clear view of Lord Roxton's home, a home he had purchased shortly after dropping his suit. It had been like rubbing salt into an open wound. She turned her head to the left instead.

The rational part of her knew her brother's argument held merit. But she could not let go of her outrage, or the hope of repairing the damage done her family. It was the only thing holding her together. The singular purpose that helped her put one foot in front of the other each day.

Turning back to her brother, she motioned to the ledger he had been hunched over before she stormed in. "How are the accounts looking?"

He made a face and returned to his desk. "Dismal, I'm afraid. We are coming up short again and the hole we have sunk into only becomes deeper with each passing day. Just when I think all of Uncle's creditors have shown themselves, another one arrives at our door. Letting out the country estates has helped, but not enough. We may have to sell some of the unentailed land."

A soft scratch sounded at the door. Benedict and Abigail looked over as it opened and their mother slipped through. A vellum envelope fluttered in her hand and a brilliant smile lit her features. For a woman nearing fifty, Lorena Laytham had held up remarkably well. Her beauty had not faded with the years or the hardship and heartbreak she'd endured. Even the most recent scandal had not dimmed the inner light that shone through her. Was it any wonder Abigail's father had risked his family's wrath and censorship to marry her?

"I have good news children," she said, though both of them had ended their childhood long ago.

"We could use some," Benedict muttered.

"What is it, Mother?" Abigail crossed the room to meet her half way.

"A dear friend has requested our attendance at her country

estate. She is throwing a party and very much wishes us to be there."

Abigail stood stunned. Could it be the tides had finally turned? Had society decided to forgive and forget? Though the forgiveness part was a sham. They had done nothing requiring anyone's absolution.

"The best part," her mother continued, "is both Caelie and Edythe have been included in the invitation."

This news shocked Abigail even further. Neither Caelie nor Aunt Edythe had been invited anywhere since Uncle Henry's death with the exception of the Doddington's masquerade. Aunt Edythe had declined on both their behalf, finding the event distasteful. Just which dear friend did Mama have up her sleeve and where had they been for the past months?

"Do you think Aunt Edythe will accept?" Her aunt had stopped going out into society well before Uncle Henry's death and her acerbic temperament did not make her a sought-after guest.

Mother shook her head. "No."

"And what of Caelie? Will she allow her to go?"

"I will do my best to convince her. Perhaps if I suggest it will further Caelie's chances of making a good match it will sweeten the request."

The barely restrained irritation in her mother's voice spoke volumes. Aunt Edythe had never taken much interest in her daughter, never forgiving her for not being born a son. Caelie bore the rejection stoically, but Abigail could see the pain it caused reflected in her eyes. She did not deserve such treatment. Perhaps the idea of a party would brighten her cousin's spirits. Though she never complained, Abigail knew Caelie had suffered horrible loneliness since the scandal and her broken engagement to Lord Billingsworth.

"Who is hosting the party, Mother?" Benedict asked.

Abigail hoped he wouldn't try to beg off, claiming he couldn't possibly leave. The break would be good for him. He needed to get away from barking creditors and ledgers that never balanced in their favor.

Mama lifted her chin, her smile never faltering. "It is from Lady Blackbourne."

Chapter Ten

A bigail's heart slammed against her breast.

Lady Blackbourne? Lord Roxton's mother? Despite the countess's warm reception of them at the masquerade and her attempt to rekindle the friendship with her mother, she couldn't possibly have gone so far as to invite them to their country estate for a fortnight. They were still pariahs amongst society. Obviously, Abigail had heard wrong.

"I beg your pardon?"

Her mother reached out a hand and placed it on Abigail's arm. "I know how you feel about Lord Roxton, Abigail; you have made that perfectly clear to anyone who will listen."

Had she really been so vocal? And why did it sound as if her mother chastised her? Lord Roxton deserved her derision, despite what everyone else seemed to think. She opened her mouth to say so, but her mother cut her off.

"Lady Blackbourne has been a good friend to us since we returned to London after your father and Roddy passed. She has been quite upset over society's treatment of us and wishes to set things right. Is that not what you have wanted?"

"Yes, but—" She shook her head. That such an opportunity should come from Lord Roxton's family made her nervous. "But how will Caelie feel attending a party thrown by the family of the man who orchestrated Uncle Henry's downfall?"

"Orchestrated is a strong word, Abigail," her mother said, making it clear she, too, did not agree. "I have spoken with Caelie. She is amenable to the idea of attending."

"She is?" Abigail could not hide her surprise. She'd practically had to beg, cajole, and plead Caelie to join her in the park the other week. Given the disastrous results of that outing, her cousin surprised her with her willingness to try again on a much more public scale.

"Yes," Mother continued. "Now if we are to attend, I must have your word you will be civil and courteous. There can be no embarrassing outbursts like the one yesterday at Lady Perth's garden party."

Abigail looked down at the floor, unable to hold her mother's pointed gaze.

"I would not call it an outburst, exactly," she muttered. "More like a private conversation, and I merely inquired about Lord Roxton's acting ability, nothing more."

"I am sure." Her mother's dubious expression indicated her doubt that Abigail's inquiry was as innocent as she portrayed it to be. "This so-called private conversation occurred in front of Miss Caldwell, and she in turn relayed it to Lady Blackbourne. Your unrestrained behavior made the young lady most uncomfortable."

"All I said was—"

"It matters not what you said. What matters is that you must have a care, Abigail. If you continue down this path, you will turn into a harpy. And no one wants to marry a harpy."

Abigail doubted Lord Tarrington would care one way or the other. He never listened to her anyway and so long as she had a functioning womb, she doubted he would even notice she had an opinion to harp upon.

"It was not my intention to make Miss Caldwell uncomfortable." Although someone as stiff and tightly wound as Miss Caldwell could probably benefit from a little discomfort now and then.

Her mother took both of Abigail's hands in her own, the lines around her mouth softening in sympathy. "Abigail, I know you want to save this family. Ever since your papa and Roddy died you have blamed yourself, as if you held the power to save them, yet somehow had failed."

Tears pricked the corners of Abigail's eyes. She shook her head, more because she did not want to revisit that time in her life than out of disagreement. Her mother hit the mark with startling accuracy. Abigail did feel responsible. How could she not? She had fallen ill first. She had brought the sickness that killed Papa and Roddy into their home. Then she had recovered, as had her mother, but Papa and Roddy had succumbed. Thankfully, Benedict had been away at school, or perhaps she would have lost him too.

"It was my fault."

Her mother squeezed her hands. "It was nothing of the sort. You were ten years old. There was nothing you could have done. I am only grateful I did not lose you as well. You cannot blame yourself, nor can you hold yourself responsible for not stopping your uncle from the path he chose. He lost himself in his own desperation and was beyond all our reach. If you want to help this family, behave as the lady I know you are and accept Lady Blackbourne's invitation in the spirit in which it was given. If not for yourself, then for your brother. And for Caelie."

Her mother's words, while not absolving her guilt over the past, settled upon her the importance of the present, and the possibilities of the future. Had she been going about this all wrong? Her mother and brother, even Caelie, had come by their forgiveness with grace and ease, while she had clung to her anger and need for vengeance. Was it time to choose a different path? The idea felt foreign to her and she was not convinced it was the right one.

But if Mother thought attending this party would aid in the reparation of their family, she would do it.

"I promise to be on my best behavior. I hear Sheridan Park is quite vast. Surely, I can manage to avoid Lord Roxton for the most part. And I have no doubt Lord Roxton will go out of his way to do the same."

Her mother nodded, satisfied, then turned to Benedict. "Do we have any funds for new gowns for the event, Ben, darling?"

Benedict glanced down dismally at the ledger in front of him. Abigail knew his sharp mind tried to calculate any possible way he could accommodate his mother's request, but in the end, one could not squeeze blood from the stone.

"I do not require new gowns, mother. I'm sure Muri can help alter any that require it. Let us not take on an extra expense if it is not needed."

Benedict threw her a grateful look and she felt a sense of relief she could assist him at least in this small way.

"Very well then. We shall make do."

Abigail excused herself and quickly made her way up the stairs to Caelie's room to see for herself her cousin's enthusiasm at attending an event thrown by the family of the devil himself.

Granted, he had not behaved like the devil when she'd taken him to task the day before. In truth, he appeared genuinely regretful for his actions. Despite her humiliation and anger over his deception, she had to concede he had been most determined to remove her from Madame St. Augustine's party while keeping her reputation intact. And his contrition over what had transpired at the masquerade only confounded her further.

Such facts shook the foundation she'd stood on these past eight months and an unwanted truth filtered past her pain. Had her hurt feelings over his sudden dismissal of her affections prior to Uncle Henry's death made her predisposed to cast him in the role of villain? Was it easier than blaming her beloved uncle for his own actions?

While she was not ready to admit such, nor could she deny the doubt that crept in. But regardless of whether Lord Roxton had been directly responsible for Uncle Henry's death or not, nothing absolved him of the ruse he had perpetrated against her, nor the events that took place in the music room during the masquerade.

An honorable man, a good man, would never have behaved in such a manner.

But if she believed that, and she had willingly been a participant, what did that make her?

"I must see you again." Opal grasped Nicholas's arm and leaned into him.

He tried to pull away but she held fast and any movement he made only brought her closer. "I'm afraid that isn't possible. I've told you, I have left that part of my life behind. I have no desire to take it up again."

"Liar!" She hissed, her hazel eyes blazing in the waning sunlight. Hyde Park was deserted, and he'd chosen a secluded area to meet. He had not wanted to come, but her threat to show up at his parents' house if he did not, proved too much. His mother would be horrified, and he refused to subject Rebecca to a woman such as Opal St. Augustine.

What had he ever seen in her?

Her skills in the bedroom were legendary, but then again, so were his. Had she been worth it? Had he truly derived enough pleasure from their time together to make up for all the damage it had caused?

No. He could say so now without hesitation. No amount of pleasure was worth the pain he had caused. And after his run-in with Abigail at the tea, seeing all he had done reflected in her eyes, her determination to make him pay regardless of the risk to her own reputation, he wished he could take it all back.

But what was done could never be undone.

Nothing he did could bring Lord Glenmor back from the dead. But he could ensure it never happened again. He needed to keep his passions and desires in check so he didn't ruin anyone else's life.

He had made great strides in accomplishing this too, until Abigail flew back into his life in a fury. It took only one kiss to strain the tenuous control he had on his passions. She had always done that to him. While the other young ladies of the ton pranced and preened and held tightly to their sense of propriety, Abigail barely maintained her balance on the fringes. She argued opinions and politics, never afraid to speak her mind. She smiled and joked; exuding such warmth and life that being with her was like standing on the bright side of the sun and basking in its glory.

As much as he had wanted her, he knew he did not deserve her. Maybe that was why Lord Glenmor's refusal of his suit cut so deep. The truth of his inadequacy had come home to roost. Everything his father had ever said on the matter had raged to the forefront. He was a scoundrel, a pretender. A bastard.

He had not deserved her then. He deserved her even less now. Yet still—*still*—he continued to try and prove his worth, like a bad habit he did not know how to break, even though he knew the outcome he wished for would never come about.

"I have turned over a new leaf, Opal. I will no longer be attending your parties. You would do better to turn your energies toward finding a new protector instead of attempting to convince me to take up the role once again. I will not. It is over. You need to accept that."

As he had to accept that despite the passion they had shared, Abigail was beyond his reach. He must forget her. He needed to stop thinking how her kiss had tasted sweeter than the most exotic of fruits, or how her ardor and enthusiasm had frayed the fragile grip he had on his emotions and desire.

But knowing and doing were two different entities altogether. He wanted Abigail with a desperation he could not deny. When their bodies touched, the need for her overtook him. It went beyond the physical to somewhere deeper. Somewhere beyond his experience.

Opal released his arm. All around them, the quiet of an early summer's night closed in. Only a few twitters of birds remained as most had settled in for the evening. Even the squirrels, that often foraged the grass for nuts and seeds, were nowhere to be seen, as if they had sensed her wrath and taken cover to avoid it.

"You will attend my next party, and you will not leave as soon as you did the last time. No one even knew you had been present!"

"What does that matter?" Though the parties were anonymous, Nicholas had often been brazen enough to forgo the mask. He had not cared if anyone knew he attended or what he did there. He'd reveled in his newfound reputation as a depraved rake who made pleasure his calling card.

And he had paid the price for it.

"So long as you stay away, the ton believes you blame me for what took place. They look at me differently. The only way

I could amass a group at my last party was to spread the rumor that you planned a return."

"You did what?" How had he not heard about that? Surely someone in his circle—

But no. He no longer traveled in those circles. The only true friends he had were Spence and Bowen, neither of whom frequented Opal's den of inequity. Spence was too busy hunting down his next adventure and avoiding the marriage noose and Bowen was simply not the type, preferring quiet, more scholarly pursuits to the debauchery of Opal's parties.

"What else was I supposed to do? My coffers are all but empty. I need a new protector, but no one will touch me. They look at me and see Glenmor dead at my feet. It's like I am still walking around with his blood on my body!" Opal pulled at the low bodice of her dress as if trying to remove stains long since gone.

The image disgusted Nicholas. It had haunted him nightly for months. It had been at a party much like the one Opal had hosted the other night. Glenmor had burst in, and in front of Opal, Nicholas and everyone else present, pulled out a gun, held it under his chin, and pulled the trigger. Blood had spattered about. In the midst of screams and shouts, the other guests rushed for the exits. Glenmor dropped to the ground, dead at their feet.

It seemed to happen in slow motion, yet Nicholas knew it could not have taken more than a few seconds. Glenmor's arm fell away and the gun clattered to the floor, the sound echoing off the marble. Nicholas stared in horror as Glenmor's legs gave out, and he buckled to the ground in a heap, his head mangled and destroyed by the force of the shot.

In the span of a few seconds, Glenmor had become unrecognizable, while Nicholas and Opal wore the remnants of him on their clothing and their skin.

Nicholas had still been standing in the same spot when the

magistrate arrived. They asked him questions, which he believed he answered coherently, but he could not get himself to move, not even when the pool of blood seeping from Glenmor's body flowed and oozed around his boots.

The image still sickened him. The man's desperation, the words of accusation he flung at both of them just before he pulled the trigger. The horrifying sight of his face dissolving and his body crumpling lifeless to the floor. The sight greeted him every time he closed his eyes. If Opal thought reminding him of that fateful night would bring him back to her, she was sadly mistaken.

He had chased after Opal because his pride had been wounded. Glenmor had prevented him from having something he wanted and so he'd retaliated by taking away something Glenmor prized. He'd won, but at what cost? Glenmor was dead at his feet and the woman he cared for the most, now despised his very existence.

He could never have foreseen the outcome, but he could control what he did now. That night had changed him. No longer could he behave the reprobate, foolishly thinking his actions held no true or lasting consequences. Once the initial shock of the event had worn off, he'd sworn an oath to change his life.

And he had.

He would not go back. "I cannot help you."

"Oh, but you will." Loathing gleamed in her eyes. "Because if you do not, I will tell everyone your lovely neighbor, Miss Laytham, attended my party and spent a good amount of time in a bedroom alone with one of my gentlemen guests."

She smiled then, and it reminded Nicholas all over again how mercenary she could be. He had once enjoyed her aggression, her take no prisoners' attitude. Now it disgusted him.

"Don't look so surprised," she said. "I knew it was you in

the bedroom all along. I watched you all but drag her from the main room."

"Miss Laytham is an innocent in all of this. Nothing happened in that room, save me convincing her to leave at once."

Opal shrugged. "I was not in the room. You locked the door, remember? And when one locks a bedroom door it is safe to assume they wish not to be disturbed. If memory serves, Nicholas, no woman has ever entered a bedroom with you and come out of it untouched. One assumes that trend continued with Miss Laytham."

"Leave Miss Laytham out of this. Her family has suffered enough at our hands."

"Please! No one has suffered more from Glenmor's actions than me. No one will touch me! I am on the brink of losing everything, but does anyone care? No! I am just some whore to be disposed of when I am no longer useful. No one will dispose of the lovely Miss Laytham. Her family's reputation is tainted for now but that will fade and eventually she'll marry that old man and live a life of luxury, as will the rest of her family. But what of me? What do I have? Nothing! And if I do not find a new protector soon I will be forced—"

She stopped and her jaw clenched, the words too awful to say, but Nicholas knew them anyway. It was the way of life for women like Opal. They played the game until their beauty faded and they could no longer attract a protector. If they were smart, they saved enough to retire and lead a quiet life, had men who agreed to pay an annuity even after their association ended. But Opal had never been one to save a shilling. She liked pretty things and possessed the arrogance of a true beauty who believed their looks would never diminish and they had all the time in the world.

Only she didn't. Her time as London's most infamous

courtesan drew to a rapid close, and with no means of support, her prospects were dire indeed.

Still, that didn't make it Nicholas's problem. "You've made your bed, Opal. I can do nothing for you. But mark my words; if you dare try to draw Miss Laytham into your machinations to save yourself, you will have a world of pain coming your way. I will not stand for it, and I will retaliate."

Her eyes narrowed to slits. "What is that chit to you?"

"An innocent bystander who has been hurt enough. I will not cause her or her family any more pain. And I will do everything in my power to stop you if you should try."

"So, you're not so redeemed after all, are you Lord Roxton?"

He didn't answer her. He couldn't care less what she thought of him, only that she left Abigail alone.

"I will settle you with some money, to tide you over, and then I am done with you. Provided you give me your word that you will let Miss Laytham alone."

Opal licked her lips and her eyes lit with hunger. Nicholas knew it had nothing to do with her want of him, and everything to do with the financial carrot he dangled in front of her.

"How large a sum?"

Their arrival at Sheridan Park went without incident. Abigail held no animosity toward Lord Roxton's family. Day by day, seeing Caelie's nervous excitement at the prospect of re-entering society, Abigail acknowledged the graciousness of Lady Blackbourne's invitation. The support of such an upstanding and well-respected member of society would go a long way to helping her family. Yet despite her gratitude toward the countess, she could not erase the sensation she had entered the devil's lair.

How strange to think only two years ago she'd enjoyed her second Season and Lord Roxton's attentions. How charming he had been. Had she only known then what she did now, perhaps she would have given him a wide berth. Bringing him into their lives had been like bringing the sickness that killed Papa and Roddy into their home all over again.

Sheridan Park, while vast, maintained a sense of warmth to it that surprised Abigail. Thick ivy climbed its way up the brick walls and flowers bloomed in the numerous lush gardens. Hints of the garden traveled inside the marbled main hall, with amaryllis and Calla lilies set in vases and paintings of glorious landscapes lining the walls in gilded frames. It was ornate without being ostentatious, homey without feeling worn. The countess's enthusiastic greeting only added to the welcome.

Lady Blackbourne's daughter, Lady Rebecca, emulated her mother with her warmth, though it disconcerted Abigail somewhat to see those familiar silvery eyes and inky black hair on another, but the resemblance stopped there. Lady Rebecca's fine, delicate features were the picture of her mother. While Lord Roxton, aside from his silvery eyes, bore no resemblance to Lady Blackbourne or his father, the earl.

It brought to mind the rumors of his true parentage. The whispers had existed for as long as Abigail had been in London, but most people shrugged them off. Lord Blackbourne had claimed him to be his son and none other, putting the matter, if not the rumors, to rest. Indeed, as they climbed the stairs to the third floor and walked the wide hallway to their rooms, Abigail did not see even the smallest hint of resemblance in any of the ancestral paintings to match Nicholas's.

What if the rumors were true? What must it have been like to be raised by a man who, every time he looked at you, was reminded of his wife's infidelity? Lord Roxton had rarely ever spoken of his father when they courted, but on the few occasions when he had, his manner and words showed no love lost between them.

"Oh, how lovely." Caelie did a slow spin as they stepped inside the beautifully appointed bedroom. Large cabbage roses papered the upper half of the wall, while a soft spring green colored the bottom. Accents of both were placed throughout the rest of the room and the two large windows filled it with light and overlooked the sumptuous gardens below that already showed hints of the beauty that awaited full bloom.

"I'm so glad you like it," Lady Rebecca said, her hands clasped at her waist. Despite her pleasing manner, Abigail noted the young woman seemed ill at ease in their presence. Hardly surprising. If Abigail had to act the hostess to those who blamed her brother for ruining their lives, she undoubtedly would be nervous as well.

Abigail wondered if things had turned out differently, if Lord Roxton had not dropped his suit, would they have become fast friends? She suspected they would have, as Lady Rebecca seemed a most pleasant sort, with a fiery look in her eyes Abigail recognized in her own.

"It is absolutely lovely. Thank you, Lady Rebecca."

"You must call me Rebecca. Please. We are to be friends, I think...I hope, and I would so much prefer it."

Caelie crossed the room, her hands outstretched to Rebecca who quickly took them. "I would like that very much. We both would."

Rebecca blushed and looked down at their clasped hands. "You are very gracious. Both of you." She glanced over at Abigail and smiled. "It is no wonder my brother was so smitten with you. Well, I will leave you for now. You may want to rest, but if not, the gardens are lovely this time of day and the meadow beyond even more so. If you're anything like me, you'll prefer to stretch your legs after such a long journey, instead of resting."

Abigail gave a perfunctory smile, shocked speechless by Rebecca's suggestion that Lord Roxton had been smitten with her. It was pure insanity of course. Lord Roxton had dropped his suit as if she had contracted the plague, hardly the action of a man struck by Cupid's wayward arrow.

Why would Rebecca suggest such a thing?

"Shall we take that walk?" Caelie asked once they were alone.

Abigail nodded, thankful for any activity that rid her mind of Lord Roxton and Rebecca's suggestion he may have held strong feelings for her at one time.

"Yes, I believe I could use a breath of fresh air."

Chapter Eleven

A bigail's breath froze until she could not remember if she had been in the process of breathing in or breathing out. As their hostess indicated, the meadow and gardens were indeed lovely, but it wasn't their beauty that swept the air from her lungs.

Lord Roxton pulled on the reins of the beast he rode and brought the animal to a stop well out of reach of Abigail and Caelie. He hesitated a moment as if he might continue on, but the brief hesitation passed and he expertly dismounted and approached them, much to her chagrin.

"Lady Caelie, Miss Laytham. I am pleased to see you have both arrived safe and sound. I trust your journey was not an arduous one."

Only in the sense that it brought us to you, Abigail thought, but she held her tongue. She had promised to be civil, and in truth, Rebecca's words pounded endlessly around her head until they trod a well-worn path between what she believed and the unpleasant possibility she had been wrong.

Caelie smiled at Lord Roxton. Her cousin's reaction, her ability to forgive, astounded Abigail. She didn't think she would ever find it in her heart to fully do so. How could she? Even if what Lady Rebecca said was true, and he had indeed been smitten with her, it did not absolve him of his actions. She gathered up her scattered anger and held it tight. Perhaps Caelie could find within her a civility that allowed her to treat Lord Roxton as if he deserved her attention or warm regard, but Abigail could not.

Her cousin took a step forward. "Our journey was most pleasant, thank you. The weather proved excellent for traveling and the scenery in this area is always most pleasing."

His shoulders visibly relaxed. Caelie had that effect on people.

"It is indeed. I much prefer it to London," he said, returning her smile.

Abigail's breath caught again. He really did have the most engaging smile. Then again, the devil was reputed to be most charming when he saw fit. She must not forget that, or allow herself to be swayed. Yes, she had promised to be civil, and she may even entertain the possibility that he did not bear one hundred percent of the responsibility for her family's current situation. But that did not mean she had to trust him in the process. He had, after all, duped her into believing he was someone else.

Granted, he had not specifically stated he *was* someone else. But he had distinctly left out the truth of his identity and allowed her to have erroneous assumptions. That, in her mind, was tantamount to a lie. For had she known she cavorted with her sworn enemy, she would never have allowed him to take such liberties, never have allowed herself to throw caution and propriety to the wind and...and...

Her face flamed.

"Miss Laytham, how nice to see you again. You are well, I trust?" Lord Roxton's intense gaze did little to settle her tangled thoughts.

"As well as one can be." In truth, his presence unsettled her and put her emotions at war. She loathed him—surely, she did! But even such loathing could not erase the memory of being held against him. Knowing the truth of whose arms had held her did nothing to lessen the perplexing need to experience it again.

"Are you on your way back to the main house? Perhaps I could escort you."

"That would be lovely," Caelie said.

Abigail glared at her. True, they were on their way back to the main house, but couldn't Caelie fib just this once and tell him it would be several hours before their planned return?

"I hear Lord Tarrington will also be in attendance." Lord Roxton looked directly at Abigail. He had the oddest way of making her feel as if he were looking into her rather than at her. "I understand he is a particular friend of the family?"

Was that concern she saw flicker in his silvery eyes? Thanks to his ruse, he knew circumstances dictated she marry a much older man, and no doubt he had enough mental acumen to put two and two together after seeing her at Lady Perth's garden party. Although, why her impending marriage should cause him any great distress mystified her.

"Indeed. Lord Tarrington is cousin to my aunt," she answered, keeping her tone neutral. "Do you know him well?"

Lord Roxton shook his head. "We have only met on a few occasions. We do not run in the same circles."

"No." Abigail failed to smother a smirk. "I don't expect you do. Lord Tarrington is an upstanding gentleman of impeccable manners." Albeit very backward in his thinking with respect to a woman's abilities and intelligence, and horribly boring when he droned on about his roses. Not to mention he made Croesus look like a young buck. But mannerly nonetheless.

"Abigail." Caelie drew out her name in warning.

Lord Roxton chuckled. The sound awakened something deep inside of Abigail despite everything he had done. She remembered a time when she'd welcomed his laughter, reveled in it. "No, it is quite all right, Lady Caelie. I'm afraid your cousin thinks the worst of me and I cannot argue her impression. Up until recently it would have been accurate."

"Until recently? Define recently? Last week perhaps?" Abigail asked, biting down before she let anything else out in front of Caelie. She had desperately wanted to confide in her cousin about her last encounter with Lord Roxton, but in the end, she feared unburdening herself would only cause Caelie more worry. It turned out she and her cousin had a secret between them after all.

"I am not the man I once was, Miss Laytham."

The gravity with which he said those words almost made her believe him. Almost. But too much had passed between them for her to be swayed by his false claims now. She had seen nothing to indicate a change in his behavior. The attentions he paid to Miss Caldwell were nothing more than a sham. If he had any true feeling for the young woman beyond what her reputation could do for him, he would never have led Abigail into the music room and seduced her.

"A leopard does not change its spots, Lord Roxton."

"Ah, but I am not a leopard, Miss Laytham," he said. "I am but a man. Are you to say a man cannot change once he has seen the error of his ways?"

For a brief moment, the sincerity behind his words made her doubt her convictions once again, but she caught herself.

"I don't believe many men ever see the error of their ways, Lord Roxton. That is the way of men, is it not? They believe whatever they do, say, or think is akin to the word of God and Heaven help anyone who has the audacity to tell them different."

"Is your brother such a man?"

She glared at him. He knew how much she revered her brother. "My brother is a wonderful man. An exceptional man. He does not need any correction in his thinking or perception."

"High praise, indeed," Lord Roxton said. A sad smile flitted across his face, then disappeared. "I hope one day my change in behavior will give my own sister cause to speak so highly of me."

She wanted to suggest he not hold his breath, but something in his expression halted her tongue and the words withered on its tip.

Look at a man's eyes. They mirror his soul, Abby, and that is where the real story lies.

Her uncle's words reverberated in her memory. She chanced a look at Lord Roxton and what she saw shocked her. For if her uncle had been right, then Lord Roxton possessed a tortured soul indeed.

Could he possibly understand the gravity of what he had done? Did he repent his actions? Or was this more trickery performed by a consummate actor who toyed with emotions like a cat did a cornered mouse?

Abigail no longer knew for sure. The uncertainty left her off balance more than she cared to admit. She lapsed into silence for the duration of the walk, letting Caelie pick up the conversation and keep it on neutral footing. She did not trust herself to take part, afraid if she steered their talk back to dangerous waters, she would find herself drowning in doubt once again.

"Grandfather feels the coffee plant will be most lucrative. The climate is perfect for growing the beans. He is thinking of sending poor Bowen back to the island to set up affairs there and get the plant running. The previous owner had been rather lax in that regard and there is much to be done to put it to rights."

Spence plucked at a passing plant and pulled the blossoming bud off with a deft snap of his fingers, then settled the trumpet-shaped flower into his lapel. "What is this flower? It's quite dashing, I think."

Nicholas glanced over at his friend as they sauntered down the pathway that led to the hunting lodge. Neither of them intended on hunting, but the lodge offered a respite from the matchmaking mamas who chased after Spence and his future title, and Nicholas needed a reprieve from behaving the perfectly mannered gentleman. To be more exact, he needed to get away from his father's critical eye. The old man watched and waited for him to revert back to his old ways. It did not help matters that the earl's mood had blackened considerably when he discovered the Laythams were on the guest list. A small fact his mother had not bothered to share until after their arrival.

"It is stinkweed, I believe."

Spence quickly dislodged the flower and tossed it over his shoulder.

"Needless to say, Bowen is not thrilled with leaving again so soon, not that he would dare say as much to Grandfather. The island life does not agree with him, though for the life of me I can't imagine why. There is such a wonderful sense of freedom there. I think you would quite like it."

"I'm sure I would." Nicholas lifted his gaze to the sky. Dark clouds scuttled across the brilliant blue though not in such abundance they threatened the afternoon's activities. His mother had planned an excursion through the pathways that led around the extensive meadows. He could stand to expend a little energy. He'd been restless and out of sorts since his arrival at Sheridan Park.

No. That was not exactly accurate. His restlessness had not begun until after Abigail had arrived.

Dinner last evening proved both a lavish affair and a torturous event. His mother had spared no expense and planned each course down to the smallest detail. For his part, he planned to avoid Abigail and her family as much as possible. He hoped the less they saw of him, the more comfortable they would be. Inviting them to the house party had been a good idea in theory, but he had not thought through the particulars. Like how it would feel to see Abigail day in and day out. How her presence would prey upon his mind—and his desires.

But he had wanted to make up for all he had done—to her and to her family. It was the main reason he had suggested to his mother they be invited as special guests to the party. His mother carried a lot of weight in society, though she rarely threw it around. And she had always held a particular fondness for Mrs. Laytham. Nicholas believed his mother admired the other woman for following her heart, regardless of the cost. How different would his mother's life have been had she done the same?

How different would his life have been?

"I believe Bowen is worried the current inhabitants of the island will take off with him as they did the last time and use him as a sacrifice to the lava gods, tossing him into a deep, dark pit in the hopes it will appease them and prevent the molten liquid from spewing over the island destroying everything in sight. A perfectly reasonable fear, I think. Don't you agree?"

"Yes, of course," Nicholas mumbled, rubbing at his chin. Perhaps he could ask his mother to re-arrange the sitting for this evening's meal. It wreaked havoc on his digestion when each bite he took had to be swallowed with a large dose of culpability.

"Bloody hell, Nick! Have you heard a word I've said? I'm discussing our dear friend's unhappy future and you are ambling along, wool-gathering as if it is of no great concern."

Nicholas stopped, realizing Spence had halted several paces behind him. He turned and offered him a contrite smile. "My apologies. You're right. My head is somewhere else today. Perhaps you could speak to your grandfather, convince him to send someone else in Bowen's stead. Although I would leave out the part about the potential lava god sacrifice. That may be stretching it."

Spence caught up with Nicholas. "I cannot ask my grandfather for anything, as you well know. If I do, he will merely place the condition of granting the favor contingent upon my marrying some proper chit. And you know how I feel about that."

"You'd rather be sacrificed to the lava gods?"

"A hundred times over."

"Then perhaps you can go to the island with Bowen, and offer yourself in exchange for him when the lava gods come calling."

Spence flashed a bright smile. "A capital idea, old boy. Perhaps I will do just that. It seems a less painful end than a lifetime of being shackled to a wife who loves my title and properties more than she does me."

Nicholas nodded. He knew full well his own future mirrored Spence's sentiment once he proposed to Miss Caldwell.

How had his life come to this?

But he already knew the answer to that. He had coveted a prize he was not fit to possess, and in losing it, he reacted with the petulance of a child whose toy had been taken away. Yet, unlike the tears of a child that quickly dried, his petulance had inflicted far greater damage. Lives were destroyed, fortunes changed, futures altered.

He wished now he had been a braver man, that he had defied Lord Glenmor's claims of his inadequacy. But he hadn't. Instead, he had stomped away and vowed to make Lord Glenmor pay. A vow he'd made good on.

———

L ady Blackbourne had outdone herself. Abigail looked beyond the ballroom, through the French doors to the garden beyond. Candlelight twinkled and wavered in the light breeze. The full moon shone down from above casting an ethereal glow over the shimmering gowns and jewels of those outside enjoying the warm air. It reminded her of a scene from A Midsummer's Night Dream. She half-expected Puck to pop out from behind one of the hedges at any moment.

Smiling at such fanciful thoughts, Abigail glanced down at her silvery blue satin gown adorned with tiny pearl beading across the bodice. It lacked extravagance, but it suited her coloring well and brought out the blue of her eyes. Muri, who had proven quite adept with the needle, had sewed a new ribbon around the hem, adding a nice bit of detail. It was the one expense Abigail had allowed Benedict to indulge her in. He had been adamant to the point of threatening not to come if she did not allow him to spoil her just a little.

Having Benedict accompany them filled Abigail with relief. It had taken some doing to convince him to leave behind the stresses of nagging creditors and unbalanced ledgers, but eventually she had managed to wear him down. Or rather, the creditors had, until he deemed it a good idea to leave town for a period and get away from it all. Though Abigail doubted such a place existed.

She knew he felt guilty he could not do more for her, but she understood. They did not come from wealthy beginnings, and though it had been over ten years since Uncle Henry had taken them in, Abigail had not forgotten their humble origins.

Besides, her mother had oft reminded her that sometimes the best way to enhance one's beauty was to let it shine through on its own, rather than trying to compete with a bunch of shiny bobbles or overdone fripperies. Abigail hoped she was right. She patted the pearls where they threaded through her upswept hair. Her dress was a far cry from many of the ensembles she saw moving about the marbled dance floor.

"It all looks so beautiful," Caelie breathed. The small orchestra played a lively tune and the men and women moved in tandem with the music. The spectacle took her breath away and it thrilled Abigail that she could share it with Caelie.

Benedict leaned in and whispered in Abigail's ear. "A far cry from the lion's den you expected?" She couldn't help but grin. Benedict did not share her animosity toward Lord Roxton—it seemed no one in her family did, save Aunt Edythe. Though, her aunt held everyone in contempt, so perhaps that was not a true measuring stick.

Despite his brotherly ribbing, lines of tension and worry still pulled at Benedict's eyes and made her determined not to burden him with her bad behavior. What good would it do? Even if Lord Roxton publically took responsibility for his actions, it would not change the one thing she wanted most.

Uncle Henry would not become less dead.

"I see some old friends from school," Benedict said, giving her hand a squeeze.

"You should say hello." Benedict's title helped insulate him somewhat from the scandal, but even he had not been immune to the distancing of old acquaintances. It saddened her. Over the years, as the scandal of their parents' elopement and estrangement from the family lessened and they became more accepted by society, Benedict's easy-going demeanor and handsomeness were much sought after. More so when it became apparent that her aunt and uncle would not be delivered of a son and heir, making Benedict the future earl. Perhaps now, with Lady Blackbourne's public acceptance, Ben could reclaim some of what he'd lost.

"I don't want to leave you. Mother is quite involved in a conversation with the Dowager Blanchard—about what, I cannot imagine—I should stay and keep you—"

"Nonsense." Caelie patted his arm. "Your sister and I will be perfectly fine on our own. This is not our first trip around the ballroom."

Benedict looked at them both uncertainly, his lips pursed as he wrestled with his choices. Abigail knew he worried about leaving them unprotected, given how many still felt about their presence here. While Lady Blackbourne's invitation and acceptance had helped thaw some of the ice, it did not melt the hearts of all.

"If you do not leave us, I swear I will hike up my skirts and run around the perimeter of the room, singing at the top of my lungs like I used to as a child," Abigail threatened.

Benedict sighed, but a smile edged at the corners of his mouth. "Somehow I don't doubt it."

"Off with you then." Caelie nudged him with her arm. "I promise to keep her from doing anything too foolish."

They watched him go. He looked over his shoulder as if to see they kept their promise, or perhaps to ensure no one had yet accosted them with their opinions. Knowing her brother, it was a little of both.

"Oh bother," Abigail muttered as her nemesis threaded his

way through the crowd making a beeline directly toward them.

"It appears, Abby, that Lord Roxton has an uncanny way of finding you, whether in a lake, a wide-open field, or a crowded ballroom. Do you not find that odd?"

Abigail forced a smile and spoke through gritted teeth. "I find it proves once and for all the only luck I have seems to be of the bad variety."

"Good evening, ladies." Lord Roxton executed a perfect bow. He exuded enough masculine charm in that one small gesture to make the other dandies prancing about pale in comparison. It irked her to no end. At least he had not tried to kiss her hand. She did not want to explain to her cousin why her face turned crimson and her knees shook.

Caelie responded to Lord Roxton's greeting with one of her own, while Abigail fought to hold her smile firmly in place. She would not give others the satisfaction of witnessing her discomfort.

"Please tell me I am not too late to claim a dance."

Abigail squirmed. She could keep up her charade of politeness for the length of a greeting, but the length of an entire dance in such close quarters was another matter entirely. But Caelie's eyes lit up at the idea. It had been too long since her cousin had enjoyed herself. If Lord Roxton chose her as his partner, perhaps others would follow suit. She stiffened her backbone. She would do what she must to ensure Caelie would not be designated a wallflower tonight.

"It would be our pleasure, Lord Roxton." Abigail said.

Chapter Twelve

"Shall we?"

Lord Roxton held out his hand and Caelie accepted, joy imprinted across her features. Caelie loved to dance, even more than Abigail did. Despite the animosity she held toward Lord Roxton, for this one concession she was thankful for his presence.

"Perhaps I may ask you for the next, Miss Laytham?"

Abigail accepted with a nod of her head, unable to speak past the lump in her throat at seeing her cousin happy. She watched as he led Caelie to the dance floor. Several gazes turned their way, their surprise obvious. Caelie's natural poise and her newfound ability to keep her emotions well hidden, made it difficult to tell if her cousin noticed the attention their entry onto the dance floor created.

Abigail looked around. Her mother had moved on from the Dowager and was now lost to her sight; her brother had joined old friends. Only she stood alone, left behind to watch the others. No one approached her for conversation. No one asked her to dance. She found herself counting the steps until the end of the quadrille.

A sense of relief filled her as Lord Roxton and Caelie returned. The light laughter of her cousin made the interminable wait worth it. But before she could reach them, Benedict interrupted their progress and whisked Caelie off for the next set.

Unfortunately, Lord Roxton continued on his way, directly toward her.

"Would you care for some punch? We have a few minutes before the next set begins. Let me fetch you a cup."

"Certainly." Abigail needed the time to collect herself before the music started and she must endure being held in his arms. Her gaze followed him through the crowd, watching his broad back and trying not to think of how she had clung to those shoulders in passion only a short time ago.

"Did you see who Lord Roxton danced with?"

Abigail froze as the tidbit of conversation floated past her from behind. She did not dare turn around.

"Lady Caelie, if you can believe. How chivalrous of him to do her such an honor. Why only a true gentleman would overlook such scandal and pay her attention."

Another lady chimed into the conversation. "I'm certain Miss Caldwell will not be pleased to know he has done so."

"Nor should she. It is quite disconcerting. I must say, I am most surprised Lady Blackbourne would go so far as to invite them. And even more surprised Lady Caelie would agree to come. Especially after the ghastly rejection she experienced from Lord Billingsworth. Though one can hardly blame the man. Why her family did not even seek recompense for the embarrassment."

"As well they shouldn't. A gentleman as eligible as Lord Billingsworth should never be forced to continue an engagement when the circumstances were so egregiously altered after he'd made his proposal."

Abigail could stand no more. She knew she had promised

her mother to be on her best behavior but their comments went beyond her limits. Satisfaction filled her at their shocked expressions when she spun on her heel to face them. The ladies turned beet red and their eyes widened in surprise.

"Miss Laytham," Lady Martin said, her mouth stretching into a tight smile. "We did not see you there."

"Obviously. What a shock it must be to both you and Lady Portsley to be talking about someone behind their back only to discover they were standing in front of you the whole time. Takes much of the fun out of it, does it not?"

Both ladies sputtered, their mouths agape. Any true lady would likely have ignored the slight and walked on, but Abigail had never been the type to let such remarks go, especially when they were directed at Caelie, an innocent bystander in all that had happened.

"And tell me, Lady Martin, how is anything my family has experienced much different than yours? Was my uncle any different from your own Lord Martin and his string of mistresses?" She leaned in and dropped her voice to a whisper. "Actresses, I hear? Oh, I know it's not the thing to mention, but since you both seem open about airing others' business, I thought you wouldn't mind a bit of your own as well. And you, Lady Portsley—"

"—it is gambling, I believe, is it not?" Abigail started at the sound of Lord Roxton's voice next to her. He gave her a conspiratorial wink, handing her one of the cups of punch he had returned with. "Hers, not his."

The ladies gasped in unison. Lady Portsley's face burned an ugly red that did little to enhance her already ruddy complexion. Her hand groped blindly for something to hold onto and found Lady Martin's. Lady Martin pulled away and snapped her fan, waving it rapidly in front of her.

"This is all too much. Too much. How dare you—"

"How dare you, Lady Martin. And you too, Lady Portsley," Lord Roxton said. "My mother has graciously invited you into her home and you repay such a privilege by insulting her guests? She will be most displeased to hear of such behavior. I know I am."

Abigail wanted to resent Lord Roxton for jumping to her rescue when she already had things well in hand. But the sense of victory at seeing the gossips squirm at the implied threat of Lady Blackbourne's censorship made up for it.

"We meant no disrespect." Lady Portsley scrambled to restore the good favor she had lost.

"What did you mean then?" Lord Roxton inquired, his intense gaze burning into both ladies until even Abigail felt the effect of it.

"Forgive us, Lord Roxton." Lady Martin curtsied, as if the motion were enough to satisfy. It was not.

"It is not my forgiveness you should seek."

Both Lady Martin and Lady Portsley paled as their gaze slid from Lord Roxton and onto Abigail. Obviously, the notion of apologizing to her for voicing thoughts everyone else present echoed was akin to having a hot poker stuck in your eye. Still, neither wished to be dropped from Lady Blackbourne's invite list and self-preservation could make one do things once thought unfathomable only a moment before. A fact she knew only too well.

Lady Martin cleared her throat and straightened her spine. "Miss Laytham, we are sorry if our words caused you any great concern."

"Indeed," Lady Portsley echoed.

Thin as far as apologies went, but Abigail did not expect more. It was all a farce either way. Neither of them experienced one iota of regret over what they had said, only that Lord Roxton had overheard and took them to task for it.

Lord Roxton took the cup of punch back from Abigail

and shoved both into the hands of the other ladies, caring little for politeness.

"If you'll excuse us," he said, turning to Abigail and offering her his arm. "The next dance is starting and Miss Laytham has been gracious enough to agree to be my partner."

Abigail took Lord Roxton's arm and allowed him to lead her out onto the dance floor. She wanted desperately to laugh at the stunned faces of the two older women who stood equal measures aghast and humiliated. They had been properly set down, first by her and then, even more effectively, by Lord Roxton.

He had come to her rescue once again. As much as she wanted to deny it, she couldn't. Any more than she could deny the unwelcomed thrill that shot through her as she placed her hand upon his.

The truth of it, and what it meant, left her unsettled.

N icholas pulled Abigail into his arms. The candlelight caught the pearls in her hair and made them sparkle, enhancing her regal beauty. Had he realized the next dance was the waltz, he may have rethought holding her to it, but he had been so incensed to come upon Abigail being spoken to thusly that his ability to think had been left somewhat muted. He wanted to toss both ladies out on their well-heeled behinds and wash his hands of them, and anyone else who shared their opinion of Abigail and her family.

"If you had done that, your mother would have no one left at her party save for my family and a few servants," Abigail said, startling him. He had been quite unaware he spoke his last thought aloud.

Her words were so matter of fact, so accepting of how things were. Is this what his actions had subjected her to? Did she have to put up with such treatment day in and day out? No wonder he rarely saw them out in society. His estimation of her rose significantly, having witnessed firsthand what she endured on a regular basis.

Yet still, she carried herself with such dignity, refusing to bow her head or hide away. He admired her courage. She may be a mere slip of a thing, but it did not stop her from taking others to task if they dared hurt her family. She possessed a sharp mind and even sharper tongue and she did not back down from using either.

The late Lord Glenmor was right. He did not deserve her.

If only he had realized this earlier, perhaps he could have altered his behavior to affect a different outcome. He would never know.

"Better your family and a few servants than a ballroom filled with two-faced sycophants," he said.

"Otherwise known as society."

How could she be so cavalier? Each word spoken against her stabbed his heart. Rage and helplessness warred within him. He wanted to protect her from it, shield her from the barbs and pointed remarks and stares, but how could he, when the reason they existed lay with him.

He spun her around, the other dancers nothing more than a haze of softly colored gowns and shining jewels set off by candlelight. Holding her in his arms, everything else faded into the distance. She brought him a sense of calm. A peace he had sought for most of his life. Yet, at the same time, she agitated every one of his desires, causing them to strain against the confines he had placed upon them. The dichotomy left him off balance.

She left him off balance.

"How can you ever forgive me for putting you in such a position?" The words escaped him before he could think better of it. When he was with her, his thoughts flowed freely from his mind and out his mouth. It had always been that way. It was one of the main reasons he thought she would make the best wife. He could be himself with her, and she did not hold it against him.

Abigail arched one blonde eyebrow and the hint of a smile played about her pretty mouth. "Who says I intend to?"

"Touché." He could not help but smile in return. When no answering glare came, an absurd amount of joy filled him and with it came a small sliver of hope. Could he gain her forgiveness? A ridiculous thought for reasons they both knew too well. "I am a despicable human being."

"A fact I do not dispute."

He wished she did not agree so readily but he could hardly blame her. He had done nothing to give her reason to think otherwise.

"Perhaps I could redeem myself in your eyes."

"Doubtful. Besides, I cannot imagine why you would care one way or the other." Her gaze drifted somewhere past his shoulder. "I am nothing to you."

She was everything to him. The thought came swift and unbidden. He clamped his jaws together tightly to keep the words inside and prevent mortifying them both. Where had *that* come from?

But he knew. He had always known. His feelings for her were there from the first moment he'd laid eyes on her and had lurked beneath the surface ever since their courtship ended. He should have ignored Lord Glenmor's refusal of his suit. He should have pressed on until the words came from Abigail's mouth only. Would she have issued them? Did she consider him unworthy of her affections as Glenmor had? She had never given him that impression when they were together. He thought it had been a mutual attraction.

They spun around again and Nicholas could not stop himself from inching her closer as they turned. Her scent, a mixture of honeysuckle and rose, surrounded him like an aphrodisiac. Even now, after everything he had done to prove Lord Glenmor's opinion was true, he wanted her still. The need for her entrenched itself within him and planted roots so deep they tangled around everything else.

"Is it always like this when you go out in public?" he asked, trying to distance his morose thoughts with conversation.

"Do you really want to know?"

"Yes."

"Then yes. It is always like that."

"I am sorry," he whispered, closing his eyes. Something in his tone must have caught her attention, for when he reopened his eyes she stared at him, but then glanced away before he could fully read her expression.

"My mother was most pleased to receive Lady Blackbourne's invitation."

It was the only acknowledgement he received for his woefully inadequate apology. It mattered not. Redemption and absolution were too far beyond his grasp. His past actions had made certain of it and his most recent ones threw more dirt on the grave.

She was lost to him forever.

He thought he had accepted this truth, but holding her now, he knew he had not.

Across the dance floor he caught a glimpse of Miss Caldwell standing near his mother, a bland look on her face as if nothing around her attracted her interest. She was his future. The notion left him cold.

He pulled Abigail a little closer still as the strains of the waltz rose and fell. It would end soon, and he would have to let her go. He wanted to savor this moment; certain it was unlikely to come again.

"Is there nothing I can do to convince you of my regret for what I have done?"

She looked at him, her mask of indifference cast aside, letting him see the pain she lived with every day. It grabbed his heart and squeezed with a painful grip, her next words shredding what was left to bits.

"Can you turn back time, my lord? Can you give me back my uncle?"

He shook his head. "I cannot. I sincerely wish I could."

"What of the past would you change if you could? How far back would you go?"

How far back? He had considered the question on a regular basis since the night Lord Glenmor stood in front of him and ended his life. Would he change that one night, or would he go back farther—to the first night he set his sights on Opal St. Augustine? Perhaps he would go even farther still, to the night Lord Glenmor cornered him and demanded he drop his suit. How far did one have to go to change the course of their life?

"As far back as I needed to."

His words were empty consolation.

"A pity you didn't think of that before your actions made it impossible to do so."

"I would—" He started, and then stopped, gathering his thoughts before he spoke again. He didn't know when, if ever, he would have her as such a captive audience again, and he did not want to waste this precious opportunity. "You have every right to revile me."

She lifted one eyebrow. The brilliant blue eye beneath it let him know she agreed.

"But I have changed," he insisted. "I *am* changing."

"Perhaps you are," she said, "and perhaps you do regret your actions and the pain they caused. Unfortunately, Lord Roxton, regret does not change my family's circumstances.

And while I no longer believe my uncle's death was what you intended; the outcome remains the same. And my family must bear the weight of that every day, while you do not. Such a fact makes it difficult to accept your apology, as such is easily given, then afterwards, you can walk without so much as a mark."

He wished she knew how wrong her claim was. His actions *had* left a mark, profound and indelible. The scars hidden deep inside where no one could see them.

"My apology is too little too late, but it is all I have to offer. All I have left. I was young, stupid, and selfish. I took my hurt and anger, and behaved every inch the fool. If I could change it all and give you back what you have lost, I would do everything in my power to see it done. I cannot, but know I live with that every day, though it pales in comparison to what you have suffered."

"Hurt and anger? Over what?"

The music ended, but Nicholas continued to hold her in his arms, staring at her, at the confusion wrinkling her brow. Could it be she did not know of her uncle's insistence he end their courtship? He had assumed she had. Was he wrong on that account?

"Over losing you." He left the words plain and undressed.

"Whatever are you talking about?"

"You do not know?"

She shook her head. Bewilderment filled him with equal parts joy and horror. Joy that she'd had no part in his rejection, and horror at the hurts he'd perpetrated thinking she had.

Only a few guests remained on the dance floor. They stood near the middle, a spectacle for all others to see. From the corner of his eye, he saw someone approach.

"Lord Roxton."

Nicholas pulled his gaze away from Abigail to rest it on her brother, hovering near them like a guardian angel, one with a dark enough expression to warn off the devil himself.

Nicholas let his arms fall away. Emptiness invaded his soul and bled through him like poison. Nothing could be done about it now. Too much time had passed. Too many hurts committed.

"Lord Glenmor, I was about to escort your sister to her mother. Perhaps you would prefer to do the honor?" He had to let her go.

"I think it best. People are beginning to stare." Abigail's brother held out his arm, but his warning gaze remained on Nicholas a moment longer, before lightening and shifting to his sister. "Would you like some punch, my dear?"

"Yes," she whispered, allowing him to pull her away. She glanced over her shoulder once, questions and uncertainty marring her expression. He wished he could explain, but would it even matter now?

He turned away and strode across the dance floor, seeking solace in the fresh air, away from the crowds and the gay laughter and jovial music. But, no matter how far he walked, he could never outdistance his guilt-stained soul.

He had driven a man to kill himself—and for what? A rejection that had never happened?

It was all too much.

Chapter Thirteen

The day dawned warm and sunny, perfect weather for the planned picnic. Abigail had expected the subversive shunning they had experienced over the past eight months to continue, however little by little the other guests warmed to their presence, or at the very least did not shy away from it. A change precipitated by Lady Blackbourne's open welcome of them, and enhanced by Lord Roxton's dancing with both she and Caelie last evening.

It gave Abigail hope all would be well, but she doubted hope would speed up the process soon enough to save her from marriage to Lord Tarrington. Still, at least it boded well for Caelie's future, if the welcome continued beyond the party. Before the scandal, Caelie's beauty and bright spirit had made her much sought after. Abigail saw a hint of that old spirit last night. It did her heart well.

She bent to pick a daisy growing near the large pond filled with lily pads and croaking frogs and the buzz of other things she couldn't name or see. She had left the others to their entertainments, most choosing to partake in or watch the ensuing cricket match. She needed a few moments of solitude.

Her mind refused to rest. It continued to reflect upon the things Lord Roxton had said to her during their dance. *He* had lost *her*? How could he make such a claim when he had been the one to leave? What did he have to feel hurt or angry about?

She'd not had the opportunity to ask, and in truth, she did not know if she wanted to—afraid the answer would cause more pain than the knowledge was worth. She closed her eyes, and for a brief moment allowed herself to relive the moments they'd spent in the music room at the masquerade, when he had given her the pleasure she'd asked for, knowing who she was the whole time. Afterward, when she discovered his identity, she'd assumed it had been another callous action from a man who cared little about who he hurt. Did she have it wrong? Could his motivations have been something other than what she'd imagined? Had the desire shared at the masquerade been mutual, as she'd originally believed?

She shook her head and reopened her eyes. No, she could not allow her thoughts to drift in such a silly direction. Such ludicrous ideas only served to muddy the waters. Perhaps it would be best if for the remainder of their stay here, she avoided Lord Roxton and any further conversation with him.

As she turned to rejoin the others, however, her plans of avoidance met instant resistance.

Lord Roxton approached, making a steady path toward her, his intent clear. Unless Abigail considered jumping into the lake to avoid him, she was stuck. And with her luck, he would only dive in and save her.

She braced herself and reined in the foolish giddiness her heart exuded at the mere sight of the man.

"You are not partaking in the cricket, my lord? I thought you would take such an opportunity to show off your prowess on the field to Miss Caldwell."

He stopped within a few feet of her. Abigail glanced over his shoulder to the hill beyond to avoid his gaze. Miss Caldwell watched the game, though she was too far way for Abigail to see the expression on her face. Boredom perhaps? Miss Caldwell did not strike her as the type to get excited over a cricket game.

"I am not in the mood today, I'm afraid," he said.

Abigail did not request clarification on whether he meant impressing Miss Caldwell or playing cricket. "I see."

"I thought I would join you down by the lake instead and see if you would care to take a stroll."

"With you?"

Nicholas—it grew increasingly more difficult to think of him as Lord Roxton—glanced around them. "Did you have someone else in mind?"

Most of the younger guests had moved farther up the hill to watch the game, cheering and jeering, depending on where their loyalties rested. The remainder of the guests had spread themselves about. Some lounged on blankets beneath the shade of the elm trees while others sat in chairs brought down from the manor. She and Nicholas were far enough away from the crowd in either case to enjoy a modicum of privacy while still being within view for the sake of propriety.

Unfortunately, it also meant no one would rescue her. Rebecca had invited both she and Caelie to watch the game with her, but Abigail had declined. She had needed time to herself. Time to reflect upon Nicholas's partial confession of the night before and what it meant, if anything at all.

Nicholas had shown her a side of himself she'd no longer believed existed and, while she had tried to tell herself his remorse was likely just a ruse, she was no longer certain she believed that.

"Fine," she conceded. What harm could there be? It would do her family good for her to appear to be on better terms with Nicholas. Or so she told herself as he swept a hand in the direction of the pathway and she turned to follow it. At least he had not offered her his arm. The less physical contact she had with him, the better.

"It's a lovely day for a picnic," he said, glancing upward to the sky.

Abigail lifted her gaze. Puffy white clouds drifted across the azure blue, lazy from the warmth of the sun's rays and in no hurry to get where they were going.

"Indeed."

Were they really going to discuss the weather? She remembered a time when they would talk about any manner of subjects. Politics, gossip, books. They had shared a wonderful relationship, short-lived though it was. He had treated her as an equal, not some simpering female that needed to be coddled and led.

She had thought him perfect.

She should have known it was too good to be true.

"Perhaps it will last for the duration of the party, do you think?"

"One can hope."

She glanced over and caught his eye as he looked down at her. The hint of a smile pulled at the corner of his mouth and a tiny flutter endangered her heart. "Shall we progress on to some other prosaic topic? I can think of nothing else to say about the weather."

Abigail stifled a grin and looked quickly away, frantically searching her mind for something—anything—to talk about. She and Nicholas had rarely engaged in small talk before, preferring broader topics, but to venture back there would be to claim nothing had changed, when everything had. She searched for a safe topic, but her mind drew a depressing blank.

"It is sad that this is what we have come to," she said. "We were friends once, were we not?"

Nicholas fell silent for a moment. "We were much more than friends, I think."

The reminder resonated deep within her. She did not like to remember. It made what he did to her family so much worse.

"Tell me something..." She hesitated, unable to look at him or acknowledge the truth of his statement. She kept her gaze fixed firmly on the ancient oak in the distance, its bright green leaves moving gently in the breeze, feathering against the blue sky.

"Yes?"

"Last evening when we danced, you said you were hurt and angry over losing me."

She ventured a quick glance up but he kept his gaze straight ahead. He too seemed mesmerized by the old oak.

Abigail took a deep breath, gathering her courage. "I'm curious. How did you lose me when you were the one who left?"

This captured his attention and brought it back to her. "*I* was?"

She stopped walking and turned toward him. "Indeed, you were. One day we were courting and the next...the next... well, there was no next, was there? You simply disappeared. What reason did you have to feel hurt or angry? You didn't lose me, you tossed me aside like a piece of old news."

Nicholas shook his head, disbelief stamped into the hard planes of his face. Her fingers itched to reach up and smooth it away. Instead, she curled the offending digits into her palms and held them tight.

"I stopped courting you because when I broached the subject of marriage, your uncle refused my suit. He said he would never countenance a union between us. That I wasn't worthy."

Nicholas's words rocked her. Marriage? "That can't

possibly be true. Uncle Henry knew I held great affection for you. He would never hurt me in such a way. He would not have made such a decision without consulting me first."

Nicholas ran a hand through his hair, ruffling its already mussed appearance. He looked around them, as if the answer he sought could be found amongst the foliage dotting the meadow. "I cannot say what he did or did not discuss with you. All I can tell you is when I broached the subject of a union between you and I, he refused me outright and would not listen when I wished to plead my case. He insisted I drop my suit altogether and that I would not be welcomed in your home after that day."

Abigail took a few steps away from him, needing to find a place in her mind where the things he claimed made sense.

"Why would he refuse you? You are Lord Blackbourne's heir."

"But I am not his true born son."

Abigail swayed; her balance compromised as revelations buffeted her from all sides. Then the rumors were true. But still, when it came to parentage, there were any number of the ton who could be questioned in such a way. If one began casting stones, how soon before the impact rocked their own house?

"Who is your father, if not Lord Blackbourne?"

"Your guess is as good as mine. My mother loved another before her family forced her to accept a more suitable marriage to Blackbourne. When her old lover returned after her marriage, they had a brief affair. Shortly thereafter, I arrived. My mother never revealed my true father's identity, nor do I expect she ever will. It was an agreement she made with Blackbourne to have him recognize me as his own."

He shrugged as if it was of no consequence, but Abigail knew differently. She could see it in his eyes. His past and future were built on a lie. The truth he would never be privy to. How could such a secret not torment a man?

Still...why would Uncle Henry refuse him? Lord Blackbourne's true son or not, the earl recognized him and so did society. Eventually he would inherit the title and all that came with it.

"There has to be more to it than that."

"To my parentage?"

"To my uncle refusing you."

Nicholas cleared his throat and straightened. He lifted a hand and rubbed at his smoothly shaven jaw. "There might have been some mention of my, uh, somewhat reprobate behavior."

Abigail lifted an eyebrow unable to help the sarcasm that dripped off each word she spoke. "Is that what they call it?"

"Your uncle feared I would not change my rakish ways and he refused to see you hurt because of it."

"And you did not change your ways, did you? In fact, you became worse." It was said the man had committed enough sins to make even the devil blush.

"I would have been faithful to you," he said, the words so soft on the air Abigail thought she had imagined them. But she hadn't, and they lingered between them like a broken promise.

She looked away. His eyes teemed with possibilities never fulfilled. It hurt to look at him. He stirred things within her, a need she couldn't place, or didn't want to, afraid if she did it would knock down her defenses and resurrect all the hopes and dreams she had placed upon him two years ago.

"How can I believe such a statement when, while courting Miss Caldwell, you show up at Madame St. Augustine's party and kiss me?"

"I was there because of you."

"I beg your pardon?" She stumbled back a step.

"Madame St. Augustine informed me of your intentions to go to the club that night. I followed you."

"Followed me? She told you?"

"With great pleasure. The key was not meant to be delivered to your address." He looked at her. "But you knew that, didn't you?"

Abigail looked to the placid surface of the lake. "I was certain you would be in attendance and I thought it the best way to corner you. To convince you to take public responsibility for what you had done to Uncle Henry."

"At such risk to your own reputation?"

"What risk? My costume kept me fully covered. No one knew of my attendance."

Nicholas took her hand and held it against his chest. "Opal knew. She knew and she used it against me."

Abigail cast a furtive glance at the other guests, then pulled her hand back before anyone took note of the improper contact. But she failed to stop the sizzle of sensation that danced up her arm.

"Used it against you how?"

Nicholas had frequented Madame St. Augustine's parties with alarming regularity after he'd stopped courting her. Why would he need to be coaxed back?

Nicholas dragged a hand down his face. His chest lifted and fell on a deep breath.

"Opal—Madame St. Augustine—has suffered a downturn since your uncle's death," he said.

"As well she should. She bled him dry and then cast him aside," Abigail said, her voice laced with the bitterness that had been burning inside of her these past eight months.

Nicholas did not refute her opinion. "After your uncle's death, I..." Emotions raced across his chiseled features, darkening his eyes to a stormy gray and haunting his handsome face. Remorse, guilt, regret?

"You what?"

"It changed me," he said finally. "In ways I'm not sure even now I am fully aware. It made me look at my life, at my behavior. What I saw disgusted me."

Remnants of hurt clung to the air around him like a dark cloud. Abigail sensed it. Her own anger and pain had made her blind to it before, but now she could no longer deny its existence.

"When your uncle died, the way he died, I held myself responsible. Both Opal and I carried on our affair with little regard for your uncle. We laughed over his obsession with her, never truly realizing its depth. We thought it amusing. It fed both our egos—me to have taken something of value away from him as he had me, and Opal for being so valuable a man would torture himself for not being able to have her. I thought in time he would find another mistress and move on."

"But he did not," Abigail said. She remembered those months. Her uncle's increasingly erratic behavior. His complete lack of propriety and good sense as he made a spectacle of himself in public over this woman. It had left Aunt Edythe humiliated, Caelie devastated, and the rest of the family helpless to stop him. He became a man possessed.

"No, he did not. And when he...died." She appreciated he did not use a more descriptive word. "Men in our circle began to view Opal in a different light. They blamed her for your uncle's downfall, as if she had lured him into it. They closed ranks and shut her out, willing to attend her parties but not to take her as mistress. She has been unable to find a new protector and now finds herself in dire straits."

Abigail wondered if he meant for her to feel pity for this woman. If so, he was to be sorely disappointed. Opal St. Augustine had brought this on herself. Abigail's forgiveness did not extend that far.

"What does any of this have to do with you following me to the party?"

Nicholas held up a hand, a silent plea for patience. Abigail bit her tongue and waited. She wanted to tell him she did not care to hear it, but the lie would not come. She did care. More than that, she needed to know, to understand how he could have done what he had.

"Opal hoped if she could lure me back to her parties and advertise my return as such, it would show the others she had been forgiven. It would pave her way back into the good graces of the men and women she catered to. When she realized the invitation had gone astray, but that you had answered it anyway, she informed me if I did not attend, she would ensure the ton would hear of your presence there, effectively ruining you and showing the ton that debauchery runs through your entire family, thereby absolving her of any guilt in your uncle's demise."

Abigail stood stunned, unable to fathom how one woman could be so devious and cruel.

"So, you came to the party to...save me?" She found it difficult to wrap her mind around the idea. For so long she had reviled him, blamed him for every heinous act she could. He was a debaucher, a rake of the first order, a man with no conscience or soul.

Yet when her virtue and reputation were on the line, he had stepped up and kept her safe. Even at the masquerade, she had been the pursuer. He had tried to avoid her, sending Lord Huntsleigh in his place. But she had tracked him down, demanded he help her. Practically begged that he kiss her.

"I owed you that much at least," he said, pulling her from her chaotic thoughts. "I could not stand by and allow her to ruin you when I had it in my power to prevent it. Your family has suffered enough."

"You tried to convince me to leave."

He nodded.

An ironic smile pulled at her lips. "How shocked you must have been to discover you were the reason I was there."

"Shocked would be an understatement. You had always been impetuous, but I did not think you would be so bold as to endanger yourself or your reputation."

"I wanted to help my family. I didn't think I had anything left to lose. Why did you agree to help me then? Why carry on the ruse?"

"I feared you might proposition another man with the same proposal. I knew you would at least be safe with me. I hoped to convince you that confronting me and demanding I restore your family's good name would only make things worse. Once I had accomplished that, I would simply disappear."

Again, he had saved her.

The man she reviled. Hated. Adored. Whose touch she craved and whose kisses made her knees weak and sent her senses reeling. He may have saved her from another man's dishonorable intentions, but there had been no saving her from her own.

Heat flushed her chest and face, her fair skin no doubt making her embarrassment readily evident.

"And that is why you told me you were leaving England."

"I could think of no other way to make a clean break. I couldn't allow our contact to continue, especially after what happened at the masquerade. I didn't want you to discover who had..." He looked over her shoulder to the lake behind her and shook his head. "I should never have let it go so far. I had no right. How you must despise me for it."

Torment darkened his handsome features and Abigail sensed the demons he wrestled with. His confessions shocked, angered, and humbled her. So much of what he had done in the aftermath of her uncle's death had been out of guilt and remorse, two emotions she had convinced herself he did not possess.

She had been wrong.

Seeing him now, the anguish deeply embedded in his silvery eyes, she knew the truth. He had suffered as well. Perhaps the knowledge he could have prevented it all only made the suffering worse.

"I did not try to stop you the night of the masquerade." If confessions were in order, she may as well be honest. She had welcomed his touch, reveled in his kiss, wished for more. "I requested that you kiss me."

"It matters not. I had a responsibility. I had promised myself—"

"Do you regret it?"

"I regret hurting you."

"But do you regret *it*?" She couldn't say the words of what they had done, or even be sure what the appropriate words were.

He glanced at her quickly, surprised. After a brief hesitation, he shook his head. "No. I do not."

His answer both scared her and thrilled her.

"There you are!"

Abigail looked around Nicholas, her nerves jumbled by the emotions racing through her. Caelie, Rebecca, and Miss Caldwell walked down the path along the edge of the lake. Rebecca had called out the greeting. At the sight of Caelie's concerned expression Abigail forced a smile to let her cousin know all was well.

Even though it wasn't.

Nicholas's revelations had turned everything she'd believed upside down.

"Can we join you on your stroll?" Rebecca asked, linking her arm into her brother's.

Nicholas allowed himself to be pulled along, glancing only

once in Abigail's direction. They would have no further chance to discuss the unfinished business hanging between them.

Perhaps it was for the best. After all, what good would it do either of them? Abigail glanced at Miss Caldwell's back. She had walked past her without so much as a nod of recognition and slipped her hand through Nicholas's other arm.

Their fates were sealed. Everyone knew Nicholas planned on offering for Miss Caldwell. And she...well, she had marriage to Lord Tarrington to look forward to.

For lack of a better word.

Chapter Fourteen

"What did you and Lord Roxton discuss?" Caelie sat on the blanket Abigail had spread out earlier. Lord Roxton had left, walking Lady Rebecca and Miss Caldwell back to the main house.

Abigail busied herself with tearing the shards of grass in her hands into tiny bits before she opened her palm and let the breeze whisk them from her hand. "Oh. You know. This and that, I suppose."

"You looked rather serious for a simple this and that conversation."

Abigail glanced over at her cousin. Caelie's warm gaze invited confidence, but Abigail hesitated. If she told Caelie about Nicholas's part in Madame St. Augustine's party, it would lead to the incident at the masquerade. Caelie, who always strove to behave in a proper fashion, would be scandalized and Abigail did not want to put any more on her cousin's narrow shoulders.

"Did you know Lord Roxton had offered for me?"

"Offered for you? But I thought he and Miss Caldwell—"

Abigail shook her head. "No, not today. Before. Two years ago. He asked Uncle Henry for my hand in marriage."

"Oh." Caelie's gaze dropped away and her slim fingers traced the pattern woven into the blanket.

"Uncle Henry refused him."

Caelie pursed her lips but said nothing.

Abigail pulled back a little, taking in her cousin's lack of response to news that had left her floored. "You're not surprised. Did you know then?"

Caelie took a deep breath and looked up. "I suspected. Lord Roxton had been so smitten, but his attentions toward you caused Father great concern. Mother made it known she found the association most scandalous and you know how she feels about even the merest hint of scandal. I don't believe she would have countenanced the marriage, even with the lofty Blackbourne name attached to it."

"Then he did care for me?"

Caelie smiled. "Of that, I have no doubt."

The idea settled around her, finding cracks in her armor where it could seep through. How she had longed to hear those words two years ago. To discover them now, when it was too late...but was it?

"Do not raise your hopes, Abigail."

Caelie's advice caught her off guard. Was she so transparent? She forced a light laugh. "Whatever do you mean?"

"I know you once hung your hopes on Lord Roxton and I know your feelings linger still." She held up a hand when Abigail tried to protest. "You would not have been as angry with him as you were, if your heart had not engaged. But he has made it very clear he plans to offer for Miss Caldwell. His mother and his sister have said as much."

"But he does not love her."

Caelie shrugged. "What is love? It seems everyone has their

own definition of the word and they toss it about as it pleases them."

Abigail had the distinct impression they were no longer speaking about Lord Roxton. "Did you not love Lord Billingsworth?"

Caelie's cheeks turned pink. "I thought so. And I thought he loved me, though in hindsight, he had never said the words. As it turns out, I was wrong. He did not love me, or at least he did not love me enough to stay. I placed my hopes where they did not belong. I don't want you to do the same and experience the hurt and humiliation I did as a result."

Abigail reached out and took Caelie's hand. "Lord Billingsworth did not deserve you, Caelie. You will find your love one day. I know it. Why, you danced with any number of gentlemen last night."

Caelie offered a weak smile. "And after each dance, did any of those gentlemen linger? Did they make any effort to engage in conversation or flirtation? No. I know you think Lady Blackbourne's support will change things, but my path is set, I'm afraid."

"Don't you still hope for love?" It broke Abigail's heart to think her cousin had given up.

"I hope for many things," Caelie said. "But mostly I hope that you will tread carefully. I do not wish to see you in the same predicament as me because of foolish choices you cannot take back."

"I promise I will be careful." She would promise anything if it would put a smile on Caelie's face. And for a brief moment, it did.

"Very good, then." Caelie looked up at the sky. "I think I will return to the house. Will you join me?"

Abigail shook her head. "I think I will stay here a little longer."

Caelie's words had given her pause. She needed time to think, to consider all she had learned over the past day.

"We did not get a chance to finish our conversation earlier." Nicholas had returned and held out a hand to assist Abigail once she had gathered up the blanket she'd sat upon. The weather had started to turn, and many were headed back to the main house to escape the dark clouds and strong winds that had kicked up. She straggled behind, enjoying the last bit of freedom before she must return to acting the proper lady once again.

"Did we have more to say?" She'd mulled over what had been said for the past hour, dissecting every word, turning them over in her mind again and again. His confessions had stirred something in her, memories of how things used to be, of dreams she'd held for the two of them, the hurt and confusion when he'd suddenly dropped his suit. Now her questions had been answered, and the answers left her at odds, torn between what she'd once believed and the truth.

"I think there is always something left to say between us, don't you?" He looked down at her as she took his offered hand, his devastating charm firmly in place as he helped her to her feet. Abigail decided then and there his most atrocious sin was simply being too handsome to bear. She could gaze into those silvery eyes until she lost herself in their depths.

She let go of his hand and reached for something to say to divert her mind. "I have not seen much of Lord Blackbourne. Is he not well?"

"His health has declined this year."

"Can I assume he was not at all pleased to hear we were included on the guest list?"

"I would not take it personally," he said as he offered his

arm. "He cares little for anything or anyone affiliated with me. One of the main reasons I set up my own home was to escape his constant censure."

His own home. Across the street from her. "And why did you choose that particular address?"

He glanced down at her and smiled. "It has the most beautiful view in the city."

Abigail blushed, his meaning clear as he stared into her eyes. She looked away and quickly changed the subject. "How does Miss Caldwell feel about your current location?"

"I believe Miss Caldwell is more interested in my fortune than my living arrangements."

Abigail breathed deeply and took in the scent of wildflowers and new beginnings. "I think it a shame a marriage should start with only that as its foundation."

"Is that not the basis for your own impending marriage?"

Abigail stopped walking. "Lord Tarrington has not officially proposed as yet, though it is expected. I know it prudent I accept when he does, for my family's sake, but—"

"But what?"

She glanced up at him. "I had hoped to find love before it came to that."

"And have you?" He turned to face her and caught her hand as it slipped from his arm. The wind whipped around them. It tangled her skirts about her legs and pulled at her hairpins until several curls slipped free. She cared little. She saved her concern for the man standing in front of her, so much like the one she'd originally fallen in love with, and so different from the monster she had created in her mind. How wrong she had been, so blinded by her own pain and sorrow.

"I thought I had found love once." Despite Caelie's dire warning, she could not help but take the chance that maybe he shared her feelings. What if he did? What if they could save themselves from the horrible fate of being married to people they did not care for, and instead spend a lifetime with someone they could? What if, in the end, they could make something good come out of all the bad?

He smiled and something inside of him seemed to ease. He closed his eyes and squeezed her hand tighter.

"You have no idea how much I wish I could kiss you right now," he whispered.

His unexpected admission shocked her. A thrill raced from tip to toe. She wished it too, but they were so close to the house and a few other guests still milled about. He could not kiss her, not even on the hand without causing talk. But knowing that did not stop the deep longing inside of her.

"I wish you could too," she admitted.

He opened his eyes and a hint of the rake he'd once been sparkled within them despite the lack of sunlight.

"I *will* kiss you," he said. "Properly this time. Not here, and not now, but I will. And when I do there will be nothing left in this world but the two of us."

His words robbed her of breath. But would one last kiss be enough?

"You say the most scandalous things."

"I have the most scandalous thoughts. Would you like to hear some of them?" Humor curved his mouth into a slow grin.

His offer tempted. Her chest tightened and good sense balanced on a slippery edge. He had always done this to her, made her want to throw caution to the wind. Perhaps Uncle had been justified in his worry over her virtue where Nicholas was concerned.

"I think you should escort me the rest of the way," she whispered. "Because if you do not, I may say yes, and then there is no telling the path it will lead us down."

His smile deepened and Abigail feared her heart would burst. How could it have come to this? She had come to this party with such trepidation, fearful of the cost of being around him, and now...now her anger had been proven erroneous, and once gone, it left in its wake the strong feelings she'd nursed in the beginning of their relationship.

Had he ever been the true enemy? Or just the easiest place to spend her pain? Perhaps, in the end, her true enemy had been her own anger. It had blinded her to anyone else's pain but her own. Somehow, somewhere, Nicholas had lifted the veil from her eyes and suddenly things became much clearer. *He* became much clearer.

He stepped away and held out his arm once again. "My lady."

She slipped her hand through his arm and sighed. This was how it should be, she realized. How it should have always been. How different their lives would be now had Uncle Henry and Aunt Edythe not interfered.

But they had, and everyone had paid the price. She could not reverse time. It marched forward and took them all along with it whether they liked it or not. But the question remained —could she change the path she traveled now?

N icholas hesitated outside the earl's rooms. He had been summoned. Never a good sign. His father rarely had anything to do with him, and when he did, it never ended well. He took a deep breath and knocked at the door. His father's valet appeared and let him in.

"He is in his bedchamber." The valet indicated the door beyond the sitting area with a sweeping gesture. "He is expecting you."

Of course, he is, Nicholas thought. One did not ignore a summons from the Earl of Blackbourne if one knew what was good for them.

Still, every time the man called for him, Nicholas toyed with the idea of doing just that. He could not help the childish fantasy, but in the end, as always, he put his feelings aside and entered into the earl's lair.

The room held a sweetly fetid smell. It reminded Nicholas of decay, and in a sense, that was what was happening. The earl had been deteriorating for the past year, but it had grown worse over the last three months. He spent most of his time in his rooms, no longer having the energy he'd once possessed. Though never a large man by any means, Blackbourne had shrunken to a fraction of his former size. Skin hung loosely from his bones as if its grip grew tenuous.

The running of the estates had fallen almost entirely to Nicholas, a task he found himself surprisingly adept at. It galled the earl to no end. Nicholas knew the man had expected him to fail miserably. In truth, so had Nicholas. But putting his mind to it helped him escape the guilt of his past and the misery of his future, if only for a little while.

"Sit." The earl nodded to the chair near the side of the bed. Again, Nicholas fought the urge to turn and leave, to walk away and never look back. Perhaps if his mother and sister did not count on him, he would do just that. An appealing thought, especially if his escape included Abigail.

Nicholas pulled the chair away from the bed and sat down.

"Is there something I can do for you, Blackbourne?" He never called him Father to his face. Blackbourne would not bear the mockery of such an address, and Nicholas could not stand the hypocrisy of it. It was the only point they agreed upon.

Yet Blackbourne would allow another man's bastard to inherit his title and lands if it meant his daughter would be safe. Despite what the earl thought of him, no one questioned Nicholas's loyalty to his mother and sister. Even Blackbourne knew that under Nicholas's protection, they would want for nothing. Had he produced a male heir, however, Nicholas would have been cast out years ago.

The pretense disgusted them both. Yet both allowed the charade to continue.

"I am not well," the earl began, twitching a hand at his wasted form. "My time will be coming soon."

Nicholas waited for a sense of sadness at this news.

It never came.

"As such, I need to ensure things are in order," Blackbourne continued.

A sense of unease crept up Nicholas's spine. "What kind of things?"

The earl glared. His rheumy eyes bored into Nicholas. "Before the end of this party, you will announce your betrothal to Miss Caldwell."

Nicholas started. Every nerve in his body recoiled. Foolish, to react so. Wasn't that the plan all along? The reason he had courted her in the first place had been to find a wife beyond reproach, a wife who would show the ton he had reformed.

Abigail's face flashed in his mind. Her fiery blue eyes. Her head tilted back as she peered up at him. The intense need— the promise he'd made only yesterday—to kiss her once again. From the very beginning of their short-lived courtship until now, she had been the constant in his life, the catalyst for everything he had done, good and bad. He could not let her go. He knew that now. Understood it. She was everything to him.

"I cannot."

Anger flushed Blackbourne's pallid face with color. "You defy me?"

"I need more time. I need—" What? What did he need? To convince Abigail? He felt her teetering, her forgiveness almost within his reach.

"There is no more time. You will propose—"

"I cannot marry Miss Caldwell."

Blackbourne clenched his gnarled hands into fists. Blue veins popped along the back of his paper-thin skin. "You *will* marry her. This is not up for debate."

Nicholas stood. The squalid air in the room closed in on him. He needed to get out, to feel the fresh summer breeze on his face. To escape his future and the earl's building wrath.

"I will not," he said. "I will marry when I am ready and I will marry a woman of my choosing."

"You gave up that right when you killed a man. It is bad enough your mother saw fit to invite the Laythams into my home, but I will not have you mooning over Abigail Laytham like a lovesick calf. I will not allow you to soil this family's reputation further. The reason Lord Selward has been so reticent in his attentions toward Rebecca is because of your past behavior. The man is averse to any type of scandal."

"A perfect match for Miss Caldwell. Perhaps I should introduce the two."

"Silence! Rebecca will have what she wants. Selward is a good match and I will see it happen. I will not have you behaving like the bastard you are."

His words pummeled Nicholas, each one beating against his skin like actual blows. He had heard this speech before, too many times to count. He was worthless. He did not deserve the title. He was a scourge on his family's honor and reputation. He had taken this abuse for years without giving any back, but today he'd had enough. He had his own money now, and while it did not compare to the earl's substantial holdings, it would suffice. If need be, he could support his mother and sister, title or no. He did not need the Earl of Blackbourne's largess any longer.

Nicholas glared down at the old man. Years of pent-up

anger burned in his chest. "You are a pathetic old man who had no other choice than to buy a wife who never loved you."

The earl growled. "And what are you, if not that? Do you think any woman would have you without my fortune and title waiting in the wings? Do you honestly believe even your precious Miss Laytham would look at you twice for any other reason? Her family is on the brink of financial ruin. It isn't you she finds of interest. It is your title and fortune."

The earl's bald suggestion hit its mark and pierced with efficient accuracy. Was that the explanation for Abigail's sudden turnabout? Did she simply see him as the lesser of two evils when forced to choose between the man responsible for her uncle's death or a life spent with a man old enough to be her grandfather? The suggestion left him disheartened but he refused to let Blackbourne see the wound.

"At least I know how to keep a woman satisfied so she doesn't seek affection elsewhere."

"Your mother is a whore," the earl spit out. "The apple does not fall far from the tree."

Had Blackbourne not already been knocking at St. Peter's gate, Nicholas would have reached forward and gripped the man's neck to escort him the rest of the way. He used the last bit of his newfound restraint to keep his hands clenched at his sides.

"You'll die soon, old man. And then we'll all be free of you. I, for one, cannot wait until that day comes."

Nicholas turned and strode from the room. He slammed the door behind him with enough force the pictures on the wall shook and the earl's valet jumped to prevent any from falling off their hooks.

"Lord Tarrington sends word, miss."

Abigail turned in her seat at the window of her bedchamber where she had been gazing out over the view of the gardens below. Her thoughts had been so firmly buried in the events of last night's dinner she hadn't heard Muri's knock. Not that the events had been anything remarkable. The food had been wonderfully prepared as always, the conversation lively, and the company acceptable. Save for one glaring absence—that of Nicholas. Lady Blackbourne had made her excuses for him, but Abigail could not shake the sense his mother had expected him to be present, and when he did not appear, she scrambled for a plausible explanation. The one she'd decided upon had included a sick tenant and hot soup. Though why Nicholas would tend to the individual was beyond her. Such things were usually left to the women, who were generally more adept at administering to the sick and providing comfort to those ailing.

She reached up and took the note from her maid. "Thank you, Muri. That will be all."

"Hmm. I'll just wait, 'case be you want to send word back to the old codger."

"Muri." She forced a note of warning into her tone. Her maid's behavior had bordered on brashness ever since Abigail had taken her into her confidence the night of the scandalous key party. She'd meant to speak to Muri about it, but there had never been time.

"Well, come now, miss. It isn't as if we both don't know you'd rather knot your knickers than spend a night with the doddering old fool."

Abigail pursed her lips and turned fully away from the window. A warm breeze touched her back. It held a hint of dampness, though the skies were a mix of bright blue and white fluffy clouds.

"Muri, I must speak to you about your behavior." She rose and walked to the center of the room. "While I appreciate one's need to speak their mind, I really must caution you to use better judgment when picking the proper moment, and audience, when doing so. You've been rather pert of late, and altogether too familiar in your manner."

Muri's round face flushed. Defiance, mixed with anger, sparked in her pale brown eyes. "Beg your pardon, ma'am. Silly of me to forget my place among you higher ups. Shall I bow down before ya, not meet ya in the eye when's I look upon ya?"

Her impertinence passed the line of acceptability, but Abigail reined in her anger and bit her tongue. She could not at this juncture afford to let Muri go, or chance her walking out. With their finances what they were, finding someone else willing to take the pittance they offered was slim. Although, she realized now why they had been able to hire Muri at such a low wage, and why her list of references had been so short.

Abigail took a deep breath and locked her hands in front of her, squaring her shoulders. "I expect you to do nothing more than behave in a manner appropriate to our relationship, Muri, as I always have. In future, you will be more respectful. Not just of me, but of the others with whom I deal. I am not telling you not to have an opinion; I am simply requesting you keep that opinion to yourself. Your thoughts on Lord Tarrington are not something I care to discuss with you. Please temper your behavior while you are in my family's employ."

Muri's gaze narrowed and she executed a short curtsey. "Yes, miss. As you wish, miss."

Abigail watched in frustration as Muri huffed from the room. The conversation had gone nothing like she had planned. She let out a deep breath and broke the seal on the note, grimacing at the shaky words written on the expensive paper. Lord Tarrington requested her presence for an afternoon walk, a request he had already cleared with her mother and brother. This day continued to go downhill.

Abigail shot another glance at the sky and offered a quick request to the heavens to pour down rain. The breeze brushed against her face like a kiss, but nothing changed.

With a deep sigh, Abigail went in search of Caelie to help her change. She had no wish to call Muri back in and deal with her maid's injured feelings.

Chapter Fifteen

Abigail stepped over a root that had edged its way out onto the narrow path. The meadow burgeoned with a blanket of newly budded wildflowers but Lord Tarrington's statement had left her too stunned to appreciate its beauty.

"Will we spend no time in London at all?"

The thought of being exiled to the country, far away from her family, palled. It wasn't that she didn't like the country, she did. In small doses, with her family around her to keep her occupied and entertained. But Lord Tarrington lived on a large estate several days ride from London. He did not court the company of his neighbors, had virtually no family left, save for Aunt Edythe, and heavens knew he did not go out of his way to entertain.

"I rarely come into town, my dear," he said, patting her hand he had taken and looped through his arm. "The air bothers my lungs and the noise is more than I can bear. We will spend the majority of our time at Maynerly."

"Oh." Her future unraveled before her, one long,

monotonous stretch of time, each day rolling into the next until she could no longer tell one from the other.

All the while, she would have only Lord Tarrington for company, and he thought more of his stupid roses than he did her. They were his true loves, while she was just a means to an end.

The gentle breeze that had mocked her earlier in her room ruffled the curls poking out from beneath her bonnet and the clouds she had wished for now filled the horizon with an imposing gray hue. The promise of rain scented the air.

"Perhaps we should turn back," Abigail said. She didn't want to be caught in a downpour. She wanted even less to prolong her discussion with Lord Tarrington. It depressed her to no end.

He ignored her suggestion.

"I would hope for two sons, though more would be bene-ficial. One can never be too certain. I am the youngest of four boys, and the only one to live into adulthood. Had my mother stopped at two, the title and lands would have gone to a distant cousin."

They traveled farther down the path away from the main house. Abigail looked back, worried about going too far from sight. Not so much for propriety's sake—the other guests were well aware she and Lord Tarrington were all but affianced—but because she did not want to spend any more time with him than necessary. The farther away they walked, the longer it would take them to return.

"Do not worry, my dear. No one will find it untoward if we try to steal a few moments for ourselves."

He laughed and the sound grated on her frayed nerves. Did he honestly think she wanted to be alone with him? She found his manner overbearing and his touch made her skin crawl.

Unlike Nicholas.

Abigail put an abrupt halt to her wayward thoughts. The stoppage lasted a few heartbeats before thoughts of him sneaked back in. She could not help it. Ever since their conversation of yesterday, she had been unable to stop.

He had promised he would kiss her. She had all but granted him permission. The thought thrilled her, while at the same time left her confused. Her renewed feelings for Nicholas were in stark contrast to the anger she had harbored. If she were truthful, she would admit not all of those negative feelings had dissipated. She missed her uncle horribly, and the way in which he had died cut deep.

But Nicholas appeared truly penitent, the impact of her uncle's death on him clear. The reasons behind his actions now brought to light. She had painted Nicholas with a callous brush, only to realize her own misery had distorted the canvas.

She needed time to sort through her feelings, to find a place for the new ones cropping up.

"You are a virgin, of course," Lord Tarrington continued, his proclamation jolting Abigail away from her thoughts. "I can't expect you to be aware of what goes on between a man and a woman, but suffice to say, I expect you will please me well enough."

Lord Tarrington's eyes drifted over her and she recoiled inwardly, extricating her arm from his. She stopped on the path. Her legs itched to run away.

"I beg your pardon, Lord Tarrington, but I do not think this topic of conversation is at all appropriate. I would like to return to the house now."

He grabbed her arm with a speed she had not expected and held her in place. Stale breath brushed her skin. Her stomach lurched in disgust.

"I will let you go this once, my dear," he said. "But make no mistake, you will not turn away from me once we are married. You will be willing in my bed until I have the sons I desire. Do I make myself clear?"

She yanked her arm away and took a step back.

He smiled, his hard gaze a testament to his expectations. Acid burned in her belly. "Good day, my dear."

He waved a hand at the path toward the house and dismissed her as if she were nothing more than a servant.

Abigail picked up her skirts and hurried back down the path. Once out of Lord Tarrington's sight, she took off at a run and headed away from the main house and meadows. She ran for the hills and the forest surrounding them. Her feet pounded on the beaten path in tandem with her heart, her lungs screamed for a reprieve, but still she kept running. She needed to escape, to outrun Lord Tarrington's demands and the future he had mapped out for her.

Abigail did not know how long she ran for, following a well-beaten path in the hopes it would eventually lead her back to the main house. Droplets of rain splashed against her skin. She slowed and looked around. The trees were sparser on the hill, leaving her little protection against the coming storm. Her chest heaved with each struggled breath. Above her, the forbidding clouds had swallowed the last of the blue sky. How far was she from the main house?

She had no idea. She glanced around. In the distance, farther up the hill, a plume of smoke stretched above the tree-tops. She headed toward it; hopeful the occupants would offer her shelter until the worst of the rain spent itself.

Soon the trees gave way to a small clearing that revealed a small cabin. An unwieldy garden grew up around it, taking over one side where vines crept upward and meshed with the thatched roof. Smoke billowed from the chimney and filled the wet air with its inviting scent. There were no other signs of life.

The rain came with more force now, and beat its way

through the trees until the muslin dress she wore plastered to her skin and left her chilled. She picked up her heavy skirts. Dark mud stained the hem. Why hadn't she returned home and sulked in her room like any normal young lady in distress?

A horse whickered somewhere behind the house, but she could not see the beast. Every fairy tale she had ever read as a child came back to haunt her as she lifted her hand to knock.

"Please do not let it be some ogre, witch, or any other such monster," she whispered and knocked with three successive raps. "Hello! Is anyone home?"

A shuffling sound came from the other side of the door, but before she could peer through the window to her left to look inside, the door swung open.

The sky rumbled ominously and opened up in earnest, coming down in heavy sheets as a strong hand wrapped around her wrist and yanked her inside.

"What the devil are you doing out here alone in this weather?" Nicholas sputtered the words out as he stared at a drenched Abigail. Had the few shots of whiskey he'd taken to warm his bones caused him to hallucinate?

"I...I..." She stuttered, apparently sharing his surprise.

"This is no place for a lady." This far into the forest, the paths were narrow and winding, often running out or twisting around each other. One had to be very familiar with the lay of the land to know where they were going. How had she found him? Too remote for walkers and too well hidden for hunters, the cabin remained unoccupied unless he was in residence.

"I was out walking," she finally said, her shoulders slumping. "And when it started raining, I knew I had ventured too far to return to the house and outrun it. I saw the smoke above the trees and hoped to find refuge."

"It's a little far out for a walk." However, from the state of her skirts, she had not strolled along at a sedate pace. Mud splashed the front and stained the hem. Wherever she had been, she had left swiftly. He suspected if he lifted her skirts and peered underneath, he would find a pair of ruined slippers and silk stockings.

He purged the thought from his mind. He had no intentions of lifting her skirts.

"Were you alone?" He led her closer to the fire to dry off.

She peered out the small window near the fireplace. He followed her gaze. The world around them was awash in shades of green and brown, made more brilliant by the downpour.

"What is this place?" She turned in a circle to peruse the cabin's interior. There wasn't much to see. He had used it as an escape from his father as a boy. It had been rundown when he found it, abandoned in the woods, but over time, he had made the necessary repairs and restored it to good order. Then he'd brought in the furniture, much of it made by his own hand.

"It is nothing. A place to escape."

She raised one perfectly sculpted blonde eyebrow. "And what are you escaping from today?"

"Blackbourne."

"I see," she said. She crossed the room to the narrow bed. He tried not to look at the bed or her near it. It conjured too many thoughts in his head. Thoughts he had no right having. It didn't help that the soaked fabric of her dress stuck to her body in a most enticing manner. Water dripped from the stained hem and puddled on the floor at her feet. Abigail shivered and wrapped her arms around herself.

"You need to get out of those clothes," Nicholas said. She

spun to face him, her eyes widened in surprise, "You'll catch your death otherwise."

"I'm fine."

Nicholas twisted his mouth and walked to the bed, pulling the quilt from where it draped over the footboard. "Your claim would be more convincing if you could say it without your teeth chattering."

Her jaw set at a mutinous angle. "I am not about to undress with you in here, my lord."

My lord. He longed to hear her say his name.

Outside, the rain continued to teem down and the dark gray clouds indicated it would be some time still before they wrung themselves dry. "I'm hardly about to step outside in this weather to preserve your modesty. I will hold up the blanket and promise not to look. When you are done, you can wrap yourself in it. It is large enough to keep you fully covered."

"I—I cannot." Another shudder caused her to stumble over her words.

"Have you considered what may happen if you catch a fever?"

"If I catch—what does that have to do with anything?"

He had forgotten how she never looked ahead, always barreling forward without a thought to the consequences. He had been like that too, once upon a time, but no more. He'd learned the hard way that some consequences were too severe.

"If you catch a fever, I will have no choice but to remove your clothing myself in order to keep you warm and dry and fight the illness. Once you are able to be moved, I will then have to convey you back to the main house, where upon I will need to explain to all present how and where I came upon you and why you are in such a state of undress. You see, while I may be adept at undressing you, the redressing will likely not go as well. You can imagine the damage to your reputation if such an event were to occur."

Rosy buds erupted in her cheeks, bringing a hint of color to her pale complexion. "You wouldn't dare."

"What choice would I have? Let you die of a fever to preserve your modesty?" Nicholas unfolded the blanket and stretched it out the length of his arms, holding it above his head to block his view of her. Unfortunately, the quilt did not block the unsolicited visions racing through his mind. "I promise I will be a complete gentleman."

A snort of derision came from the other side of the blanket. They may have reached an understanding of sorts over the past few days, but he obviously still had a little way to go to earn back her full trust.

"This is insane."

"So is catching your death because you are too stubborn to listen to reason."

Reason indeed. There was nothing reasonable about his suggestion. The very idea she should disrobe with him anywhere near her was the height of lunacy. She shivered again and a droplet of water dripped down the length of her nose and tumbled off its end. How had she ended up here?

She had set out that afternoon to walk with Lord Tarrington in the hopes she could find something about the man to recommend him. Instead, she'd run off to escape him and wound up jumping from the pot into the fire.

Despite the dimly lit interior, the sparsely furnished cabin had an inviting quality about it. The furniture, though rudimentary, was well made. The shelves held only the most necessary of items. And the bed...

Her gaze skimmed over it, then quickly away. Madame St.

Augustine's party had been the only other time she'd ever stood in a bedroom with a man unrelated to her. The same man who held the quilt in front of him now. He hadn't exactly acted the perfect gentleman that night, kissing her as he had. Then again, she'd hardly acted the part of the proper lady, meeting and matching his ardor.

The memory scorched her brain and refused to leave. It came back to her at the most inconvenient of times and caused her no end of embarrassment. Although it paled in comparison to the night at the masquerade, when he had kissed her again in such a scandalous fashion she ached whenever she thought about it.

"My arms are growing weary," Nicholas said, shifting his shoulders so the quilt wavered in his grip.

Abigail swallowed. Did she dare? Could this be another ruse? Yes, he had explained himself the other day down by the lake, but could she believe him? A part of her wanted to. She wanted to believe the man she had once known would never have done something so cruel and callous without proper provocation. But did any provocation justify what he had done? Did such a confession mean she could trust him now?

"Do I have your word you will not look?"

After a brief hesitation, he answered. "You have my word."

It was the best she could hope for. Her clothing was not getting any warmer and the shivering now went on unabated. She had to do something or risk the eventual outcome Nicholas had described. She did not want to imagine the humiliation her family would endure if she were carried home wrapped in a quilt and nothing else in full view of all the guests. It would be the end of them, just when they were on the verge of turning things around.

Abigail reached up and untied her ruined bonnet. It had done precious little to keep her hair dry at any rate. The strings proved difficult to undo and took several tugs before they came free. Next came her slippers, also ruined. Perhaps, if she set them by the fire they might recover, but she doubted it. She issued a silent curse to Lord Tarrington.

Her pelisse proved a more taxing item to remove. The wet sleeves required much struggling on her part to peel away from wet skin until she felt a little like a dog chasing its tail. If Nicholas could see her twisting and turning, he'd think her a proper fool. Her gown proved no easier. She managed to undo the first two buttons at her neck, but she could not reach the third. Where was Muri when she needed her?

"How are you coming along?"

Abigail glared at the spot on the quilt where she imagined Nicholas's face to be. "This is an impossible task. If you have so much experience disrobing ladies as you claim, then you must be aware of the intricacies of our wardrobe and know we require assistance. My dress consists of a row of buttons I can neither reach nor undo. I told you this was a foolish idea."

"I confess, I had not considered that." The quilt dropped suddenly. Nicholas's dark brows knit together as he stared at her.

"Do not look at me so."

"How am I looking at you?"

"Like I am a puzzle that needs to be solved."

A brief smile flitted across his handsome features and an answering tingle erupted in her chest. "It isn't you that is the puzzle, it is the problem of getting you out of your clothes."

"A dilemma I'm certain you've never encountered before." She could not keep the sarcasm from her voice.

His eyebrow arched upward. "You flatter me."

"Be assured, I did not mean that as flattery."

"I will have to assist you."

She blinked. "I beg your pardon?"

"I will play ladies' maid."

"You most certainly will not."

"What other choice do you have? You're shivering, cold and I suspect somewhat miserable—"

"I can assure you any misery I am currently suffering has nothing to do with how wet my clothing is and everything to do with the situation I find myself in."

"But it is a situation neither of us can change. Step closer to the fire."

She had no choice but to obey as he ushered her back with a shooing of his hands. The warmth from the flames touched her bared skin but failed to penetrate the sopping wet garments. Nicholas was right, she had to get out of her clothes, but the idea of what that meant caused her no end of vexation. It was one thing to allow him to have his way with her at the masquerade. For one, she had not known his true identity, and secondly, what had happened came upon her suddenly with no time to think or consider or debate. This—this was a deliberate decision on both their parts and while no amorous overtures were included with the proposition, it did not diminish the fact she would be naked in front of him. Worse, he would be the one undressing her.

"Turn around," he instructed, swiveling his finger in the air.

She obeyed, determined not to look at him, to block what was happening. She would imagine Muri to be the one—

She jumped as his strong hands rested on her shoulders. A bolt of heat pulsed down her body. No. That would not do. Her imagination did not stretch that far.

"Relax."

She glanced over her shoulder and glared at him. Did he truly expect, under the circumstances, she would be able to achieve such a state?

She returned her gaze to the fire as his hands slid from her shoulders to the buttons lining her back. One by one, he worked them free. Abigail held her hands to her breasts to keep the loosened dress from slipping to her waist. An ache developed at the juncture of her thighs when his hands brushed against her bottom as he undid the last few buttons. She shivered, but this time it had nothing to do with being cold.

"Here," he whispered. His hands returned to her shoulders and slipped the cap sleeves of her dress down to her elbows. "Abigail, you need to straighten your arms."

His soft tone glided over her, touching her in places even his hands couldn't reach. He had called her Abigail. Such an intimate thing to hear him say her name, as if it belonged on his lips. Oh, this was a dangerous situation. She tried to conjure up the anger she had carried for the past eight months and use it as a shield, but only remnants remained, no defense against the depth of need roiling inside of her.

Did she dare trust it? She had done so once and been egregiously hurt.

"Abigail."

She straightened her arms and let him pull the dress downward until it fell of its own accord and landed at her feet in a wet heap. Her petticoat met a similar fate until she stood before him in her underthings. She wished suddenly she had prettier ones, rather than the plain cotton she wore, but she pushed such recalcitrant thoughts away, afraid of where they would lead.

"These are quite wet as well," Nicholas said, his finger brushing along the back edge of her stays. His touch penetrated the flimsy cotton of her chemise and scalded her skin. "We should remove them also."

Abigail nodded, barely aware of answering him. He didn't sound any happier about this than she.

Outside, thunder rolled across the hillside and the rain strengthened in its intensity. The fire had warmed the small cabin, holding the dampness at bay. The gentle glow of light chased away the worst of the shadows. Behind her, Nicholas's nimble fingers made quick work of the laces on her stays.

"Lift your arms."

She did as instructed, and he pulled the loosened contraption over her head. She could finish the rest herself, but when he slowly lifted the hem of her chemise upward, she didn't stop him. Inch by treacherous inch, her body responded to being laid bare before him until the dull throb between her thighs became an intense ache. He removed the chemise and tossed it aside, then his hands returned to touch her bare shoulders. Modesty forced her to cross her arms over her breasts.

Nothing but her stockings and drawers remained.

Her breath caught as his hands slid down her back. His knuckles grazed the curve in her spine and skimmed over her rounded bottom. He knelt behind her and untied the garter holding up her left stocking, then eased it down, caressing her knee, her calf, her ankle. His touch was slow and torturous, his manner silent, almost reverent as he slid the stocking from her foot.

Her entire body trembled. He had not said a word to her, save a brief instruction here or there, though now even those had ceased and any communication came through his fingertips. When the last stocking had been removed, Nicholas stood once again, closer than before, so their bodies almost touched. Abigail longed to lean back and rest against him. Her knees trembled and she did not know how much longer she could withstand this sweet agony. She had no idea what had happened to the quilt he had promised to wrap around her to preserve her modesty. It hardly mattered now. She had no modesty left.

"You're the most beautiful creature..."

She wanted to tell him no. Caelie was the beauty of the family. Everyone knew that, but the words did not come. She wanted to be beautiful to him. In that moment, she wanted to be everything to him. Their past, their present, even the future had been stripped away, leaving only the two of them. The only world that existed lived within the four walls of this cabin.

He pulled the pins from her hair and raked his fingers along her scalp, freeing the chignon Muri had carefully constructed. Her hair fell, heavy against her back. She closed her eyes and leaned into his ministrations. The rhythm of his movements lulled her and her muscles relaxed until she rested fully against him. His need pressed against her and an answering thrill rushed through her. She wiggled just enough to elicit a sharp intake of breath from him and he pulled her closer.

"Can I touch you?"

Desperation edged his request and Abigail realized she was not alone in what she felt. She nodded her assent and held her breath, waiting. His hand slid over her belly and made a slow descent downward. She took in a quick breath then stopped breathing altogether when his fingers found the split in her drawers and slid inside.

Chapter Sixteen

"Oh!"

Abigail was slick from wanting and his fingers glided over her with ease, back and forth with slow intent until she thought she would lose what little remained of her mind.

She arched, her bare back rubbing against the superfine wool of his waistcoat. His other arm came around her, his calloused hand finding her breast, cupping it gently and brushing her nipple with his thumb. Spirals of ecstasy weakened her legs further until she didn't know how much longer she could stand.

His lips touched her neck and her pulse jumped. "Tell me to stop."

Again, the desperation in his voice, as if he needed her to be the one to put an end to this madness. But it was too late. Her need for him left her unable to form the words. She shook her head. His fingers worked their magic until the need built to a frenzied pitch.

"If we don't stop—"

"Don't stop." She could manage nothing else. If he

stopped now, she would surely expire on the spot. And then, a white-hot heat pulsated through her body and poured over her in waves, leaving her limp, yet far from satiated. Even as the tide of pleasure ebbed, she wanted more. Needed more.

Her breath came in gasps and a sheen of moisture dotted her skin.

"You have haunted every one of my dreams since the first night I danced with you," he said.

Abigail remembered that night as if it had happened only yesterday and not two long years ago. He had shown up at Almack's. The stir of his entrance swept the room like a wild-fire across dry wheat grass. She'd never seen such a reaction and had known little about Lord Roxton at the time, though it didn't take long for the gossips to fill her in. He was an unrepentant rake with the ability to make even the most sensible of women turn wanton by his attentions. When he asked her to dance, she told him no. Instead of being angry, he'd been amused and had stuck by her most of the evening. When she'd danced with others, he'd insisted on telling her everything wrong with each man. Foolish things, really. Thick ankles. A badly tied cravat. A propensity to over-chew their food. By the end of the night, she realized she had quite enjoyed being with him. He was different than the other men she'd met. He lacked the airs and artifice, his manner most genuine and honest, if not borderline inappropriate.

She had missed his company terribly when he went away.

She turned in his arms and gazed up into his silvery eyes. "I find you horribly overdressed, my lord. It puts me at a disadvantage."

He touched her face with a reverent hand. Want and regret etched into his handsome features. His head fell forward and touched hers, a gesture so intimate, so telling, Abigail could only hold her breath and wait. "I have compromised you beyond all reason. We need to stop this now before—"

"If you have compromised me beyond all reason then there is no going back. Stopping now will not uncompromise me." She placed her hands on his chest and undid the buttons of his waistcoat. He did not stop her, as much a slave to what grew between them as she. The knowledge made her bold.

"Make love to me," she whispered, slipping her hands inside his waistcoat and pushing it down his arms. The warmth of his body enveloped her, chasing away the chill.

"Abigail, I—"

"Do not tell me no. Don't deny me this. I do not expect you to offer for me. I have no expectation or claim on you, nor do I intend to make one. But soon Lord Tarrington will make his offer and I must accept. Before that happens, I want something for myself. I want to know what it is to be with someone who wants me for who I am, and not for how many sons I can bear him. Please. Let us have this time, then we can go back to the way things must be and no one but us will be the wiser."

She gave her impassioned speech, then pressed her cheek against his chest and slid her arms around him. He stroked her back, stoking the flame yet to be fully extinguished.

After a moment, Nicholas swept her up into his arms and carried her to the bed behind her, kicking the blankets back with his boot and laying her gently upon the cool sheets. He stood over her, looking down, his intense gaze never leaving hers as he pulled off his shirt, revealing his strong chest. Abigail longed to reach up and let her fingers trace the rigid muscles in his stomach but she dared not move. His gaze broke and he sat on the edge of the bed to yank off his boots. Then he stood once again, his back to her as his trousers were removed.

She held her breath as his backside was revealed, sculpted and round. She stared like a wanton fool. He was truly beautiful. A piece of sculpture come to life. And he was hers, at least for this moment. He turned, his need for her evident. For a brief moment hesitation gripped her, but curiosity tossed it aside.

With a tentative hand, she reached out and touched him, surprised by how silky smooth he was.

Nicholas gasped at her touch and his head fell back. "Dear God."

For a moment she thought she'd hurt him, but the expression on his face told her different. Emboldened, she touched him again and let her hand slowly slide down the full length of him. His hands clenched at his sides and she smiled.

"Does it feel good?"

He swallowed and dropped to his knees onto the bed, forcing her hand to fall away. "You have no idea. Shall I return the favor?"

A thrill of expectation made her quiver. "Yes." There was no going back.

Nicholas crawled over her, like an animal stalking its prey. His movements were graceful and calculated. "I have longed for this moment. Did you know that?"

Abigail shook her head.

"Every night when I was not with you. Every day, when I paid you court. I wondered what it would be like have you beneath me. To look down and see you smile up at me with invitation."

"Your thoughts were highly improper, my lord."

He grinned, and the tension eased from his face. "I know, but I could not help myself. Your uncle was right to refuse my suit of you. I was a reprobate."

Sadness colored her happiness. "I wish he hadn't. How different things would have been—"

"We cannot change the past." He leaned down and his lips grazed hers. "I wish we could. If it were possible, I'd do so in a heartbeat. I'd make you my wife and we'd have a passel of babies and make love every evening until dawn." His lips traveled down across her jaw. "Your laughter would fill our household and our home would be a place of joy and love."

Abigail's fingers slid into his thick hair as his mouth trailed a line of kisses down her neck sending spirals of pleasure through her body until they pooled low in her belly. It occurred to her Nicholas had likely never had any of those things. As much as Lady Blackbourne and Rebecca loved him, Lord Blackbourne despised him. Even in the week she'd spent in his family's company and the limited contact where the two men shared the same space, the animosity crackled around them. How must it have been to live so?

She held him to her breast and he kissed it reverently until all coherent thought raced away; replaced with only the physical need to give him all the things he longed for, to be the home he needed.

Abigail slid her hands along his broad shoulders, marveling in the way his muscles shifted beneath her touch. He left her breast and found her mouth, kissing her with such tender devotion, any last bit of anger and resentment she'd harbored melted away and she saw clearly the way things were. She understood now. He had been driven by hurt, rejected once again as not good enough.

"I do not want to hurt you," he said, when his mouth left hers, both of them breathless. "A woman's first time can be painful."

"I am certain you will take the utmost care with me." She did not even question it. Despite her attacks on him, through every angry word she spouted in his direction, he had never once retaliated. Yes, he had lied to her about his identity, but had he revealed the truth to her the night of Madame St. Augustine's party, she would never have allowed him to remove her from the party unharmed and undiscovered. While she had tried to destroy him, he had done nothing but protect her.

Nicholas stretched out next to her, half covering her body with his. His erection pressed against her hip, so close to the center of her own need the ache only increased. His hands explored her body, touching every inch of skin until nothing was left unattended save for the incessant longing. It became difficult to lie still beneath his teasing ministrations.

When she thought she could not stand it another moment, Nicholas shifted his weight and settled between her thighs. With one hand, he touched her face.

"Are you certain?"

Strain tightened his skin and made his cheekbones even more prominent. She knew what it cost him to stop, knew he would anyway if she said the word.

"I am certain."

Nicholas leaned down and gave her a languorous kiss. The storm raged and swirled like a tempest outside before he shifted yet again and eased into her, giving her a moment to adjust to the newness of the sensation, then with one brief thrust, he breached the barrier of her innocence and held still once again. Abigail tensed as a sharp pain stole her breath, but as quickly as it came, it calmed and the unfamiliar pleasure of him inside of her overtook it. She wanted more and pushed her hips into him, taking him in fully.

"Sweet Lord," he uttered and tightened his hold around her. He moved once again and each stroke built the need growing inside of her, pushing her to a point she couldn't quite reach. Closer and closer it grew as the wind outside whipped against the walls of the cabin. Their bodies moved together in a natural rhythm.

Abigail's hands caressed the smooth planes of his back feeling his muscles shift with each thrust. With her legs clasped around his hips, tension gripped her body each time he filled her, deeper and deeper until the tension peaked and broke, washing over her in undulating waves of pleasure. She had a vague awareness of Nicholas's body stiffening as he found his release, his groan of pleasure echoing in her ear and sending a shiver straight to her core. She tightened her grip around his hips and held him there, as he collapsed on top of her, reveling in the last few moments of pleasure.

N icholas could scarcely believe what had just happened, certain at any moment he would awake and realize it had been nothing more than another one of his dreams. But he could not deny the reality of the warm body wrapped around his. Her scent enveloped him. He hadn't dreamed it. She was with him. Abigail.

She had explored his body, given herself to him with a bold fearlessness that had surprised and entranced him until he could not hold himself in check. All his promises of squelching his desires were lost the moment he touched her.

Nicholas held her tighter and rolled to his side, bringing her fully against him. She snuggled in as he reached down and pulled the blankets around them. Outside, the rain had abetted to a light smattering of drops. Soon, it would be safe to leave, to return to reality.

But how could he? He had found his own Eden here in this cabin with Abigail. How could he return to the hell of his real life and survive, knowing he had walked away from this, and for what? Everything he did was to show Abigail he had changed, that he understood the enormity of his actions and would atone for them.

He had wanted her forgiveness. If she had willingly given herself to him, did that not mean he had it? Could they have the life together he had always dreamed of? Though many expected he would make an offer to Miss Caldwell, he had already told Blackbourne he had no intentions of doing so. Perhaps many believed an understanding to be in place, but he had made no promises. There was still time, still a chance he and Abigail could find the happiness that had eluded them the first time around.

Hope soared through him as the last of the raindrops were squeezed from the clouds and a weak shard of sunlight peeked through the window and lit a path across the wide slatted floors to pool at the rug next to the bed.

"Abigail?"

"Mmm..." She nuzzled her nose into his side and pressed closer to him.

"I will make this right. If you will allow me, I will make this right."

Though she kept her eyes closed, he sensed the change in her body as she shrugged off the warm lure of satiated sleep.

"Do not feel you need to. We made no promises to each other," she told him. But he had made a promise to himself, to protect her, to never allow her to be hurt again the way she had when her uncle died due to his callous actions.

"It is not a matter of need." He kissed the top of her head and breathed in her sweet scent. Their lovemaking had left her hair tousled. It fell around her shoulders in disheveled waves. She had never looked more beautiful to him. "At least not in the way you think. I am not doing this because I feel the need to make something right. I am doing it because I cannot imagine letting you go."

Abigail shifted and looked up at him, her blue eyes clear and sharp. "It is not necessary. You do not—"

"Do you not want to?" He had not even asked. A horrible sense of falling overcame him. What if it had been as she had said—just one night, with no expectations? Had he simply been a way for her to experience pleasure without worrying about repercussions? Without engaging her heart?

"I do not want to be a duty you need to fulfill," she said.

"You are not a duty. You are the only thing that gives my

life any meaning, any sense. I do not want to lose you again. I will find a way for us to be together."

He leaned down and kissed her, knowing soon they must part. Their precious time together had run out. He needed to leave her, to establish an alibi of having been elsewhere, for her sake as well as his. When he married her, he did not want anyone to think he did so because he had to. He did it because he loved her. He had never stopped. He *would* never stop. Abigail snuggled into his side once again. Her lack of an immediate answer to his proposal left him unsettled. He held his breath and waited, forcing himself not to prompt or prod.

"Then I am yours," she said, finally. He could hear the smile in her voice.

Nicholas's heart soared, but reality tempered it. There were still obstacles to overcome. His father's dictate that he marry Miss Caldwell the most immediate. Despite his own insistence otherwise, Blackbourne did not give up easily. He would have to tread carefully there.

Chapter Seventeen

I will make this right.

The words echoed in Abigail's head until she could think of little else. It had been two days since Nicholas had whispered them into her ear, before they parted. He had headed to the stables and she to the main house, their stories firmly intact so as not to arouse suspicion.

For two days, her head swam with possibilities. Would Nicholas regret what they had shared and change his mind? She had told him from the beginning he owed her no promises for taking her innocence.

No. Not taken. She had given it willingly, lured by the warmth and yes, the torment that clung beneath his charming surface. But could she marry him after all that had transpired? She thought of the afternoon in the cabin. His hands on her naked skin. The pleasure he'd given her. The promises he'd whispered. How perfectly right it felt being with him.

How could she not marry him?

If he proposed.

In the time since they had made love, they'd had no contact save for longing glances across a room. Fate conspired against them, devising activities that prevented them from stealing any time alone. Even now, as she sat with an unread book propped in her lap, the men were off hunting, while the women drank tea and chatted over needlepoint or cards. From across the room, Caelie's soft laughter drifted as she and a few other young ladies played a game of whist. It did Abigail's heart good to hear that sound again. It had been too long since her cousin had known joy.

She herself should feel joyful as well. If Nicholas proposed, her worries were over. Not only could she avoid marrying Lord Tarrington, but her family's fortunes would turn around as well.

If...

The word nagged at the back of her mind, mingled with the worry Nicholas had regained his senses and decided marrying her was a foolish proposition. It wasn't as if she had anything to offer him, save a family name in tatters and no dowry to speak of. Not that he cared about those things, but the Earl of Blackbourne did, and the earl held the largest portion of Nicholas's wealth in his tight fist.

Her hand left the book and rested against her flat stomach. What if their tryst had resulted in her carrying Nicholas's babe? If he did not propose, should she tell him? Or carry on and marry Lord Tarrington, passing the child off as his, knowing all the while it belonged to another man? She thought of Lady Blackbourne, of Nicholas's life living with a man who despised him for just such a scenario and she knew she could not do it.

Fear rooted deep within her. She was in a fine pickle, but pride prevented her from going to Nicholas and begging him to address her concerns. *If* he proposed, then he must do so out of love, because he truly wanted to be with her. She could not bear the thought of marrying the man she loved, knowing he did not return the sentiment. It was one thing to say the words during the intimate encounter they had shared, but something else to mean them and be ready to commit your life to them.

Was Nicholas ready for that kind of commitment with her?

Abigail's thoughts were interrupted as Miss Caldwell sat down next to her at the window seat without invitation, a cup of tea carefully balanced on her lap. She took a moment to carefully arrange her skirts, smoothing out any wrinkles without spilling so much as a drop of tea.

"Good afternoon, Miss Laytham. I trust you are enjoying the book?"

Abigail glanced down at the thick tome in her lap. In truth, she hadn't even looked at the title when she pulled it off the shelf. It could be on animal husbandry for all she knew.

"It has failed to capture my full attention, I'm afraid."

"Hm." Miss Caldwell lifted the teacup to her lips and took a dainty sip. The movement appeared practiced, as if she'd spent hours in front of a mirror perfecting it. "Are you enjoying your time at Sheridan Park?"

Abigail could feel the heat of a blush creeping up her neck. "I am indeed."

Miss Caldwell smiled. "It was quite generous of Lady Blackbourne to have invited your family."

"Yes, it was." Abigail set aside the book and reached down to the basket at her feet. She picked up her needlepoint. She needed something to distract her thoughts.

"I must admit the invitation surprised me." Miss Caldwell gazed about the room. "Your family has not exactly been in the public eye since...well, for the past little while."

Abigail followed Miss Caldwell's gaze. Caelie and Lady Rebecca had moved to the pianoforte, smiling and talking. The two had gotten along famously since their arrival here. At first, Abigail wondered if it hadn't been due to Nicholas's coaxing, but in truth the two seemed to genuinely like each other and Abigail found it difficult to imagine an ulterior motive.

"We have been in mourning," she pointed out. "It would not have been appropriate to attend a string of parties."

"Yes, of course." Miss Caldwell took another sip before turning her dark brown eyes on Abigail. Her unwavering gaze unnerved her, the intelligence lurking behind it making it even more potent. "And I am certain your financial situation does not make it any easier. It is obvious you have not purchased new gowns this Season."

Heat pulsated beneath Abigail's skin. "I beg your pardon, but—"

"There is no need," Miss Caldwell cut off Abigail's indignation and turned to face her. "I merely state the obvious. Certainly, I do not mean any harm in doing so. It is merely a prelude to my point."

Abigail reined in her anger and tried to stay calm. "And your point would be?"

When Miss Caldwell spoke, her tone remained soft and even, but a core of steel lay beneath it. "My point is, it would make perfect sense for you to play on any misplaced guilt Lord Roxton may feel for your family in the hopes of reeling him in and forcing a proposal. His wealth would certainly be a boon, and I understand it is much needed. But make no mistake, Miss Laytham, yours is not the only family in need of a fortune, or with debts to pay. I too have a responsibility to marry well. I have two younger sisters. My marriage to Lord Roxton will help secure them the most suitable of husbands and alleviate my father's worry, not to mention the financial strain a houseful of daughters can put upon a man."

"I was not aware—"

"No, of course you weren't. You have been too busy with your own wants and needs to consider those of others. But do not think I will stand idly by and let you use whatever hold you think you have over Lord Roxton to ruin my plans."

Abigail had spent the past week watching the other woman strategically place herself with Nicholas or his family members at every turn. She did nothing to attract attention, heaven forbid, but instead maintained a quiet grace, like a marble statute one could not help but admire. There was much more to Miss Eugenie Caldwell than met the eye.

Miss Caldwell's assessment of her character stung, partly because it held a grain of truth. She had been blind to the pain of others. She hadn't seen Nicholas's suffering and she hadn't considered Miss Caldwell's motives to be any more than a her plan to latch onto a husband of good fortune.

"I have no intentions of setting my cap for Lord Roxton," Abigail said. The lie tripped off her tongue and self-reproach wrapped around her heart. She had always thought Nicholas and Miss Caldwell an odd match. She had never considered Miss Caldwell would have her own motives in marrying him. The knowledge set her back. She understood the desperation Miss Caldwell alluded to. If she were to marry Nicholas, she put Miss Caldwell and her family in the same precarious position hers now experienced. It did not sit well.

"I know Lord Tarrington hopes to make a match with you. If I were forced to choose between a man thrice my age and a handsome, young man such as Lord Roxton, it would be no contest. We may be forced to marry for financial gain but there is no law indicating we can't make the best choice possible."

"Why do you believe I have chosen Lord Roxton?" Were her true feelings toward her former enemy so obvious? Did others suspect their mutual attraction as well?

"I am aware of your past attachment." Tension pulled at the edges of Miss Caldwell's mouth and her eyes turned to dark obsidian. When she spoke next, her words were absolute.

"But I warn you now, I will be the next Lady Blackbourne and I will brook no interference on your part. My family is counting on me and I will not let them down."

The words, so familiar to Abigail, set a torrent of fear whirling in her stomach. Miss Caldwell may have the reputation of a proper young miss, but Abigail sensed a will of iron beneath her poised veneer. Miss Caldwell would fight until her dying breath to get what she needed.

And what she needed was Nicholas. Or at least what his title and fortune could provide.

Abigail had underestimated the obstacles standing in the way to her future happiness with Nicholas. Yes, she had suspected Miss Caldwell would be disappointed, and his father likely enraged, but she thought Miss Caldwell would understand in the end what a horrible match they were and, ultimately, be relieved to have avoided making such a life-long mistake. As for Nicholas's father, when was the man not in a rage over something Nicholas had done?

But as Miss Caldwell determinedly sipped her tea, her gaze fixed on the current Lady Blackbourne, Abigail realized Miss Caldwell had no intention of going down without a fight. And it appeared Miss Caldwell had a lot of fight left in her.

N icholas took a deep breath and chose his words carefully. For several days, he had worked this conversation through in his head, discarding several versions and abandoning even more. He did not want to hurt her. He simply did not want to marry her, and the more thought he put into it, the more he realized the truth of it.

He wished he had been able to spend more time with Abigail, to gauge her level of interest after what had transpired between them. Had she experienced a change of heart? Did she regret the rashness of their passion? Knowing her mind would have made what he had to do easier, but the fates had conspired against them. For three days now, he had been unable to get her alone. He wondered if the earl had something to do with it, or if perhaps it was Abigail's own way of letting him know she had changed her mind.

Either way, he took a chance, made a decision, and now sat in his mother's private receiving room on the second floor. He prayed he would not regret his actions.

"I hope you can forgive me. I did not mean to lead you on or give you false hope. In truth, I had hoped we would be well suited, but as time has passed it has proven to me that such is not the case, and—"

"Well suited?" Miss Caldwell's dark brows knit together, the only hint of expression on her placid face. It always struck him as odd how one so beautiful could be so lacking in emotion. Nicholas straightened in his chair, the stiff back most uncomfortable. His mother said she often sat the guest there if she wished their stay to be brief. He hoped, in this case, his visit would follow suit.

"Yes. Of course. Did you not hope to have an affection for the man you marry?"

Didn't most women hope for that? Granted the chances of such a thing were not always in their favor, but still, one would hope over time affection would grow. But he simply did not see that happening with Miss Caldwell, even if he had not already given his heart to another. How could he? Miss Caldwell, for the entirety of their acquaintance, had not once displayed even the smallest hint of interest in him personally.

At times, he had wondered if a well of passion hid behind the veneer of propriety that she showed to the world. If so, he had never been able to access it, and in the end had to assume it simply did not exist. She did everything that was expected of her, said what a young lady of impeccable manners would say, and behaved in a way completely acceptable to society. What Nicholas would have given to have her stumble just once. Or say something inappropriate or unexpected. Or to laugh.

Unlike Abigail, whose emotions rippled across her beautiful features with alarming clarity giving her features life and interest, Miss Caldwell's own face remained a stone wall, her thoughts and feelings carefully concealed behind it.

"My duty does not allow me to wallow in such frivolous pursuits," she told him. Her brow smoothed out; her expression, once again, unreadable. They could have been discussing the weather for all the sentiment she put into the conversation. "I am to make the match my parents feel is appropriate and settle myself into being the best wife I can be."

Nicholas sat back in his chair. "Would not being the best wife you can be entail having an affection for your husband?"

"No," she stated flatly. "It would entail keeping his house to the standards he wished and providing him with the heirs he required and seeing to their well-being. It would mean behaving in an appropriate manner at all times so as not to bring embarrassment and strife upon my husband."

Nicholas tried to imagine Abigail providing such a role for Lord Tarrington and his stomach churned. She would die a slow death married to the elderly lord. She possessed far too much passion and intelligence to live within such stringency.

"But what of passion?"

Sharpness edged Miss Caldwell's features and her eyes turned cold. Strange, he thought. Up until now, he had always considered brown a rather warm color. He would have to adjust his perspective in that regard.

"Passion?"

"Yes, passion. Do you not have a passion for anything?"

Her back stiffened, her spine ramrod straight. "Passion is

for those who do not have the strength of character to conduct themselves with decency and decorum."

It sounded to Nicholas as if she were quoting words from a book. Did she honestly believe such nonsense? "What of painters who have a passion for their art? Is that indecent?"

"If shown outwardly in their behavior, yes."

Nicholas shook his head. There were no gray areas with her. There never would be. It was either black or white. Night or day. But he lived in a world of dawn and dusk and he could not reconcile himself to spending the rest of his life with someone who could not see or experience the brilliant colors and shifting shadows.

He stood. "Forgive me, Miss Caldwell. I did not come here to argue with you. I simply meant to convey my feelings with respect to any hopes I may have given you regarding the prospect of a future engagement. I am afraid, in this regard, I must disappoint."

She did not move, did not blink. She reminded Nicholas of a fine marble statute molded by the masters into a hard kind of beauty.

He made a fruitless attempt to explain his reasoning. He owed her that much. "When I vowed to turn my life around, I thought to turn my back on passion and desire. I realize now that is impossible. I have no wish to return to the life I had lived previously, nor do I wish to live a life void of those two things. I don't think I would survive it."

"It is inappropriate for you to mention such...things to me." She said the words as if the very notion of them mortified her.

"Forgive me. I do not mean to cause you discomfort." Although in truth, he thought she could use a healthy dose of it. Her corset was laced so tightly he marveled she could breathe at all. "I only mean to illustrate to you my feelings—"

"Feelings are irrelevant, Lord Roxton. The only thing of

importance is that our respective parents expect us to marry, and marry we shall."

Nicholas shook his head. "No," he said. "We won't."

Surprise registered in her eyes, but it quickly faded, replaced by something harder. For a brief instant, she reminded him of Opal and the sensation did not sit well. He knew what his former mistress was capable of.

"And what, pray tell, has brought on this change of heart?"

Nicholas turned and gazed at the fire. It burned low in the hearth and chased away the dampness that permeated the air around them. It had rained again last night, and while it had since stopped, the clouds lay low and heavy in the sky giving the afternoon air a heavy, oppressive feel.

"I have an affection for someone else," he admitted, turning to face her. "It is an affection that has long-existed and that I can no longer deny."

"Miss Laytham, I presume," she said, each syllable brittle and angry. Had she suspected all along? Did others?

"Yes," he said, unwilling to deny it. What did it matter? Once he finished speaking with Miss Caldwell, he planned on tracking down Glenmor to inform him of his plans to propose to Abigail. If all went as planned, he would be announcing their betrothal at tonight's ball, and then everyone would know.

"You will not marry her."

The words were clipped and completely, utterly, final.

"I beg your pardon, but I have every intention of doing just—"

Miss Caldwell stood abruptly forcing Nicholas to take a step back. The placid expression Miss Caldwell had worn since she arrived altered. The change was subtle, almost imperceptible. Something one felt as opposed to saw. The air in the room took on a chilled aspect.

"You will not marry her and I will tell you why." She clasped her hands in front of her as she spoke, a slight tremor affecting her tone. "It appears your Miss Laytham is not so different from her uncle, the late Lord Glenmor."

"I beg your pardon?"

"It has been brought to my attention Miss Laytham has recently attended one of Madame St. Augustine's parties."

Nicholas tried to respond, but words failed him as the enormity of what Miss Caldwell suggested dawned on him.

"Do not look so surprised. I am not so sheltered I do not know of such things. It was your own disgusting habits that brought them to light last year upon Lord Glenmor's death. I have chosen to overlook your past despite this. I have every intention of marrying you, Lord Roxton. I will become the next Lady Blackbourne. I will elevate my family's status, alleviate their financial strain, and ensure my sisters marry well. And I will not let Miss Laytham or your own misguided needs stand in my way."

Nicholas's heart pounded in his chest. "How did you know?"

She waved the question off as if that part were inconsequential. "Servants are a wealth of information. It does not say much about the loyalty Miss Laytham engenders that her own maid would come to me with such information, laying it at my feet. I'm not sure what she expected from me. Certainly, I would never employ such an individual, knowing their loyalty changes with the wind. Regardless, I will not allow Miss Laytham to ruin my plans."

"What do you mean to do?"

She shrugged. "Nothing, if you do what is expected—which is to announce our betrothal. If you do not, then the ton will witness yet another horrible downfall of a member of the Laytham family. Society will discover that Miss Laytham is not the innocent she portrays herself to be, but instead is nothing more than a cheap doxy given to insidious passions."

Nicholas couldn't breathe. The air in the room suffocated. This couldn't be happening. It couldn't.

"You wouldn't dare." Cold sweat prickled the nape of his neck.

She looked at him sharply. "What choice do you leave me? Naturally, I would never appear to be the one who divulged the information, but it would get out nonetheless. She would be destroyed, as would the rest of her family. The Laythams may have risen from the ashes once, but it will not happen a second time."

"What would you have me do?" But he already knew the answer to that. She had stated it from the beginning and had not wavered.

"You will forgo any affiliation with Miss Laytham. You will set aside this silly notion that a marriage between the two of you. At tonight's ball you will announce our betrothal, and you will look quite pleased to do so as if this unsavory discussion had never occurred."

Nicholas swallowed. "And if I do not?"

"Then Miss Laytham will be completely and utterly ruined. Not even Lord Tarrington would touch her then. I'm certain you can surmise the outcome for her family if that were to occur."

Financial ruin, along with everything else.

"I thought you a decent person, but you had me fooled. You are cold and heartless. How could I not have seen it," he muttered.

Her mouth tightened, as if his harsh words hit their mark, but she quickly recovered. "I am what I need to be for the sake of my family. It matters not what you thought you knew of me, but know this. I will do what is necessary to secure my family's future."

The unspoken threat of what that meant hung heavy in the air. Nicholas had no doubt Miss Caldwell would carry out her threats. His guts churned. In order to save Abigail, he must break her heart. And his. He must spend the rest of his days tied to a woman who now held their futures crushed in the palm of her hand.

He did not know if he had ever hated someone more than he did in that moment.

"Fine. You will have your announcement," he said.

Pain tore through his heart as he watched his happiness disintegrate before his eyes.

Relief settled on Miss Caldwell's features. It was the most emotion he'd seen from her during their entire association. "Thank you."

Nicholas stood rooted to the spot as he watched her walk from the room in carefully measured steps expected of a proper lady, her posture giving no indication she had just ruined two lives without even the smallest hesitation.

In that moment, he wished Glenmor had not used the bullet on himself, but had aimed it at Nicholas's heart and pulled the trigger.

Surely, death was a better alternative than life with a woman he now despised.

Nicholas could scarcely believe how their lives seemed destined to intertwine and unravel. Each time happiness hovered within their grasp, it was yanked away. And each time it was Abigail's family that suffered. Maybe it was the best thing to remove himself from their lives for good, to give Abigail a chance at a happy life, instead of a cursed one with him.

Except he had taken her innocence. He had let passion overwhelm him.

A passion he would never feel again.

And she would be consigned to a similar fate with Lord Tarrington.

What if she carried his child? What then? How would he live, knowing another man raised his child? If Abigail even went through with the marriage. His head ached with the mess he had made of things.

The clock ticked on his betrothal announcement this evening. The earl had been informed and the bastard had gone so far as to plan to attend the event—likely to ensure Nicholas went through with it.

He needn't have worried. Under any other circumstances, nothing in the world could force him to marry Miss Caldwell, but these were not normal circumstances, and he would do everything within his power to keep Abigail safe.

Even if it meant breaking her heart.

He needed to meet with her before the announcement, to explain to her as best he could, and to do so without alerting Miss Caldwell, for fear of what she might do if they were discovered. But he had to take the risk, to slip away with Abigail and warn her.

It was the least he could do.

The very least.

It was all he had left.

"Desmond," he called into the other room where his valet prepared his suit for this evening's festivities.

"Yes sir?" Desmond appeared in the doorway.

"Have this delivered to Miss Laytham's rooms," he said and handed over a folded note, sealed with his crest.

"Yes, my lord." Desmond took the note and disappeared from the room. All that was left for Nicholas to do was wait.

Chapter Eighteen

"Who was at the door, Muri?" Abigail called from the dressing room where she luxuriated in a warm bath, secretly dreaming of the night ahead and swirling around the dance floor in the arms of the man she loved. Not even Muri's sullen mood could dampen her spirits.

"T'was nothing, miss. A servant with the wrong room. Can't find good help these days," she muttered as she returned to the dressing room and busied herself with brushing out the deep lavender silk Abigail planned to wear to the ball.

Muri had been in a snit since Abigail had reprimanded her for her inappropriate behavior. Perhaps she expected an apology, and, had Abigail been in the wrong, Muri would certainly receive it. But she hadn't been in the wrong. Muri had overstepped, assuming a familiarity reserved strictly for family and close friends.

The water from her bath reached her chin as she sunk down farther. She hoped she and Muri could put this unfortunate incident behind them and return to a more stable relationship.

"You are still in your bath?" Caelie came into the room and sat on a cushioned stool near the tub, careful not to wrinkle her dress. Her hair still needed to be attended to and she had come to Abigail's room to make use of Muri's services in that regard.

"I will hurry," she said. "Muri?"

The maid picked up a towel and helped Abigail wrap it around herself as she rose from the bath and stepped out. Excitement for the night ahead filled her with giddiness. Would Nicholas propose? Perhaps under a blanket of stars?

"You are grinning like a fool, Abby." Caelie's voice contained an edge of suspicion. "What are you up to?"

Abigail cleared her throat and tried to rein in her emotions. She should not get ahead of herself. "I am simply excited about this evening."

Caelie's eyebrow lifted. "Is that all?"

"Is that not enough? I've heard the final ball is a most spectacular event." Lady Blackbourne had invited the local gentry. And being close enough to London, several prominent families had made the trip from the city, filling the local inns or opening their own summer homes to guests. Few who had received an invitation to the event turned it down.

"I suppose." But her cousin didn't sound convinced.

"Have you seen Benedict?"

Abigail had it on good authority an important announcement was to be made by Nicholas's family that night. She smiled to herself.

Caelie glanced at Abigail through the mirror's reflection. "I have not. I believe he spent part of the afternoon with Lord Roxton and Mr. Bowen viewing the stables."

A thrill shot through Abigail and she sat on a stool next to Caelie. She had not spoken to Benedict. Had Nicholas broached the subject of their intended marriage with him? And would Benedict accept? She knew her brother wished to find another way to rescue their finances and save her from going through with marrying Lord Tarrington. If he could find a better alternative, surely, he wouldn't hesitate.

She wished she'd had the time to find Benedict and question him about the nature of their conversation. The anticipation had left her stomach riddled with unruly butterflies. She did not know how much longer she could wait.

"It will be a fine time, you'll see." Abigail turned to face Caelie, concerned with her cousin's lack of enthusiasm. Once upon a time, such a night would have had her over the moon. "Are you enjoying yourself at least a little?"

"Of course. The break from Mother was worth the trip alone," she said, but something lurked beneath her claims.

"What is it?"

Caelie hesitated as if weighing her words with care. "I have noticed the way you look at Lord Roxton."

"It is nothing, really. We have called a truce of sorts, that's all." The description paled in comparison and she disliked hedging around the truth. She hated lying to her cousin. They had always shared everything. But Caelie had counseled her against doing anything rash or foolish and she didn't want to worry her now by admitting she had blatantly disregarded her sage advice. "Caelie, are you all right? I had so hoped the party would lift your spirits."

Is it possible her cousin's advice to act with caution was more than just concern? Did the idea of Abigail becoming involved, possibly betrothed to the man who she once believed had been instrumental in Uncle Henry's downfall leave her unsettled? Caelie had once suggested Abigail not judge him so harshly, but forgiving Nicholas and bringing him into the family were two vastly different things.

"It has. Truly. I just..." Her words drifted off, then she took a deep breath and shook off whatever melancholy that held her in its grip. "It's nothing. I'm being silly. The party will be wonderful. I promise to enjoy myself immensely."

Abigail relaxed and returned Caelie's smile. Everything would be fine. It had to be.

N icholas searched the crowd frantically. He had tried to find Abigail, thinking the announcement would come later, after they were certain most guests had arrived.

How foolish of him. Frail and exhausted, his father would make the announcement early on, accept congratulations and then retire to his room, leaving Nicholas to face the devastation of decisions beyond his control.

Had she not received his note? He had gone to the designated meeting place, a private alcove off the balcony, and waited, but she had not shown. Had she changed her mind? Realized she could not forgive him after all? But no. She would never have given herself to him with such passion had her heart not been fully engaged.

Again, he searched the room, looking for the pale blonde head and pretty face that had haunted his every moment.

But it was too late. Time had run out.

Lord Blackbourne motioned for the band to stop playing and the crowd quieted. "Ladies and gentlemen." Many moved closer to hear what he said, his voice weakened from illness. Next to him Lord Caldwell stood, his round face filled with proud joy. "It gives me great pleasure to announce the betrothal between my son and Miss Eugenie Caldwell, eldest daughter of the Right Honorable Lord Caldwell and his wife, Lady Caldwell."

Nicholas heard the words like a barred door being slammed in front of him, the lock firmly set in place.

It was over.

Done.

He closed his eyes and prayed for Abigail's forgiveness. Or at the very least, to be given the opportunity to explain. He needed her to know he had not made the decision lightly. He had never intended to hurt her. His words fell short, but it was all he had left.

Abigail pushed through the crowd and made her way to the front as Lord Blackbourne said the words that turned her world upside down. The lords and ladies around her clapped. Their enthusiastic congratulations drowned out her gasp as the impact of what had just happened sunk in.

There had to be a mistake. There *had* to be!

But as she stared in disbelief, Nicholas's gaze found her, and she could see in his eyes the truth. Miss Caldwell stood on the dais with him. Her father escorted her over to Nicholas's side, forcing him to look away from her and into the smiling visage of his newly betrothed.

Abigail's knees faltered beneath her.

"Steady." Benedict's calm voice cut through the blood rushing in her ears. His firm hand held her elbow.

Abigail shook her head. It couldn't be true. It was a dream. A horrible nightmare she would wake from at any moment. It had to be. Benedict had met with Nicholas earlier. What other reason could he possibly have had to do so if not to offer for her?

"Ben..."

"Come with me." He slid his arm around her waist and gently led her away, holding her up while propelling her forward. She took one last, fleeting glance back to the dais, to

Nicholas. His eyes met hers and, in that split second, she saw an apology within their depths, but then the crowd of well-wishers converged and her love was swallowed up by the crowd, her heart trampled beneath their well-shod feet.

Chapter Nineteen

❧

"I do not understand." Abigail sank into the chair in front of the fire of her bedchamber.

Benedict stoked the fire once, letting the flames leap to life and lick the stone hearth before he took the seat across from her.

"What is there to understand, Abby? Roxton has courted Miss Caldwell for several months now. Everyone expected a betrothal announcement."

"But you met with him at the stables this afternoon. Did he say nothing to you?"

"We discussed horseflesh."

"And he said nothing...else?" How could this be happening? Why was she not waking up from this horrific nightmare? Her mind whirled and a deep wound penetrated her chest until she ached all over.

Benedict leaned forward and rested his forearms against his knees. His expression registered concern as he searched her face, for what she did not know. Finally, he let out a long breath.

"Roxton indicated he thought you might have developed

an affection for him. He expressed concern your feelings might be hurt when they made the announcement this evening. He asked that I stay close to you in the event you were upset and needed support. He swore me to secrecy, however, and I—"

"An affection...?" Abigail could not believe her ears. He thought she had developed *an affection*? She had given him her innocence. He had boldly stated his feelings for her. He had promised to make things right. He loved her. She knew he did.

Yet now, just days after sharing such intimacies, he told her brother he feared she had *developed an affection for him*?

Horror filled her. Had he simply used those words to trick her? To seduce her into his bed? Bile roiled in her stomach as the possibility grew like a weed in her mind. He had tricked her twice already. Once at Madame St. Augustine's party and again at the masquerade. Was it possible...?

Horror twisted into humiliation. She had been duped again by a master manipulator. Fooled and disgraced and left ruined in the process! What other explanation could there be for him to do such a thing? Had he offered to make things right only to keep her quiet while he secretly made plans to marry another?

"Abigail?"

Benedict had continued speaking but she had missed most of what he said. "I'm sorry, Ben. What did you say?"

"I said, I told Roxton his concerns were unfounded, but..." He leaned closer and his hand touched hers where it rested limply in her lap. "Looking at you now, I wonder if I spoke out of turn. Do you have feelings for the man, Abby?"

She shook her head, unable to form the words to lie. She took a deep breath and reached deep down inside of her to find the strength she needed. Only scraps remained. The past year had sorely depleted her reserves.

"I have become reacquainted with Lord Roxton over the

244 • KELLY BOYCE

past fortnight and realized that what you had told me is true. He is not the one to blame for Uncle Henry's downfall."

"I see," her brother said. His hand squeezed hers.

"Perhaps in seeing him in this renewed light, my feelings changed and I saw the man I once knew." Or thought she'd known. She blinked away tears, hating the break in her voice she could not prevent.

"Abby..."

The compassion in her brother's voice nearly proved her undoing. She pulled her hand away and fisted it into her stomach, giving a quick shake of her head.

"Perhaps I only wished to think he shared the same sentiment. I was merely caught up in the moment though."

Benedict's expression turned hard. "Did he do anything to make you believe he shared these feelings? Did he lead you on?"

For a fleeting instant, anger surged in Abigail and she contemplated turning him in for the cad he was. But she could not. Her heart refused to hear the words spoken aloud. To fully believe any of this had just happened.

"No," she said. "He did not."

She gazed at the fire. The bright flames danced and entwined around each other like lovers. Her bleak future stretched out before her. She could avoid it no longer.

She turned back to Benedict. "Please inform Lord Tarrington I would be most receptive to his proposal should he choose to make it."

"Abby, it's not necessary. We'll find another way. Things are beginning to change. In time, I am certain I can—"

She shook her head. "There is not enough time," she told him. Resolve strengthened her words. "You know that. The creditors are at the door and our reserves are all but empty. The time for frivolous notions has passed. We are on the brink of ruin, Ben, and I have the ability to prevent it and the willingness to do so. Speak to Lord Tarrington. Broker a marriage deal and let us be done with it."

The words broke her heart and somewhere deep inside of her the last embers of hope were smothered beneath the loneliness of her future.

T he expression on her face would haunt Nicholas the rest of his days. He could not shut it out, could not close his eyes and erase the look of hurt and horror rife in her blue eyes.

Because of him.

He had become the monster she had always claimed him to be.

He leaned against the stone mantel in the earl's study, his head resting in his hand. Heat from the fire beat against his legs but it barely registered. He had gone numb. Body, mind, and soul.

How could it end this way? He had been desperate for a chance to find her, to explain. Though, God help him, what did he think an extra five minutes would do? What explanation could he give? That he loved her so completely he must sacrifice what they had to save her reputation? He shook his head. Perhaps it was best he had not seen her first. Five minutes, hell, five days would not be long enough to explain to her, to make her understand. Knowing Abigail, she would tell him the threats mattered not, that they should throw caution to the wind and face the storm together.

The old Nicholas would have agreed with her. But he had reaped the consequences of such impetuous behavior and watched a man die for it. He could not be so cavalier a second time. Not when Abigail's reputation, and her family's, hung in the balance once again.

"Congratulations, my boy. You have managed to do something right," Lord Blackbourne said as one of the footmen wheeled his creaky chair into the study and stationed him in front of the fire next to Nicholas.

Nicholas reached for the brandy he'd set on the mantel and took another long pull on the liquor wishing the burn of the fiery liquid would clear his mind.

It didn't.

The earl waved the footman away.

"I will hasten the marriage along," Blackbourne said. "I do not want to waste any time. There is no telling how much I have left and I will have things settled before I go."

Nicholas glared down at the earl. "You think I would renege on the engagement without you here?"

"I think you would do whatever suited you and care little over who it affected. Much as you always have. You have been a thorn in my side since your conception. I see no reason for you to change now."

"Indeed," Nicholas muttered. No doubt he could save a boatload of drowning children from the lake and still Blackbourne would see him as nothing more than a scourge on the Sheridan name. It had always been that way. It would never change.

The realization hit Nicholas square in the chest. As a young boy, he had tried to win his father's favor and failed. By the time he became a callow youth, he'd become jaded by Lord Blackbourne's disregard and went out of his way to live up to the man's ill impression of him. He took great pride in embarrassing the earl with his rakish behavior, retribution for each hurt he'd been caused. If he could not earn the man's love or respect, then damn it, he would make his contempt worth his while.

Then he'd met Abigail. Her quick acceptance of him broke down his barriers. She saw within him the good he'd gone to great lengths to bury. With her, he saw a different future and realized how much he wanted it. How much he had longed for a life filled with love and laughter and acceptance.

When he'd thought she had rejected him, it solidified everything Blackbourne had ever said about him. He'd slipped off the edge and dropped so far into the dark abyss that a man died. Only the hope of reclaiming Abigail's good opinion and, God willing, her forgiveness, kept him from losing himself completely. His father's opinion of him no longer mattered.

Only Abigail's did.

Now, even that was lost to him.

He emptied the snifter of brandy and left it on the mantel, then turned and headed toward the door. He could not spend another minute in his earl's company.

"Where do you think you're going," Blackbourne barked.

"Wherever you're not. My days as a bachelor may be coming to an end, but I'll be damned if I'm not going to make the most of the time that is left by immersing myself in every depravity I can find!"

The words the earl hurled at him were lost against the study door when he slammed it shut behind him. Nicholas strode to the steps and took them two at a time. It had been an empty threat. He wanted none of it. He only wanted Abigail. His head pounded and his heart ached. He found his bed, shucked his clothing, and crawled into it, hoping to forget this day had ever happened.

But he couldn't. His fate was sealed.

And it was a miserable one.

"Dead?" Abigail pulled herself up from her bed into a sitting position. Her blonde hair tumbled over her shoulders and down her back. Everything hurt. "Lord Blackbourne? Are you certain?"

Her eyes burned, a result of crying herself to sleep last night. Sleeping being a gross exaggeration. Most of the night had been spent tossing and turning as she tried to make sense of what had transpired. How could she have been so stupid to fall, once again, for a jade like Nicholas Sheridan?

No answers came. Her foolish heart remained as much a mystery to her this morning as it had the night before.

"Yes, miss. Below stairs is all a buzz with it. They found him in his study. Footman thought he was asleep, but when he tried to wake him, he was stiff as a poker."

Abigail waved off Muri's detailed description. She did not require a fully painted picture.

She tossed the blankets aside with a sweeping gesture and climbed out of bed. Her muscles protested. How strange that heartbreak could make you feel pain all over. As if it didn't just break your heart, but broke you everywhere.

"Does Mother know? And Benedict?"

"Can't say. Didn't ask." Muri gave an inconsequential shrug and stared at her reflection in the oval mirror above the vanity.

Abigail had had enough of Muri's insolent attitude and lacked the patience this morning to deal with it. "Then I suggest, Muri, that you do ask. They should be informed with all due haste. See to it now."

Muri huffed and spun around from the mirror. "Miss Caldwell was right about you. You may be a lady but you ain't proper *or* decent."

Ice trickled through Abigail's veins. "I beg your pardon?"

Muri froze, as if realizing her words. She pursed her lips together.

"What did you mean by that? When would you have spoken to Miss Caldwell?"

Muri backed up. "I didn't mean nothin'. Just that—"

Abigail advanced on Muri. Her anger rose with each step. Intuition screamed at her to pay attention, that Muri's words provided the missing piece of the puzzle of this living nightmare.

"Explain yourself!"

Muri's mouth moved but no sound came out.

Abigail came nose to nose with her maid. "Tell me now, or you will be dismissed on the spot without references."

The color drained from Muri's face and the indignation she had worn over the past week crumbled.

"I—I like it 'ere. I thought maybe if I offered her some information she could use, she'd give me a position once she was lady of the house. Surely it would provide more quid than what I get from your family." The last words came as an accusation, as if Muri had been forced to take their offer out of no fault of her own.

Queasiness roiled in Abigail's stomach. "What did you do?" But she already knew. And it sickened her.

"I told Miss Caldwell about the key party." Though she whispered the words, they thundered through the bedchamber with a deafening roar.

"No."

"I didn't mean to hurt you. Ain't nothin' wrong in tryin' to elevate one's circumstances. I just—"

Abigail cut her off with a cold glare. She did not care what Muri's motives were. It changed nothing.

"Get out."

"But miss—"

"Out!"

Rage poured through her, pure and unadulterated. She *had* misplaced her trust, but it hadn't been Nicholas who had broken it. Instead, her future with the man she loved had been traded away for the hope of a few extra quid.

Everything made sense now. Miss Caldwell must have used the knowledge of Abigail's own impropriety to force Nicholas's hand. He did love her, after all. He had only been protecting her, keeping her reputation, and her family's, intact by sacrificing his own happiness.

Stupid, stupid man!

If he had only come to her. If he had only told her, she would have convinced him it didn't matter. So, what if there was a scandal? Once they married, all would be forgiven. The ton had a strange sense of morality in that regard. So long as Nicholas married her in the end, the details of their bizarre courtship would be reduced to a tasty little bon mot for a short time then fade into myth.

But no. He had chosen another path. He had chosen to marry Miss Caldwell instead.

Abigail sunk to the edge of her bed and dropped her head in her hands.

What was Nicholas thinking?

And what did it mean now with his father dead and he the new Earl of Blackbourne?

No doubt Miss Caldwell's talons would sink even deeper into his flesh now that she stood on the precipice of becoming a countess. Quite the elevation from a mere miss.

Abigail leaped from her bed and rushed to the armoire. She had to find Nicholas. She needed to know if they could avert this impending disaster before it ruined both their futures.

But by the time she had picked out her outfit and attempted to dress without Muri's help, her movements slowed and her determination waned. His family would now be dealing with the death of their father and all that entailed. They would not have time to deal with the meddling of a broken-hearted young woman. She would have to wait. And in the interim, provide the family whatever support they needed during this trying time.

If they needed anything from her at all.

Dead. The words rang in Nicholas's head. The earl was dead.

Nicholas walked to the large window that overlooked the gardens. Clouds covered the sky, blocking the sunlight and shrouding the world in shadow, as if the earl reached from beyond the grave to cast a pall over them.

He shook off the maudlin thought. The earl wasn't even in the ground yet, though that would soon be remedied. In the distance, the spire of the old stone church stabbed the sky. In a matter of hours, they would arrive there, listen to the ceremony, and watch them bury the man who'd acted as his father for his entire life.

He tried to feel something, but only regret floated to the surface.

Regret that he didn't feel more.

Regret that the earl hadn't been a different kind of man, and he, a better kind of son, even if it was in name only. Maybe then their lives would have been easier, different. Maybe then, he wouldn't have wasted half his life trying to live up to a reputation the earl had labeled him with as a child.

But he couldn't blame it all on Blackbourne. He may have laid the groundwork, but Nicholas had done nothing to knock it down. Instead, he had embraced it, determined to verify the earl had been right in every respect and to prove he didn't care.

Except that he had.

All he had wanted was the earl's acceptance. To feel he belonged. Yet all he had ever received was rejection.

Now the man was dead. Amends would never be made.

His valet approached him. "Is there anything I can do for you, m'lord?"

"No, Desmond. I'm fine." It was the standard response he'd given since Lord Blackbourne's passing. He didn't even know what it meant any longer.

Many of their guests had stayed on to attend the services. Nicholas wished they would all leave. The constant slew of sympathy and condolences made him feel like a charlatan. And being referred to as Lord Blackbourne made him uncomfortable, as if he had woken up one morning to find he'd become someone else. It didn't sit well. He wanted to run away, back to the cabin, back to Abigail. Back to the one perfect moment when he lay entwined with her in the small bed and placed his heart in her hands. In that moment, he had been accepted. Loved. Hopeful.

Those sweet emotions had now been replaced with numbness and misery. He was not fit company for anyone.

"Perhaps you could set out my suit for the service?"

"As you wish, m'lord." Desmond nodded and left him in peace.

He took a deep breath and slowly exhaled before he turned and followed Desmond from the room. He had a funeral to prepare for.

Reverend Barnaby kept the service brief and thankfully did not drone on endlessly, nor did he attempt to build the former Earl of Blackbourne into a great man who bore little resemblance to his true nature. For that,

Abigail was thankful. Being the direct recipient of the earl's machinations, she was not warmly predisposed to him. Death did not change that fact, though she kept such thoughts to herself.

Not that she had anyone to talk to about it. No one knew the true cause of her heartbreak, save for Benedict, and even he did not know the full scope of what had transpired. Just as well. Had he known, they might have been burying two Earls of Blackbourne today. Either way, he had been most solicitous toward her since the night following Nicholas's engagement to Miss Caldwell. He had offered to take her home the next day, despite Lord Blackbourne's death, but Abigail wouldn't have it. She wanted to be here to lend her support to Nicholas. She understood better than most the conflicted feelings he must have over the earl's death.

Not that they'd had any opportunity to talk. Miss Caldwell stuck to him like a burr, as if she were already the new Lady Blackbourne and took it upon herself to stay latched to his side every minute of the day.

Most of the guests had left and taken up residence elsewhere nearby to allow the family privacy while they mourned the earl's passing. Only a select few had stayed at the estate at the request of Lady Blackbourne. Miss Caldwell and her family, Lord Huntsleigh and Mr. Bowen. And finally, her family. It did not surprise Abigail. Her mother and Lady Blackbourne had reignited the friendship they'd lost and the countess appeared reluctant to let that go at a time when she needed close confidantes around her.

Once the majority of the guests had left, the house plunged into silence. Black crepe hung on the door, symbolizing this as a house of mourning. Even now, when the guests returned briefly for the funeral service and burial, a pall of gloom remained in the air and voices were dampened to a hush. Abigail looked forward to escape, to leaving Sheridan Park behind, returning home and letting her wounds heal.

The service ended, Nicholas and five others lifted the coffin onto their shoulders and made the long solemn walk behind Reverend Barnaby to place it in the hearse that carried it to the family plot at the top of the hill, while the mourners followed along behind. Abigail wished she could find a moment to speak to Nicholas, but he had been holed up since the earl's death and his family planned to leave for London directly after the burial. It would be another week before they would accept condolence calls.

The separation wore on her. She wanted to tell him she knew what he had done and why, but an appropriate time had not presented itself.

Was this to be it then? Was this the end?

Lord Tarrington had warned her he planned to spend the majority of his time at Maynerly, which meant her time in London would be rare. And when she did see Nicholas, the idea that they would be relegated to polite chitchat at crowded social events broke what remained of her shredded heart.

Perhaps it was better this way. Seeing him, knowing he belonged to someone else would only twist the knife in the wound a little deeper. Perhaps the best outcome would be to keep her distance in the hope that eventually time would dull the pain.

She decided not to hold her breath on that account.

Chapter Twenty

"I do not miss him," Nicholas admitted. He took a drink and the liquid slid down his throat with welcomed warmth. He had come to the club, anxious to leave the house and seek the comfort of his friends. The earl had been in the ground for a fortnight and the constant barrage of condolence bearers had worn him out, and while he did not like abandoning his mother and sister, he needed out. To breathe. To wrap his head around what had happened and what it meant for his future. He needed to speak freely, without fear of judgment or censure. "Part of me is glad to be rid of him. How awful is that?"

"Not so awful," Spence said. "Blackbourne was a bastard. I doubt anyone in their right mind would miss him over much."

"Lady Rebecca will," Bowen pointed out. Nicholas nodded in agreement. His sister did indeed mourn her father, and he supposed he couldn't fault her for it. She had received the best of him, such as it was. Any love Blackbourne had inside of him, he had bestowed upon his daughter.

"She will be the only one, is my guess."

"Spence," Bowen sent a warning glance to his friend.

"What?" Spence feigned innocence.

"The man is dead. Show a little respect."

"No," Nicholas waved the comment aside. "Spence is right. He was a vile man. Death doesn't eradicate that." He sighed and leaned back in his chair. He just wished...

Well, he wished it could have been different.

Spence signaled for another drink. "So, what now?"

Nicholas shrugged. "Now I get to enjoy the rest of my life." A scowl twisted at his mouth.

Spence sat up straighter in his chair and leaned forward. "You can't seriously be planning to go through with this sham of a marriage, are you? Blackbourne is dead. He cannot force you to—"

"They are engaged, Spence. The announcement has been made. What other choice does he have?" Bowen said, though he didn't look any happier in stating the fact than Nicholas felt in hearing it. "If he does not go through with it, he will be in breach of promise. Only Miss Caldwell can call off the marriage now without reprisal. If Nicholas does, it will ruin her."

"What are the chances she will do that?"

"Nonexistent." Nicholas took another drink. If only the liquor could wash away the desolation wallowing in his gut, but it didn't. "Her family is in dire need financially. With no male heir, most of what they own will go to a distant cousin upon Lord Caldwell's passing. Miss Caldwell and her two younger sisters need to make good marriages to secure their futures."

"Can't she simply find another poor, unsuspecting sod? She's certainly not hard on the eyes, if you like that kind of cold, remote beauty." The face Spence pulled made it clear he did not.

"Why would she, when she already has one? I am a

certainty. Besides, the better the match she makes now, the better chances for her sisters when it is their turn."

"Then you must convince her marrying you would be a catastrophic mistake," Spence said.

"And how do you propose he do that?" Bowen asked. "He has already told us Miss Caldwell has few options and strong motivation."

Spence leaned forward in his chair, the leather creaking beneath him. "What does Miss Caldwell value most? Aside from your bank account and title."

"Propriety," Nicholas answered without hesitation.

"Exactly."

"What crazy scheme are you cooking up now?" Bowen asked, his voice rife with suspicion. With good reason, Nicholas supposed. Most of Spence's grandiose schemes did not end well.

Spence held up his hands to ward off Bowen's warnings. "All I am suggesting is that Nick consider which of the two she holds most dear and then find a way to ensure she does not get it, making the prospect of marriage to him so unappealing that she has ample incentive to break off the engagement."

"How would I do that? I can't very well empty my bank accounts or give away entailed lands and property."

"No. But you could stage a scandal." Spence shrugged. "It really isn't too difficult."

"From the mouth of the master," Bowen muttered.

"And how, exactly, would I do that?"

Spence sat back and grinned as Farnley arrived with his drink. "I'm sure you'll think of something."

"Abigail?"

Abigail glanced up from the mound of dirt she had been toiling over for the better part of an hour. In the past week, she had taken to the task, determined to coax her family's pitiful gardens back to their full splendor. She had no idea if what she did served any purpose other than it kept her hands busy and gave her something to focus on besides Nicholas.

She had paid a condolence call on his family yesterday, hoping to find a private moment to speak with him, desperate to convey what she knew, but only Lady Blackbourne and Rebecca were there to receive them. Thwarted at every turn, her thoughts turned desperate. She had even entertained the idea of sending Nicholas a direct missive to request a private meeting. The scandal, if word got out, stayed her hand in that regard, but the idea lingered.

She shielded her eyes from the sun and addressed Caelie. "He is here, then?"

Her cousin nodded and Abigail's shoulders slumped in response. Lord Tarrington had sent a notice the day before requesting a meeting, first with Benedict and then with her. It could mean only one thing.

He meant to propose.

Her stomach plummeted and she stared down at her earth-covered gloves. Time had run out. She pursed her lips to keep their sudden trembling under control. Much as she wanted to pound her fists into the ground and wail her frustration for all to hear, she could not.

"You don't have to go through with this," Caelie said. She had been opposed to the association from the first moment Aunt Edythe had promoted it in the hopes of recapturing their family's former glory. That she had to sacrifice her niece to do so did not even signify.

"Oh, Caelie, I wish that it were true." She stood and pulled off her gloves. "But what other options do we have?" The creditors continued to bang at their door demanding their pound of flesh.

Caelie grabbed her suddenly and pulled her into a tight hug. "I hate this," she said, her voice filled with emotion. "You do not deserve such a fate. None of this was your doing. Papa lost his mind and now you are being made to suffer for it and it just isn't fair! It should be me. He was my father. I should be the one to pay the price!"

But they both knew that could not be the way. Being Uncle Henry's daughter, coupled with her broken engagement to Lord Billingsworth, had put Caelie on the shelf, possibly permanently. No gentleman had shown the least bit of interest in an association with her now, not even Lord Tarrington. Even at the house party, though she'd had several dance partners, not a single gentleman went out of his way to pay her special attention. Despite her beauty, despite her high birth, she remained a pariah.

Abigail pulled out of Caelie's embrace and squared her shoulders. "Do not fret, Caelie. After all, it is just a meeting. Nothing is written in stone yet."

She forced a smile in the hopes of easing Caelie's fear that her closest friend marched to her doom. Even if her bravery proved nothing more than a false front, she needed Caelie to see it, to believe she made the choice freely and without resentment.

"Come," she said, slipping her arm through Caelie's. "Let me go ready myself and then we shall see what Lord Tarrington has to say."

· · ·

"Ah, my dear. You look lovely." Lord Tarrington stood, leaning heavily on his walking stick to vault himself out of his seat on the sofa.

Abigail acknowledged his compliment with a curtsey, stopping several feet away from him. She chose a chair across from him on the opposite side of the low table. A tea service and plate of biscuits sat atop it. Her stomach growled. She had spent the lunch hour in the gardens and now paid the price of skipping her midday meal.

Her mother and Aunt Edythe flanked either side of her. Her aunt rarely made an appearance to see guests, but she usually made an exception for Lord Tarrington.

Abigail glanced at her brother. He lounged by the fire but had turned slightly away from them and did not return her look. Her stomach dropped a little farther. This gathering could mean only one thing.

"My dear cousin has made a most generous offer," Aunt Edythe said, with what Abigail assumed was meant to be a smile. That is, if one could call a tight pursing of the lips a smile. In all of the years Abigail had known the woman, she had never once seen a genuine smile grace her face, nor heard her laugh. Abigail found it difficult to reconcile any relation between her and Caelie.

Benedict finally turned and came to stand behind Abigail's chair. His hands rested on her shoulders and she could feel a slight tremble. Was that from her, or her brother? She could not be certain.

"Lord Tarrington has made an offer of marriage," he said, picking up where Aunt Edythe had left off, taking control of the conversation. She reached up and placed one of her hands over his, suddenly needing his support.

"Has he?" Her voice came out light as a feather. The words ruffled the air, barely there.

"It is quite true I assure you, my dear," Lord Tarrington beamed. He seemed quite proud of himself, as if his offer made him heroic, a savior. And though it held a grain of truth, his puffed-up sense of self disgusted her nonetheless. A part of her still wanted to fight, to find another way that didn't leave her as breeding stock for an old man, and her brother, mother and cousin mired in guilt because they had failed to save her from such a fate. She had come so close at the house party; tasted freedom and happiness on the tip of her tongue only to have it turn sour.

Nicholas thought his actions would save her. In truth, he had thrown them both to the wolves.

"I will settle a large portion of your family's debts. However, in doing so, I will also take control of several unentailed properties and advise young Glenmor on how best to manage his remaining business and assets."

Benedict's fingers tightened on her shoulders. She knew how much Benedict despised the older man's interference. In truth, her brother had done a spectacular job keeping their family afloat as long as he had, finding ways to cut expenditures and improve investments. If they had more time, she had no doubt he could turn their fortunes around. But the creditors had tired of waiting.

"Where you have no dowry to speak of," Tarrington continued, "I feel this is a fair settlement. We will have a short engagement as well. I wish to retire to Maynerly Park. Four weeks should suffice. That will allow time for the banns to be read. A small service will be all that is required. Given the family's current social standing, I believe anything extravagant would just appear garish."

"I see," Abigail managed. Despite bracing herself for the inevitability of this moment and her determination to see it through for the sake of her family, desperation clawed at her insides. It took every last ounce of her will not to throw

Benedict's hands from her shoulders and bolt from the room.

"Can I take that as your acceptance of my generous offer?"

Abigail opened her mouth and tried to force the words out, but the ones that came were not the ones she had planned. "I'm sorry, Lord Tarrington. It is a very generous offer indeed, but it is also an important decision, and if it please you, I would like a week to consider it."

Lord Tarrington's face turned stony.

"Don't be foolish, girl!" Aunt Edythe lurched forward in her chair. Anger splintered from her dark eyes.

Abigail's mother stood. Her face had paled and her features were drawn tight, but her voice came strong and steady. "Taking the time to weigh such a decision is not foolish in the least, Lady Glenmor. If my daughter wishes to take a week to decide, then she will be granted a week. If Lord Tarrington is not willing to give her such time, he may rescind his offer. I am sure he has any number of young women lined up, eager to take Abigail's place."

The hard expressions on Aunt Edythe and Lord Tarrington's faces said otherwise. Though a titled lord with a bank account to match, he was an unpleasant man and not well liked. Few families cared to bind their young daughters into such a marriage if an alternative existed. And with his advanced years, Lord Tarrington's time to produce a male heir was running out.

The weight of power shifted slightly. For the first time, Abigail realized he needed her as much as her family needed his money.

"I will grant Miss Laytham the time she has requested." Tarrington pushed himself up from the sofa with the help of his walking stick. "But I will not extend it one hour past that. I will return in one week's time. By then, I will have her acceptance of my offer, as I believe we all know there will not be another one forthcoming."

Benedict squeezed her shoulders, then his grip loosened and slipped away. "I will show you out, Tarrington."

Not until the doors to the receiving room closed behind them did Abigail let out a long breath and let the tension flow from her muscles.

She had bought herself a week.

The question was—what was she going to do with it?

T he meeting was perilous despite the early hour that found most of their peers still snug in their beds. Nicholas should have dissuaded her. This was sheer folly. But Abigail's missive read most urgent, and in the end, he could not deny her. She requested no reply, simply stating she would be at the indicated spot at the appointed hour, and that he meet her there.

The thought of her standing beneath this secluded alcove of thick oaks alone did not put his mind at ease. What other choice did he have but to meet her and ensure her safety? Finally, he could explain to her why he had betrothed himself to Miss Caldwell. But not without great risk. Was it worth it?

Yes.

If he could see her, hear her voice, hold her in his arms for just a few moments, the chaos of his life would recede and things would make sense again.

And the second he let her go, it would reclaim him once again.

Oh, but for those few glorious moments...

So, he waited. Waited and hoped beyond all reason she would listen to what he had to say and forgive him. He knew his chances were slim, but when she'd contacted him with a request to meet in secret, hope had flared and he clung to it like a lifeline.

Above him, songbirds woke with the weak light of early morning sun, their warbled songs a balm to his savaged nerves.

Through the morning mist that had yet to burn away, a dark figure slowly emerged. Though faint at first, he recognized her instantly despite the dark hooded cloak she wore covering her from head to toe. He stepped away from the tree to greet her, drinking in the sight of her as she approached. The mist swirled around her legs like a specter. The maid who had escorted her stopped a discreet distance away. A different one than the maid she'd had at the country estate, shorter and heavier.

She stopped just beyond his reach. He longed to cross the space and enfold her into his arms, but he held back, unsure of her feelings. He had hoped her request to meet meant she had forgiven him, but he refused to give in to such fancy. Knowing Abigail, she had arranged the meeting to give him a proper dressing down for what he had done and to demand an explanation and apology.

"You said it was urgent," he said. "Is everything all right?"

It was a stupid question. Nothing had been right since he'd announced his engagement to Miss Caldwell.

Abigail's hands clasped in front of her and she squared her shoulders. "I know why you are marrying Miss Caldwell," she said. She wasted no time with pleasantries but rather jumped right in.

"You do?"

"My previous maid, Muri, confessed she told Miss Caldwell I had attended Madame St. Augustine's party. It appears she tried to sell her loyalty for the promise of a better position in a loftier household. As such, she is no longer employed at ours."

"Nor would such a woman ever come under my employ."

Nicholas's heart pounded in his chest. Was that all she wished? For him to ensure her maid did not gain from her betrayal? If so, it was done.

Abigail waved a hand, dismissing the issue. "It matters not. She will reap what she sowed eventually. That is not why I asked you here."

"Then why did you?"

"To confirm my suspicions. Did Miss Caldwell use the information to coerce a proposal from you? Are you marrying her to protect me?"

Nicholas tried to form words of denial but none came. He did not want Abigail to bear the burden of the decision he made. He wanted her to be free of all of this. He wanted her to carry on and have a happy life. But she did not look happy. He recognized the depth of misery in her eyes and the lies would not come.

"I would have never agreed to a betrothal otherwise." He took a step toward her, removing the divide and took her hands in his, wishing the gloves did not exist so he could feel her soft skin. "I went to her to advise her there would be no engagement between us, that I loved another. She informed me if I did not announce our betrothal at the ball that night, she would let it be known you were at Opal's party. She would ruin you."

Abigail nodded and stared down at their hands. Sadness softened her pretty features, giving her a melancholy beauty that cut deep into his heart. "I suppose I have only myself to blame. It was my decision to attend the party. Caelie warned me no good would come of it."

She lifted her head and in the early dawn light unshed tears brightened her impossibly blue eyes.

He squeezed her hands. "This is not your fault."

She gave him a knowing look. She would not be placated so easily. She did not seek absolution, nor did she shirk her own responsibility for their situation. Despite wanting to protect her, he had never admired her more.

"We both know if I had not been so foolish and pigheaded as to traipse off to Madame St. Augustine's party that night none of this would have happened."

"Perhaps. But without that night, none of *this* would have happened."

Despite the hurt, he would never regret what had occurred between them. It was the one thing he had left to sustain him. The memory of the love they'd shared would linger long in his memory to see him through the dark hours of his future.

Chapter Twenty-One

S omething in Nicholas's voice caught Abigail's attention and made her pause.

None of this would have happened.

His words rang true. She would not be standing on the brink of scandal. He would not have been forced to marry a woman he did not want. And she would not be counting the hours down before she had no other alternative but to accept Lord Tarrington's proposal to save her family from financial ruin.

She should regret attending Madame St. Augustine's party. But how could she? Despite everything, she had found love and passion with a man she had once adored then learned to despise. He had opened her eyes, made her look past her pain and see the truth. She had learned the power of forgiveness and the healing strength of love. She had experienced the intense intimacies between a man and a woman and known what it meant to be cherished and valued for who you were, faults and all. For a brief moment in time, she had been fulfilled in every way imaginable.

If she had not gone to that party, she would not have

discovered the true Nicholas Sheridan beneath the mask and realized that despite his actions, he was still a good man. A man struggling to change his life and do the right thing.

He had saved her in any number of ways since that night.

"I owe you so much," she whispered.

Nicholas shook his head. A lock of dark hair fell across his brow. Her fingers itched to brush it back, but she knew if she did, she would be lost.

"I had no right to take what I did from you. What if you are with child—"

"I am not." A wave of sadness washed over her. How she would have loved to have Nicholas's child growing inside of her. Forget the scandal. Forget the total and utter ruin it would bring down upon her and her family. For one selfish moment she allowed herself to wish, and to feel the disappointment of that wish going unfulfilled.

He hesitated. "It's for the best."

But in his hesitation, Abigail sensed he too shared the same loss as she. A profound sadness filled her.

"I wish I had not wasted so much time being angry with you. I knew well before I forgave you that you did not carry all the blame. I just couldn't bear to admit it and see my uncle in such an unfavorable light."

"That is perfectly understandable. He wasn't a bad man; he simply made some bad choices. We all did."

She nodded. "I know, but it doesn't excuse my behavior. Especially when you tried to save me from my foolishness time and again."

He lifted one eyebrow and a thrill surged through her. Oh, how that one movement affected her. Spoke to her. "I took part in that foolishness, if you'll recall. I am no hero."

"I do recall," she said, placing her hand against his chest, unable to help herself. She needed to touch him, to feel him. She slipped her fingers through the opening in his jacket and held her palm against his heart until she could feel its steady beat. "I recall every minute of it and I relive it each time I close my eyes. I crave the touch of your hand on my bare skin and the feel of your lips on mine. I can barely sleep because each time I try I can feel the weight of you upon me and when I awaken, I am faced with the knowledge that moment will never come again." Her voice caught.

"Abigail."

She shook her head, unable to stop the tears from flowing. She did not even try. They had been bottled up inside of her since the night of his betrothal to Miss Caldwell and she could contain them no longer.

"No. I have lost you. Through my own stupidity, I have rendered our situation irretrievably broken. You are forced to marry a woman who has blackmailed you into a betrothal. And I am to live the rest of my life knowing if I had only acted sooner, if I had told you that it did not matter what she did or who she told, then maybe, just maybe, we could be together now."

He pulled her to him and let her cry, murmuring nonsense into her ear that she did not even hear. She let the warmth from his body make her feel safe, as if it could hold back the future. A foolish illusion, but she gave in regardless, just for a moment, to make things bearable.

"I would never allow you to sacrifice yourself for me," he said.

A soft breeze caressed her face. Soon the sun would break through the clouds and the fog would dissipate. She must be gone before then, or risk them being seen. Their time grew short.

"It would be no sacrifice." Abigail lifted her head and brushed at her eyes with her gloved hand, sniffling slightly. Her eyes stung and she knew they were likely puffy and red. "I must look a mess."

Nicholas peered down at her and a small smile touched his lips. He cupped the side of her face with his hand and shook his head. His thumb brushed away what remained of her tears.

"You are the most beautiful woman I have ever seen."

"Ah, then I've fallen in love with a blind man."

His smile grew. "You love me."

She swatted at his chest and sniffled again. "Of course, I love you, you idiot. I have loved you longer than I care to admit." Her heart throbbed and ached in her chest. "And I will love you for longer than I think I can bear."

"I do not deserve you."

"You do not deserve Miss Caldwell. If I thought you could be happy perhaps it would not trouble me so, but—"

"I could never love Miss Caldwell," he said. "Marriage to her will be a misery. But I would go through a thousand miseries if it would keep you safe and give you a chance at a better life. Just promise me, please, that you will grasp that life. Do not sell yourself short. Do not marry Lord Tarrington. I could not bear it if you were unhappy too."

Abigail pushed away from the safe cocoon of his arms. How could he so willingly accept his fate? How could he tell her not to be unhappy when they both knew by marrying Miss Caldwell, he consigned himself to a lifetime of grief?

"Lord Tarrington has proposed and I have until the week's end to give him an answer. It will mean my family stands a chance at recovery. We could pay off Uncle Henry's creditors and start anew."

"Even at the price of your own happiness?"

Abigail looked down at the ground between them. Did it even matter? Lord Tarrington or someone else. Either way, it would not be Nicholas.

"Is that not what you are doing by marrying Miss Caldwell?"

"Abigail, please..."

She held up her hand to ward off what he was about to say. She had not come here to discuss that. She had asked him here for one purpose only—to know for certain they had done all they could do. "Am I too late then? Do we stand no chance at all of reversing this mess?"

She had scoured her mind time and again, trying to come up with a way to undo what had been done, but every idea fell apart in the face of one insurmountable fact. The engagement had been announced. Only Miss Caldwell could break it now without further scandal, and Abigail well knew the woman's desperation. Knew it and understood it, though she despised the methods used to achieve it.

She hated the pain etched into Nicholas's handsome features. His hands fisted at his sides as if he wanted to strangle the fates that had led them here. She couldn't blame him. She shared those same feelings. Fate was a cruel mistress to give them love only to snatch it away in such a calculated manner. But no, she could not blame fate. In the end, much like everyone else in this sad little tale, they had been the authors of their own downfall.

Now the time had come to pay the piper.

"It is then," she said, in the face of his silence. She swallowed the lump in her throat and spoke past the next round of tears threatening to dissolve her composure. She forced a tremulous smile. "Well do not worry about me. I will be fine. I am a survivor."

Had she not proven that already? She had survived her father and brother's early deaths, her uncle's suicide, and the scandal that followed. She'd survived losing the man she loved to another woman and she would survive marriage to Lord Tarrington.

Somehow, some way. She just didn't know how as yet.

"No!"

Nicholas stepped forward and cupped her face in a gentle

embrace. Before she could speak, his mouth was upon hers, suffocating her gasp of surprise. He kissed her with wild abandon until her knees weakened and she clung to him for support. Her lips parted and his tongue plundered, tasting, teasing, and urging her to do the same. They became entangled in each other, tongues and limbs and pain. Everything entwined together until there was no telling where one began and the other left off. Abigail wanted to disappear inside of him, let him carry her in his heart for all eternity. Maybe that would be enough.

When their lips finally parted, something wrenched from her chest as if he had taken her heart from her. It didn't matter. Without him, she had no use for it.

Nicholas rested his forehead against hers. "Promise me, you will not accept Lord Tarrington's proposal. Just give me a few days."

"A few days to do what? There is nothing to be done."

He shook his head and his bright silvery eyes caught hers. They sparkled and burned with need and hope and want and something else she couldn't put her finger on. Desperation, perhaps.

"I have an idea. It is not without risk and I do not know if it will work, but please, promise me you will not accept Lord Tarrington's proposal until I at least try. Promise me, you will not make any decisions until you hear from me."

Abigail stepped away from him and tried to ignore the small ember of hope fluttering to life deep inside her heart. "What are you planning?"

He shook his head. "I cannot tell you. Not yet."

Abigail laughed, a silly, hopeful, little sound. "But—"

"A chance. That is all I ask."

A chance was all she had wanted. "I will give you whatever you ask of me."

He rushed forward and kissed her again with determination and passion. Something in his kiss fortified her spirits, made her believe in possibilities. The ember of hope caught fire and raged to life.

"I won't let you down," he said. "I love you and I won't let you down."

Before she could change her mind, he turned and strode away. His declaration echoed in the mist and wove around her heart.

He loved her.

She smiled and hugged her arms around herself as if she could hold in the words forever and never let them go.

He loved her.

And she would risk it all to keep it.

Nicholas lifted the brass knocker on the bright red door and let it fall twice. A moment later, he stood in the receiving room, ornately decorated, yet somehow lacking the true elegance he expected its owner had wished to achieve.

"Have you finally come to your senses?"

Nicholas turned to face his old mistress, and for a fleeting moment, he wondered what he had ever seen in her. It mattered not. Not anymore. What he wanted from her now he would pay any price for.

He smiled broadly. "In a manner of speaking."

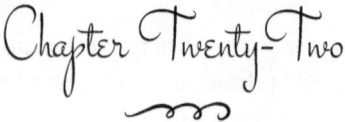

Chapter Twenty-Two

"Sir?"

An agitated major domo appeared at Nicholas's shoulder.

"Yes, Farnley," he said. "What is it?"

But Farnley did not get the opportunity to inform him. The situation snowballed far too quickly and despite being involved in the situation, part of Nicholas felt like a spectator, watching as Opal strode into the men's club, her eyes wild and her hair disheveled as if she had just tumbled from her bed.

"Is it true what I hear?"

"Madame, you cannot be in here." Farnley tried to grasp her arm, but Opal shook him off and hissed. The major domo took a step back as if she were a serpent with a lethal bite. He was not too far off in that regard. Indeed, Opal appeared as if she could spit venom and draw blood in that moment.

She advanced on him, every eye in the club firmly upon her. "Is it true you are engaged to marry your precious Miss Caldwell?"

The crowd's attention quickly shifted focus, boring into him as they witnessed the spectacle. A time had existed when such a scene would not have fazed him in the least. He had reveled in the embarrassment these incidents caused his father with a selfishness that now embarrassed him. But he intended today's performance for a different audience. "Calm down, woman. You forget yourself."

"I forget myself?" She leaned forward, her ample bosom threatening to spill out of her risqué gown. Crimson red trimmed with black lace. A whore's outfit. Nicholas silently applauded her choice of costume.

She seethed at him, then drew herself up to her full height, impressive in a woman, and enhanced by the full mane of golden hair flying freely about her head in untamed curls. She knew how to play to a crowd, to draw their attention and she did so now. The ten thousand pounds he'd promised to pay her for the performance and passage to France where she could start over had proven strong incentive. When she left London, she would leave an indelible memory in all of their minds, making her last moments here a thing of myth and legend.

"You fool. Do you honestly think Miss Caldwell will consent to the marriage when she learns you still frequent my bed?"

Nicholas's heart slowed to a crawl. He had not given Opal any particular script to follow, only the instruction that the show had to be grand, public and scandalous. He must tread carefully.

He shrugged nonchalantly. "You have me mistaken for someone else. I have not frequented your bed in nearly a year."

She laughed, a throaty guttural sound that was both sensual and threatening.

"Is that so? Because you seemed quite charmed last night as I wrapped my legs around you and rode you like a stallion. You begged me for more, in fact."

Farnley approached her again but her cold glare held him off.

Nicholas rose from his chair. "My dear, I can assure you, whoever you had your legs wrapped around last night, it was not me. But then I expect so many men pass through your bedroom it is difficult to keep track."

The palm of her hand cracked across his cheek with stinging force. He gritted his teeth and played along. "Then tell me where you were last night? Prove to me it was not you in my bed."

Nicholas swept an arm wide. "I was here, of course," he said. The lie tripped easily off his tongue. He'd made a point of staying home, despite Spence's urging that he join them.

Opal boldly faced the men present while Farnley stood nearby wringing his hands. "Which of you remembers seeing Lord Blackbourne amongst you last evening?"

Before anyone could vouch for him out of a misguided sense of solidarity and ruin everything, Nicholas grabbed Opal by the arm and dragged her in the direction of the door.

"Let me go! Are you all going to stand there as he manhandles a lady?"

Nicholas barked out a laugh and raised his voice. "I'm certain if there was a lady present, they would indeed not allow such behavior to occur. But there is no lady here, just a whore with too much imagination for her own good."

A footman opened the door as he approached and Nicholas hauled Opal over the threshold, though he propped one foot against the door to keep it open. He did not want to lose his audience.

"Go home, madam," he said, ensuring his voice carried back into the club. A club that had grown silent of droning voices, giving him a rapt audience. "This is neither the time nor the place to discuss private matters."

She gave him a sly grin and winked and he responded with a slight nod. Their business had concluded. Their story ended. She'd get what she wanted—a fresh start, a new life. Nicholas could only hope the theatrics played out here today would afford him the same.

He stepped back and slammed the door in her face, then returned to the interior of the club. Bowen and Spence stared at him, dumbstruck. He had purposely not told them of his plan. He needed their reaction to appear genuine.

He took his seat, picked up his drink, and casually waved it in their direction as if nothing untoward had occurred. The other members of the club began to murmur about the scene they had witnessed, their gazes still riveted to him.

"You were right, Spence," he said quietly.

His friend's eyes widened. "I was?"

Nicholas forced himself not to grin, wanting to look properly chagrined in front of the other patrons, so that when word spread, it would be told that despite his protests of innocence, Lord Blackbourne's reaction, when called out by his mistress in a most public and humiliating fashion, told a different story.

"It appears I came up with something scandalous after all."

He watched the realization sink in. Spence schooled his features, but an appreciative spark gleamed in his eyes. "Well played, sir. Well played."

"Not so fast," Bowen said, his voice kept low. Nicholas turned to him. "Lord Selward is sitting two tables over. He appears less impressed with the display than the two of you."

Nicholas shrugged. "Was that not the point? The scandal of today needs to swiftly reach the ears of Miss Caldwell and her family. At which point I will let her know such events will be a regular occurrence in our marriage and she should accustom herself to that fact or find herself a new groom. Selward is a particular friend of Lord Caldwell and therefore the perfect man to get the job done."

"He is also the man your sister is determined to marry.

Will he take kindly to courting your sister after today's fiasco? The man avoids scandal as if it were the plague."

Nicholas let his gaze slide toward the man in question. Selward did in fact appear quite disgusted. The younger man glared at him, then looked away.

His sister would not be pleased with him.

"Think of it as killing two birds with one stone," Spence said, finding the bright side. "Opal's theatrics will hopefully eradicate Miss Caldwell's desire to marry you and it will keep Lady Rebecca from making the hugest mistake of her life by marrying a man who has strung her along for much too long." Spence held up his drink in salute. "Job well done, I say."

Nicholas doubted Rebecca would share Spence's sentiment. When his sister set her mind to something, deterring her was like trying to run through a brick wall. Impossible, and often painful.

H er mother handed her gloves and hat to Titus as Abigail descended the staircase. She had gone out to make a few calls, their company now sought after, more so than it had been, thanks to the impression that a truce had been called between the Laythams and the Sheridans. Abigail had forgone visiting today however, as her mother intended on seeing Lady Blackbourne, and Abigail did not have the heart to listen to chatter of her son's upcoming nuptials. Despite Nicholas's promise to make things right, the odds were stacked heavily against them and as much as she trusted in his willingness to do what he could to change things, what could he really do? The engagement was set. It would take a Herculean effort to convince Miss Caldwell to give up the financial security and elevated status marriage to

Nicholas would bring her and her family and time was running out. Abigail had two more days before Lord Tarrington demanded an answer or withdrew his offer.

At the base of the stairs the tall clock ticked off the seconds, a constant reminder time passed. She had yet to hear a word from Nicholas since their clandestine meeting.

"Good afternoon, Mother," Abigail said, forcing a smile upon her face as she entered the front hall. "How does Lady Blackbourne fare today?"

"As well as can be expected." Mother motioned to the front sitting room. "Will you join me for tea?"

"Yes, of course."

Her mother turned to their butler. "Have Mabel bring us a tray, will you, Titus?"

"Right away, madam."

Once they were settled, her mother looked at Abigail and reached across to take her hands. "There has been a further upset at the Sheridan household, I'm afraid."

"Oh dear, no one is ill, are they?" Her mind immediately went to Nicholas. Fear rippled through her body. Is that why she hadn't heard from him?

"No dear, although Gloria has said her son is simply not himself since his father's death. They were never close and she is surprised by his melancholy. Still, I suppose one never knows what goes on deep in someone's heart. Perhaps he is simply mourning the missed chance to repair their relationship."

Abigail dipped her head to avoid her mother's gaze. She knew Nicholas's melancholy had little to do with repairing the past, only saving the future. Their future.

"If no one is ill, what is the problem?"

Her mother sighed. "It appears there was a scene at the club involving Lord Blackbourne and that vile woman, Madame St. Augustine."

"A scene?" Abigail head jerked up. "What happened?"

"I am not sure. Lady Blackbourne did not go into detail, but it appears Lord Selward witnessed it and was less than pleased."

"Oh." What had Nicholas done? Had he given up and fallen back into the black despair of his former behavior? No! She refused to believe it.

"As a result, it appears Lord Selward has withdrawn his attentions from Lady Rebecca. He has not graced their doorstep since the event at the club. She is quite heartbroken over the matter. More distressing to Lady Blackbourne is the idea that Lord Blackbourne has returned to his old life. She thought that well left behind, but it appears not."

"We must not jump to conclusions, Mother. There may be a logical explanation," Abigail jumped to his defense.

"Perhaps," Mother said as Mabel set the tea service down on the table.

Abigail's brain worked furiously as she poured two cups of tea. "Perhaps the gossips exaggerated the event." The ton had a penchant for embellishing the facts to make a better story as she knew all too well.

"Perhaps Lord Blackbourne's marriage to Miss Caldwell will help smooth things over, but who knows when that will occur."

The cup rattled in Abigail's hand and realization struck like a rogue streak of lightning from a dark sky. Lord Selward was not the only one averse to scandal. Miss Caldwell shared his aversion. Had Nicholas staged an embarrassing display in order to achieve the impossible? Did she dare hope? "And has Miss Caldwell given any indication she wishes to end the engagement?"

Her mother picked up a biscuit and nibbled off an end. The interminable wait while she chewed the small bite drove Abigail to the brink. "No, of course not. This marriage is a huge boon for her. I think it would take more than one scandalous event to sway her from it."

Abigail's heart deflated and sank to her toes. She lowered herself into a chair and took a sip of tea to hide the tremble of her lips. "Oh."

"It is just with the mourning period, the wedding has been put on hold. Lord Blackbourne has indicated he feels it in bad taste to host such a celebration in the wake of his father's death." Her mother looked across the table at Abigail and lifted a skeptical eyebrow. "I'm certain he is right, though it feels more like a delay tactic to me."

"A delay tactic?" Abigail studied the intricate rose pattern on the teacup.

"I think he proposed to Miss Caldwell to please his family, especially the previous Lord Blackbourne. Now with his father gone, perhaps he regrets his proposal. Not that there is much to be done about it now."

Oh, how Abigail loathed this sense of helplessness. Waiting and wishing without being able to do anything. Her stomach had been in knots since her meeting with Nicholas. How could she simply stand by and wait while the man she loved stood on the precipice of marrying someone else?

Yet, what else could she do? She had combed her mind for any thread of an idea that would aid their cause and each time came away empty handed. It was not in her nature to sit idle when something needed to be done. But now she had no other choice.

She must sit tight and put her trust in Nicholas to make things right.

Trust.

She took a deep breath. It wasn't Nicholas she didn't trust. It was fate. To date, it had not been kind.

Abigail closed her eyes and prayed this time fate would be on their side. And soon.

Chapter Twenty-Three

It had been several days since Nicholas had stepped foot inside the Caldwell home for his customary visit to his fiancée, but suddenly everything looked different. Little tell tale signs of wear and tear popped out at him while he waited in the sitting room. Signs that the Caldwell's were not terribly affluent, a reminder he had let slip from his mind when he first courted Miss Caldwell. It hadn't really mattered. He courted her for the good she could do to his tarnished reputation, and if she in turn needed him for the large sum in his bank account, it hardly seemed to matter. Tit for tat, so to speak.

But somewhere along the way, tit for tat had stopped being enough. Nicholas could pinpoint the moment with alarming accuracy. In the park when Abigail claimed she would prefer to sink to the bottom of the Serpentine rather than accept his assistance.

Even then, the difference between the two women had been apparent. Miss Caldwell would never have tried to evade him. She would have suffered in silence with a fixed demi-smile upon her countenance. She would have said all the right things and then gone on her way.

But Abigail was never one to suffer in silence. She did not possess a passive or demure bone in her body and he loved her for it all the more. She was an uncommon sort of woman and he loved her more deeply than he ever thought possible. Life with her would never be dull. It would be full of life and laughter and constant surprises.

He would be damned if he let her slip through his fingers again.

"Lord Blackbourne! I was not expecting you." Lord Caldwell walked into the room and extended his hand. Nicholas suffered a pang of regret. It had never been his intention to cause the Caldwell family grief. The baron was a good man. Nicholas would ensure Caldwell did not suffer for what he must do this day.

Nicholas forced a welcoming grin. "Indeed, I was not expecting it myself. But I was in the area and thought I would pay Miss Caldwell a visit, if it would not be too much trouble."

"Of course, of course." Caldwell made a sweeping motion with his arm. "Make yourself at home. Gordon," he motioned to the butler, "Fix Lord Blackbourne a drink. I shall see where my daughter is. Women, you know. We're forever looking for them or waiting on them, eh?"

Nicholas nodded, but knew it not to be true. For at this moment, one certain lady waited on him; pinned her hopes and her trust on his success today. The weight of it rested heavy on his shoulders.

A few minutes later, his betrothed appeared in the doorway. She moved with grace and poise as she stepped into the room, leaving the door opened for propriety's sake. Despite being affianced, he expected her mother lingered nearby.

"Lord Blackbourne." Miss Caldwell gave a brief curtsey,

always a stickler for propriety. Did she plan on doing that every time they met after they were married? He hoped never to know the answer to that question. "It has been several days. I had begun to wonder if you had forgotten my address."

Nicholas's gaze raked over her. She was a true beauty, at least in the conventional sense, with deep chocolate brown hair and almond shaped eyes. She had a pleasing shape, not too thin, not too plump. Her manner of dress was neither ostentatious nor overtly enticing.

All in all, Miss Caldwell was the perfect picture of what a man should wish for in a wife. If a man were only buying a picture. But his fiancée held no warmth for him. Nothing about her welcomed or embraced him. He was nothing more to her than a means to an end. She needed *this*, so she must do *that*. People of their station did it all the time. But he had seen firsthand with his own parents' marriage, the misery such a loveless union wrought. He could not consign himself to that. Nor would he allow Abigail to do the same.

He had once thought his passion and desires were responsible for his downfall and had wished to be rid of them. Now he saw them for what they were—an integral and necessary part of life. Without them, life became colorless. It lacked depth and meaning. It held nothing of interest.

No, passion was essential. Desire even more so. And both were worth risking everything for.

Abigail had taught him that.

He would not allow the lesson to go unacknowledged.

"Please, sit down." Nicholas motioned to the seat on the sofa next to where he stood. "I feel it imperative we speak."

Miss Caldwell crossed the room and did as he bid, arranging her skirts around her. "I expect you are going to apologize for your atrocious behavior? I heard all about your altercation with *that* woman. It is done. And if I have your word that it will not happen in the future, then it can remain in the past and we shall never speak of it again."

Nicholas's stomach turned. He had hoped she would not so easily dismiss the scandal his interaction with Opal had created. He had wanted her to be appalled. Disgusted. But if so, she chose to overlook it to meet her ends.

"I'm afraid that won't be possible," he said.

"I beg your pardon?"

Nicholas took a deep breath and plunged in. "It will not be possible for me to give you my word it will not happen again. For it shall, weekly. Maybe daily. I will scandalize you in every way I can think possible. I will drag my name through the mud and let it wallow there for as long as is necessary."

"Necessary for what?"

"For you to break off our engagement."

She hesitated for an instant then quickly collected herself. "I will do no such thing."

"Yes, you will, and I'll tell you why."

Miss Caldwell glared at him, her dark eyes cold and hard. "Please do, Lord Blackbourne. I'm sure it will be most illuminating."

"You will break off our engagement because I do not love you. You may be the perfect picture of what a man should wish for in a wife, but in truth, I find you cold and calculating. I cannot trust you and I have absolutely no desire to spend the rest of my life with you."

"This is not about what you want," Miss Caldwell said, and Nicholas knew the statement to be fact. She had never cared. He had never managed to penetrate the wall she had built around herself and she had no desire to let him in.

He forced himself to stay calm. "You will break off your engagement to me. Because if you do not, I will."

Shock registered on her features, freezing them for an

instant. Nicholas recognized a moment of satisfaction that he had finally managed to register some emotion with her.

"You will not."

"I will. And I will not be kind about it." He waited for a full moment while the ramifications of his threat settled in. She would be humiliated, possibly even shunned and ostracized. Her hopes of helping her family dashed.

"You wouldn't dare. What of your own reputation? You were so concerned with repairing the damage your past behavior had created. Do you honestly believe I would be so gullible to think you would risk that now?"

Nicholas shrugged. "My father is dead. I have no one to account to now."

He leaned back and crossed one leg over the other and affected a posture of indifference, though inside, his stomach churned and boiled. He did not want it to come to that. It would be ugly and wholly unnecessary.

But if he had to, if Miss Caldwell forced his hand, he would. He would do whatever he had to in order to be rid of this engagement she had blackmailed him into and ensure Abigail did not suffer in kind. He had no desire to hurt Miss Caldwell, but if he had to choose between her future and Abigail's, it was an easy choice to make.

"Why are you doing this?"

A small crack appeared in her calm façade and Nicholas could almost smell her desperation. He hardened himself against the sense of pity that threatened. He did not wish her ill, but nor did he wish to spend an eternity with her as his wife.

"I am doing this because a marriage between the two of us would make both our lives miserable. You think my financial status will compensate for any lack of affection between us, but I assure you it will not. The veneer of wealth will wear thin very quickly and, in its place, will live only resentment and bitterness."

"I disagree."

"Of course, you do," he said. "But you are only looking with your head and not your heart."

"What do you know of heart," she spat at him. "You, who wallowed in your own debauchery for years as if it were sweet cologne."

"And I paid the price for that," he reminded her. "I am still paying."

Nicholas stood and walked to the mantel. His fingers slid along the stone edge.

"It is because of *her*, isn't it?"

Nicholas turned and faced her. For a moment, he thought to deny it, but it seemed ridiculous now. "Yes, it is. I had planned to offer for her, but your threats and extortion prevented me and forced me into a betrothal I do not want."

Her mouth tightened but she did not deny his claim.

"The only reason I agreed to this was to prevent you from harming Abigail. I realize now this marriage would do her far more harm. It would do everyone far more harm, yourself included. We all deserve better than this."

Miss Caldwell stood abruptly and paced the floor. He could feel her desperation building, giving her movements a sharp edge. It was the first true emotion he had ever seen her display.

"You cannot do this. I will...my father will—"

"I sincerely doubt your father will care if he knows the decision was yours. Beyond that, my family has enough power and wealth that anything he says or does will be rendered moot. Do not make me do that," Nicholas said. "I have the utmost respect for your father. He is a good man. I do not wish to hurt him or his reputation. Or yours, for that matter."

"But you would."

"If you force my hand."

"For her." She said the words as if they left a vile taste in her mouth.

"I love her," he said. The words came easily as did the sense of calm their truth created. They brought everything into crisp clarity.

"And what of me? What of my family? Are we to suffer for this change of heart?"

Nicholas didn't consider his refusal to be a change of heart but he did not argue the point. "When you announce our betrothal has ended, I will settle upon your family a handsome sum as compensation. It should assist your father in offering decent dowries for you and your sisters."

Miss Caldwell clasped her hands in front of her. "What will people think?"

"They will think you are most wise to rid yourself of a fiancé whose favorite pastime is to immerse himself in scandal. I will, of course, wait a suitable time before Abigail and I announce our betrothal to avoid any hint that the decision to part was mine."

Miss Caldwell stood and paced; her movements sharp. "I cannot believe this is happening."

"What did you expect?"

She turned on him, anger in her eyes. "I expected to marry. I expected to make my family's life a little easier! To help my sisters!"

"And you will," Nicholas said. "I will see to it. The dowries, coupled with your sterling reputation and beauty, will make you an attractive prospect. I suspect next Season you will have your pick of gentlemen, provided your reputation remains undamaged by your decision here today. Say you will call off the engagement."

"This constant avoidance of your duty is beyond the pale." Aunt Edythe paced in front of the window. One hand grasped the brooch fixed at the base of her neck, the other swept through the air to punctuate her words.

Abigail sipped her tea and did her best to ignore her aunt's tirade over her insistence of waiting out the week before she gave Lord Tarrington her answer. Aunt Edythe considered her acceptance a foregone conclusion. The diatribe had lasted for the past ten minutes and showed no signs of ending any time soon.

Abigail refrained from commenting. There was no point. What was she to say? She had insisted on a week because she believed a miracle would occur, that fate would finally cast a kind eye in her direction and like magic, she and Nicholas could be together. The more she said it in her own mind, the more ridiculous it sounded.

And now, here she sat on the last day of her seven-day reprieve, no closer to that miracle than she had been on the first. There had been no word from Nicholas, no letter. Nothing. Days had passed since the scandal at White's and still... nothing. Silence.

Her heart sank deep into her satin slippers. His scheme had failed.

"If you were my daughter, I would not have countenanced such behavior. And when Lord Tarrington arrives tomorrow, you will beg his forgiveness and pray he does not withdraw his proposal."

Tomorrow.

Abigail glanced up from her tea at the sound of a carriage. A knock sounded below and Abigail's heart lurched. Had Lord Tarrington come a day early? Could she stall him for one more day?

But to what end?

The inevitable had arrived at her door. She rested the teacup in her lap and stared forlornly at the door to the sitting room. Perhaps the time had come to accept her future. To realize not every story had a happy ending.

The door opened and Titus stepped inside, announcing their caller. "Lord Blackbourne."

Startled, Abigail nearly toppled her teacup. Somewhere behind her, Aunt Edythe gasped. Abigail quickly set her cup and saucer aside and stood slowly, afraid to move lest she disturb the scene unfolding before her eyes. Nicholas stepped inside the room and Titus closed the door behind him.

For a brief moment, everyone remained motionless.

"Lady Glenmor," Nicholas said, his voice steady and quiet. "Miss Laytham."

"This is highly irregular." Aunt Edythe glared at him; horror seared into each line on her face.

Nicholas offered a small smile, but his gaze never left Abigail's. "Forgive me."

She returned his smile. It was so good to see him in the flesh. She wanted to rush across the room and throw herself into his arms, but his words kept her rooted in place.

Forgive him for what? Had he been unsuccessful? Uncertainty tempered the joy of seeing him. Was this to be good-bye, then? Tears watered her vision and Nicholas's image wavered.

"There is nothing to forgive." She held her voice steady, determined to maintain her dignity. It was a difficult battle. She wanted to throw herself into his arms and collapse like a wailing child.

"What you have done, sir, is unforgiveable!" Aunt Edythe's ire wafted from across the room. "How dare you show yourself in our home."

Nicholas ignored her and reached out to take Abigail's

hands in his own. His were warm and strong. She took solace in that small contact and wished she could hold on forever.

"Abigail, look at me."

Aunt Edythe gasped again and whirled away, the words she muttered lost on Abigail as she did as Nicholas bade and gazed into his silvery eyes. The love reflected there wrapped around her heart and squeezed.

"Do you forgive me?"

She nodded and blinked back the tears threatening to fall. "I'm sure you did all you could."

Nicholas shook his head. "No, not for that. For your uncle. For my behavior. My part in his death. I need to know —do you forgive me for that?"

She nodded. She had forgiven him some time ago. Benedict, Caelie, her mother, even Lord Tarrington—they had all been right. Her uncle's decisions were his own, and while Nicholas may have played a part, it no longer signified. If Madame St. Augustine hadn't used him, it would have been another gentleman and the outcome would have been the same. They had all become trapped in the vicious circle of her uncle's obsessive love for a woman he could not have.

Abigail could sympathize. It was a most painful thing to love someone who was once yours but never could be again.

"I forgive you," she said. "Completely."

Nicholas raised her hands and pressed his lips against the backs of her fingers.

"This is—scandalous!" Aunt Edythe fanned herself. "I insist you leave immediately. Titus!"

They ignored her.

"It appears Miss Caldwell has chosen to break off our engagement." Abigail's eyes widened. "She has deemed my most recent behavior too reprehensible for words and cannot in good conscience attach herself to one prone to such reprehensible and unrepentant behavior."

"Oh." Her breath rushed out of her as Nicholas's words sank in. Miss Caldwell had broken their engagement. He was free. And he was here. Standing—oh no, kneeling! —in front of her.

Aunt Edythe rushed over and motioned with her hands, waving them about. "What is this business? Stop this instant! Get up! Get up!"

Nicholas's grin widened, love and laughter reflected in his gaze. "I was curious..."

"Yes?" Abigail could scarcely breathe.

"Would you perhaps be interested in accepting an invitation?"

"An invitation?" Her heart pounded against her breast.

"Stop it!" Aunt Edythe swatted at Nicholas's shoulder. "Stop it this instant. Titus!"

A giggle burst out of Abigail. Was this really happening?

"To a wedding. Ours, to be more succinct. Provided you would still like to become my wife, that is." His smile tilted to one side and a gleam shone in his eyes. "I would much prefer the rest of my scandals to be played out with you."

His words sent Aunt Edythe reeling backward in dismay.

Abigail dropped to her knees in front of Nicholas, pulling his hands to her heart, caring little that they had an audience of one about to have an apoplexy.

"That is an invitation I am most willing to accept."

Nicholas let go of her hands and wrapped his arms around her, lifting them both to their feet. He swung her around, whooping with pleasure and in that moment, Abigail realized they had come full circle. Forgiveness was given, passion rediscovered, and love rewarded.

"I love you," she whispered against Nicholas's lips until she felt his smile.

"No more than I, you."

T he wedding proved a wondrous affair, though the anticipation had nearly been the death of Abigail, each day dragging slower than the one before it. They had honored Nicholas's promise to Miss Caldwell and allowed for a brief waiting period before announcing their betrothal. After which, a special license was quickly procured and a small group of close friends and family reconvened at Sheridan Park for the event.

Save for Aunt Edythe, who had declined her invitation. At least, Abigail assumed that was what was meant when Titus returned it to her torn in two. Her aunt had not spoken to Abigail since witnessing Nicholas's proposal. The silence had been glorious.

But none of that mattered now as her family and friends looked on with smiles on their faces and the vicar announced the new Lord and Lady Blackbourne. A countess. Good heavens! And, more importantly, Nicholas's wife.

"I believe you may bestow a kiss upon your bride, my lord," the vicar declared, clutching the bible against his ample belly.

"I believe I may do just that."

Nicholas grinned down at her and wasted little time in taking the vicar up on his offer, kissing her soundly to cheers from the pews. And although Uncle Henry was not in attendance, Abigail felt her uncle's presence in her heart and imagined he would have greatly approved in the end. For despite his faults, Uncle Henry had been a romantic at heart.

And Abigail could think of no better way to honor his memory than to let true love flourish.

A Sneak Peek

～～

BOOK 2: A SCANDALOUS PASSION

L ady Caelie Laytham stepped off the busy dock and onto the gangway leading up to the deck of the *Windswept*. The narrow stretch of wood wobbled beneath her feet and she froze.

"Come along." Her mother shot a swift glance over her shoulder, her gaze and purposeful stride filled with impatience. Caelie looked down at the dank, dark waters beneath her and opened her mouth to question once again whether leaving London was truly the best course of action. Then she closed it just as quickly. What was the point? Mother had made her decision and Caelie had already received an earful from her first two attempts to change her mind.

There was no turning back.

Behind her, the noise from the dock rose up and pushed against her. Wagons and carts with their iron wheels clanged against the cobbled streets and echoed in her ears only to be over-powered by raised voices and the stench of fish mingled with salt air and a bevy of other aromas she could not pinpoint nor wished to.

She had spent her entire life in London, yet at three and

twenty this was the first time she had ever seen this section of the city. To think her last vision of home was to be a jungle of spars and masts jutting upward into the grey morning sky did not seem right.

Caelie let out a breath and forced one foot in front of the other. The damp wood made for a slippery surface. Beneath her, the Thames churned and splashed between the ship and the narrow wharf. Her stomach roiled at the thought of falling into the disgusting waters below.

Then again, perhaps that would be a much more tolerable fate than the one that awaited her in Italy.

Her mother had informed her a month ago of the journey. Caelie had possessed no notion her mother corresponded with a distant cousin, Mr. Beechum. Not that Mother was in the habit of sharing personal information with her. Still, it had come as a shock when she announced they were to leave London for Italy, as Mr. Beechum had proposed and she had accepted. She claimed the union was their only chance at getting out from under the embarrassment and scandal they had suffered these past two years.

A feat, she made a regular point of mentioning, Caelie had failed to accomplish by securing a proper marriage herself.

She could not fault Mother's accounting of the situation. Society had all but turned their backs on them after Father's scandalous death. Her heart panged at the memory, a wound that was slow to heal.

"Caelie!"

She started at Mother's harsh tone and reached out a hand to grab the rope strung alongside the gangway. "Coming, Mother."

Mr. Beechum would be sorely disappointed if he expected a gracious companion to enjoy his later years with. Edythe, the Countess of Glenmor, was not known for either warmth or a genial manner.

Caelie cast one last look at the water below then stepped onto the ship's deck. A bevy of activity surrounded them. Men of all shapes and sizes moved along the deck with purpose, heavy loads hoisted onto their shoulders. Profanity peppered their rough-hewn speech, enough to turn Mother's normally sallow skin an almost pretty pink.

Caelie forced back a smile. Something she had grown accustomed to doing around her mother. Amusement belonged to the lower class, she often said. A lady comported herself in a much more sedate and dignified manner.

Beneath her, the strong sway of the ship did nothing to settle the anxiety tossing around inside of her. She did her best to ignore it. Nothing could be done about their departure. Mother had made her decree and Caelie, as was her duty, followed it. Her cousins had begged her to stay, but pride was a funny thing. She loved Benedict and Abigail dearly, but she would not be a burden to them.

Water lapped against the side of the *Windswept* hard enough to be heard over the chaos on board. Her stomach rolled as each wave mocked her choice.

Caelie glanced about the deck in search of Mr. Marcus Bowen. The ship belonged to a fleet owned by the Marquess of Ellesmere. Mr. Bowen, his man of business, had agreed to ferry them to Italy, though the ship's final destination lay somewhere well south of that.

The ship wasn't generally meant for passengers, but Mother had no intention of backing down from her plans to leave England. Caelie's new cousin, the Earl of Blackbourne, had therefore spoken on their behalf and ensured their passage. He wanted them to travel with someone he trusted, and Mr. Bowen was a close friend.

Unfortunately, Mr. Bowen was nowhere to be found.

"This is indefensible." Mother's sharp eyes searched the deck. Caelie glanced down at the small bag her mother held in her hands. Her gloves creased where she gripped the handles as if her life depended on it. A marvel the wood didn't snap from the pressure. Mother did not tolerate tardiness.

"I'm sure Mr. Bowen will be along promptly." Mother would take a strip off the gentleman if Caelie didn't intervene. It would not get their trip off on the right foot.

Always the peacemaker. Abigail's voice sounded in her head and a lonely pang pierced her heart. She blinked back the tears that pricked her eyes. Her cousins were the closest things to siblings she'd ever had. Her own brother, her twin, had not survived their birth. A fact Mother never failed to remind her of, as if she were somehow responsible.

Being an only child, and not a son, had proven a very lonely existence until her aunt and cousins arrived to live with them a decade ago. They'd brought a welcomed warmth into an otherwise cold home. She would miss them fiercely. But Abigail had married, and Benedict had his hands full as the new Earl of Glenmor upon her father's passing. They had their own lives and, as Mother reminded her, there was nothing left for her there. Her father's suicide following his scandalous affair with the famed courtesan Madame St. Augustine and her own broken engagement to Lord Billingsworth had ensured that.

Abigail's marriage to Lord Blackbourne had improved the situation nominally, but it hadn't been enough. Though she could show her face in public once again, no one went out of their way to repair old friendships or court new ones.

She remained a pariah amongst the ton. The dream she harbored of finding a husband to love, children to care for, a place to belong—remained well out of reach.

"You there!" Mother barked at a burly man with a large sack of something resting on his shoulder. The man stopped and shifted the burlap sack as if it contained nothing more than a load of feathers.

"Ma'am?" He looked her up and down and Mother's beady eyes widened in revulsion. She recoiled and held her gloved hand to her nose in an apparent effort to ward off the stink of sweat wafting off the large bear of a man.

"I demand you take us to Mr. Bowen this instant."

The large, bushy, black moustache above the man's upper lip twitched. "Might be 'ard t'do, seein' as he ain't har." His voice rolled with the thickness of an accent Caelie couldn't place. Northern perhaps?

"I beg your pardon?"

"He isn't here," Caelie translated. She smiled as she addressed the man in front of her, an attempt to soften the effect of Mother's strident tone. "Has he not arrived as yet?"

"Nah. Won't be either, lassie."

Caelie swallowed the rush of hope, afraid to let it bloom. Had she been granted a reprieve from Mother's forced exile? "Mr. Bowen will not be sailing today?"

"Not accordin' to 'is majesty." He jerked his head toward the opposite end of the ship then continued on his way without so much as a by your leave. Mother let out a huff filled with self-righteous indignation. She did not care to consort with the lower classes, but Caelie did not see how she could avoid it on this voyage. It appeared they were the only ones of high birth on board.

Caelie shifted her gaze to where the man had nodded and quickly realized the error of her assumption. She recognized the identity of the man referred to as *'is majesty*.

"Oh dear."

Also by Kelly Boyce

THE SINS & SCANDALS SERIES

THE BRIDES OF FATAL BLUFF

SALVATION FALLS

Dear Readers,

Thank you so much for reading **AN INVITATION TO SCANDAL**, Book 1 in the _Sins & Scandals Series_. I hope you have loved getting to know Nicholas and Abigail, as well as their friends and families. I know I have definitely enjoyed writing them!

If you enjoyed **AN INVITATION TO SCANDAL**, I hope you will check out the other books in the **Sins & Scandals Series.**

For the most updated booklist, check out my **website** or sign up for my **Newsletter** at **www.kellyboyce.com.** I send out notifications to all subscribers to let them know when a new release is on its way, as well as provide the opportunity to win a prize with each new edition. Be sure not to miss it!

I love to hear and connect with my readers through social media and email and you can find all of my relevant links (Facebook Page, Instagram, Goodreads, Pinterest) on my **website**! And for any of you readers who knit, you may want to check out my YouTube channel where I talk about my other passion – Loch Briar Knits.

Lastly, in addition to my Regency series, I have also

written several **western historical romances set in the Old West – The Outlaw Bride**, originally published by Carina Press and soon to be re-released by me. As well, there is my **The Salvation Falls Series**.

Again, thank you for reading **AN INVITATION TO SCANDAL** and I hope you will consider leaving a review at your favorite online retailer to help others discover **THE SINS & SCANDALS SERIES!**

Wishing you all the best,

--*Kelly*

Acknowledgments

First and foremost, thank you to my family for their unequaled love and support, especially to my amazing husband, John, who never once looked at me askew when I told him I needed to spend the weekend at the coffee shop drinking copious amounts of caffeine and typing madly in order to make my deadlines.

To the tremendously awesome trio who supported me throughout this process – Pamela Callow, Julianne MacLean and Cathryn Fox. For your unparalleled guidance and friendship, I thank you. Thank you, thank you, thank you! You three never cease to amaze me with your kindness, brilliance, and insight. I owe you a large chunk of my sanity.

Anne MacFarlane and Annette Gallant – thanks for keeping me on track. When I meet my goals, you have only yourselves to blame!

Deborah Hale – There's a reason I say, 'When in doubt, ask Deb.' Thanks for answering my questions and providing your always sage advice. I bow to your greatness.

Nancy Cassidy – thanks for working with me through the editing process. I promise next time to never add an *s* to *toward*.

To my faithful hound, Cedar – thanks for being, in equal parts, a complete clown, an overgrown lap dog, and a genuine teddy bear (in other words, the true embodiment of a golden retriever). All these things came in handy during the 5 am writing sessions.

And last, but not least, to the ladies who make up Romance Writers of Atlantic Canada. You gals rock!

About the Author

Kelly Boyce started writing stories in Grade 2 when her favorite teacher, Mrs. Matheson, showed up with a box filled with plot ideas and she was immediately hooked. But it wasn't until she read Lisa Gregory's *Bitterleaf* that she fell in love with historical romance. Once she discovered Romance Writers of Atlantic Canada and learned how to turn those stories into books, it was full steam ahead.

A life-long Nova Scotian, Kelly lives near the Atlantic Ocean with her amazing husband and a clownish golden retriever with a stubborn streak a mile wide. She loves writing stories about relationships and creating a sense of community around the hero and heroine filled with secondary characters who take on a life of their own.

Along with *The Sins & Scandals Series*, she has also released several western historical romances with Harlequin. The first two, **The Outlaw Bride** and **Salvation in the Rancher's Arms** will soon be re-released under her own banner, while the remaining, **Salvation in the Sheriff's Arms**, and two Christmas novellas: **The Cowboy of Christmas Past** and **Christmas in Salvation Falls** are still available through Harlequin.

Currently, she is hard at work developing a new three book series on the Lindwell Family, who were introduced in *The Sins & Scandals Series*.

Copyright

ISBN: 978-0-9936169-0-7

Cover design: Kim Killion
Editor: Nancy Cassidy

www.ingramcontent.com/pod-product-compliance
Lightning Source LLC
Chambersburg PA
CBHW020539020726
47494CB00006B/1828